Cover Art and Design by Viergacht © 2022 LVP Publications

The Coppergate Killings (*Tales of the Talisman* Vol III Issue 4, June 2013)
The Garretton Ghoul (*Machina Mortis*, 2013)
Unfathomable (*Steampunk Cthulhu*, 2014)
Brassworth (*Airship Shape and Bristol Fashion*, 2014)
The Etheric Dynamo (first published as 'Preserving the Integrity of the
Feminine Mystique' in *Daughters of Frankenstein*, 2015)
The Modern Woman (*NeaDNAthal*, 2015)
Rosie Red-Jacket (*Fae*, 2014)
Of the Utmost Discretion (*We Walk Invisible*, 2013)
No One of Consequence (*Insidious Assassins*, 2015)
The Terrible Secret of Tetley Hall © 2021 Christine Morgan
Cinder's Twelve © 2021 Christine Morgan

Dreadful Fancies Copyright © 2022 LVP Publications

Printed in the United States of America

Lycan Valley Press Publications
1625 E 72nd St STE 700 PMB 132
Tacoma, Washington 98404 United States of America

First Printing

ISBN: 978-1-64562-900-9

DREADFUL FANCIES

Christine Morgan

LVP

CONTENTS

THE COPPERGATE KILLINGS

Oᴜᴛ ᴏꜰ ᴛʜᴇ ɢᴇᴀʀʜᴏᴜꜱᴇ?

Toby didn't dare pinch himself, in case he woke and found it only a dream.

Why, he couldn't remember a time before the gearhouse, wrack his brain though he might. Endless hours at his work-station. Gruel in the morning, bread and sour ale at midday, soup or thin stew for supper… and a good knock of spirits at bedtime to make sure they slept through the night, boys crammed together hip and shoulder like sardines in a tin.

He looked at the man ahead of him, opened his mouth, then snapped it shut. Far be it from him to question this turn of good fortune.

Always the gearhouse, since he was a tot. He'd been a sorter, thanks to keen eyes and deft fingers. You had to be careful as anything because not only did the sharp edges sting, but red-staining the shiny metal would get your ears fair boxed.

Each gear was vital. Even the smallest component of a machine had its place. That was how cities were built, railroads and steamotive engines, airships, overocean liners and underocean

1

nautiluses! Why, to think that gears he'd sorted with his own hands helped make those—

"Still with me, lad?"

"I am, sir!"

The man chuffed a laugh. A working man like any other, he had rough clothes, rough hands, and rough lines at the corners of his eyes and mouth. Ropy knots of scars ran up under his cuffs, and down into his collar on both sides of his thick neck.

But, to Toby, he couldn't have appeared grander, because this man had come to the gearhouse, chosen him out of all the others, and brought him away.

"Bright one, aren't you? I said to myself when I saw you, I said, now there's a likely looking chap."

"Did you, sir?"

"Ah, now, enough with the sir. Donlin's my name. What's yours again?"

"Toby, s—Mr. Donlin."

Chosen out of all the other boys, wasn't it a wonder? They'd set someone else to his work-station, and taken Toby off to to be readied. Though in truth, that part he hadn't cared for. A scalding bath in a big tub, as if they meant to boil him like a cabbage— scrubbed and scoured within an inch of his life—the servant girls making fun of his scrawny nakedness, not to mention his dingle... but at the end of it, he'd been cleaner than he could ever recall. Clean, and put into a shirt and britches, into shoes that only pinched his feet a bit, into a jacket not too roomy, and a cap to cover the close-cropped ginger stubble of his hair.

"How old are you, then?" Mr. Donlin asked, as they turned down another street of grimy cobblestones and sooty brick. "Any inkling?"

"Ten, sir, Mr. Donlin, or thereabouts. Eleven maybe."

They scrambled quick out of the way as a trio of velocycles

came whirring around a corner. Each had a front wheel farther across than Toby was tall. Pipes jetted steam from their rear-mounted engines with a teakettle whistle.

The riders, perched high on their seats as they swerved through carts and passers-by, were young men, dandies, resplendent in the peacock-blue waistcoats of the Foundry Row Fellows. They whooped and shouted, waving people aside. The leader wound up a brass bell that went clang-jangle, adding to the cacophany. Dogs dashed after them, barking up a storm. Pretty girls waved their lacy hankies.

"Nuisances," Mr. Donlin said, scowling.

Toby was quick to stifle an envious grin. He made his voice solemn. "Yes, sir. Dreadful nuisances."

Oh, but what he wouldn't have given to be one of them! Speeding along, high above the crowd, wind riffling his hair, ultra-glass lenses in leather goggles keeping grit and bugs from his eyes… what fun!

As he watched, the third dandy veered his velocycle toward a plank that lay at an angle against a crate in front of a greengrocer's stall. He meant to use it as a jump-ramp, and Toby almost squealed aloud.

"Maniac!" shouted the grocer.

"He's going to break his damn fool neck," said Mr. Donlin.

The dandy hit the plank, shot up it, and the crate collapsed in a splintering wreck. The velocycle came down with a terrific crash, clipping the grocer's display bin. The big front wheel sprang loose. It caromed away, bouncing. The bin teetered, then tipped, spilling produce all over. The machine's body pinwheeled, steam-jets spouting, coils sputtering sparks and flashes. The dandy himself was thrown, limbs a-flail, onto a heap of burlap sacks. The grocer descended in a fury, beating him about the head with a bunch of leeks. Urchins scampered after apples, turnips, onions, and beets, then raced for the alleys with their shirts bulging from the unexpected bounty. Further down the street, slewed around by an ornate bronze clock-and-lamp, the other Foundry Row Fellows howled with laughter.

"Nuisances and damn fools." Mr. Donlin shook his head. "Come on. The missus will have supper ready. You look as though you could use a good feeding-up or three."

Curiosity got the better of Toby after all, not to question the fact of his good fortune but the nature of it at least. "What is it you do, Mr. Donlin?"

For that was why anyone came to the gearhouse, wasn't it? To take on lads to do work? The tall, strong boys would go work in the stockyards and lumberyards, the tanneries, the mills and factories. For slighter ones like Toby, it'd be the craftsmen and tradesmen... or shopkeepers, and this man was obviously no shopkeeper.

Oh, and if his new master was a machiner, or an inventor, or an engineer, wouldn't that be just ripping? Making delicate clockeries and jeweleries, maybe... or weapons, like lightning cannons and pepperbox guns...

Mr. Donlin looked amused. "It's not for me you'll be working. Me and the missus, we're in the employ of a lady and gentleman of means. We look after the house for them."

"And I'm to help?"

"You're to be company for their little girl. Anna. Sickly, she is. Poor health. An invalid. Confined to her rooms."

Toby went in silence for a while, trying to think what he knew of little girls. The ones at the gearhouse were dirty ragamuffins like the rest of them. As apt to kick you in the shins and snatch away your supper, if you'd let them.

"Company...?" he said.

"Mmm-hmm. Sit with her, talk to her, tell her stories. Do you know your letters?"

If he said he didn't, would he be sent back?

If he said he did, he'd be caught in the lie soon enough.

"I can do my name." He hung his head.

"That's a start, then." Mr. Donlin clapped a callused hand to Toby's shoulder. "Step lively. We're almost there."

Ahead was the high greened-metal arch that gave Coppergate Street its name.

A prickle crept the nape of Toby's neck and he felt the sudden mad urge to run.

Run? Run where? Run why?

It was only Coppergate Street. Oh, there were rumors, to be sure. Rumors of madmen and beldames... once-fine homes run to ruin since the wars... haunts... people gone missing... murders...

He glanced around, but saw only the usual end-of-day business —women with heavy-laden market baskets, men done with their shifts and headed for the gin-houses, more urchins, more dandies, a vendor hawking wind-up toys, a huckster giving out fliers for a Thrilling New Demonstration In The Advancement Of Enginecraft And Science.

No one was paying any mind to the two of them.

Well, but for a girl half-glimpsed in the shadow of a gaslamp not yet lit for the coming evening. What he saw of her hinted at black ringlets, red lips, striped stockings and white curves. A tuppence girl? But, tuppence, fourpence, sixpence or a farthing, she made no move to approach as they continued down the crooked street.

"Ah, and here we are."

Mr. Donlin stopped at a gate of spear-topped iron bars in a wall of gritty stone, acrawl with ivy of a dull-dead brownish hue. The garden beyond was likewise dull, dead and brownish, overgrown in tangles. The house looked in similar need of care—gaps in the slate roof-tiles, shutters hanging askew, the chimney seeming about to crumble—but for all that it was as grand a house as any Toby had ever seen.

He was to live there?

Being company for some tiresome girl, to be sure… but if she were as sickly as Mr. Donlin said, then she'd need plenty of sleep, wouldn't she? And during those times, he could help out with the garden and repairs.

The side door boasted an array of bolts and a great ratcheting self-lock mechanism. Toby's nose twitched as they went in. His mouth watered. His stomach gave out a grumble so loud that Mr. Donlin grinned.

"Hungry, are you, lad? Let's see to that first thing." He led Toby into the kitchen.

A short, roundish woman turned from the stove, where a pot simmered heavenly aromas into the air. Her face was red and sweaty beneath a bonnet. She wore a stained apron over a grey wool dress with a bit of shabby lace at the high collar and cuffs. "This the new one, is he?"

"That he is. Toby, he's called. Toby, meet the missus. She'll see to getting you fed while I let them know you're here."

"Sit yourself there," Mrs. Donlin said, waving a ladle at a stool.

Toby did so. Moments later, a bowl plunked down before him.

Stew! Not the thin, watery stuff he was used to, but stew thick and hearty, with beef broth and red wine, with chunks of tender vegetables, with meat! Meat, and it wasn't even Sunday!

"Is this… all this… for me?" he asked, blinking, sure that there must be some mistake.

But, instead of swatting him and calling him a ninny, Mrs. Donlin merely nodded. She gave him a spoon and a chunk of bread three times as big as he would have gotten at the gearhouse, then flapped her hand as if to tell him to go on, eat up.

He wasted no more time. Soon, he'd cleared the bowl to the dregs, scraping the sides with a crust to get every drop. Had he ever felt so full? His belly all but sloshed. He was warm and drowsy, could have gone to sleep right then without so much as a sip of spirits.

Instead, he took a better look around the kitchen, marveling at the cold-cabinet with its humming coils and chugging pistons, the frosty blue vapor wisping through glass tubings. Wouldn't it be fancy if gears he'd sorted with his own two hands had gone into the likes of that cold-cabinet? Or the chopping machine, all gleaming brass and scything blades?

"Had enough?" asked Mrs. Donlin.

His attempted answer turned into a long beefy burp.

"I gather that's a yes," Mr. Donlin said, coming back in. "Ready to go on upstairs?"

Blushing, mumbling an apology, he nodded and followed close on the man's heels, gawking about with every step. If the house was in disrepair on the outside, efforts must have gone into making the inside as comfortable as any lady and gentleman of means could have desired.

"What should I—?" he asked as they reached a door.

"You'll suss it out soon enough." Mr. Donlin drew a ring of keys.

"It's kept locked?" Not merely locked, Toby saw... a turn-bolt cranked by a wheel was set into the oaken slab, giving it a curiously daunting look.

"Can't have her wandering off."

"Is there a... a nurse?"

"No." The tumblers clunked. The turn-bolt turned.

That prickle crept down Toby's spine again, a chill-mouse of quick scurrying feet.

"I... I think I'd rather go back..."

"To the gearhouse? Don't be a fool, boy."

The door opened onto a dim, stuffy space. Before Toby could

move, Mr. Donlin's callused hand was at his back, pushing him through.

"Wait, I—"

The man gave a harder shove. Toby tripped on the edge of a rug and went sprawling.

"Oof," went Toby as he landed, getting the wind knocked out of him, almost getting the stew and bread knocked out of him as well. He gasped a breath of stale sickroom air.

The door shut. The latch and lock clicked, and the turn-bolt slid home.

"Mr. Donlin?" Toby called.

Something rustled.

He spun and set his back to the door. His eyes bugged wide, for all the good it did him in the dimness of burnished sunset filtering through a skylight's dirty panes. As his vision adjusted, Toby saw the outlines of furniture—a wardrobe, chairs, a writing desk, bedposts with heavy draperies, a desk stacked with primers and readers, a blackboard on an easel. He saw toys strewn about the rug.

The something that had rustled before rustled again.

The bed. The sound came from the bed.

"Hullo?" He did not budge from the door.

The little girl… Mr. Donlin had given him her name… what was it?

"Miss? Anna? Hello?"

Another rustle. Feeble somehow.

"I'm… I'm Toby, I…"

Had no idea what to say, that was for certain.

The skylight went from burnished bronze toward copper. Soon it would turn dusk-rose, then twilight-violet, then full night black.

Rustle, and a faint, scratchy whisper.

"Are you all right?" He sidled sideways along the wall, the back of his shirt rasping against textured paper, the seat of his britches against wooden wainscoting, until he reached a table with lamps upon it. He fumbled to light one. The flint-strikers spit a flurry of sparks and caught. Twisted spirals of wire within flame-shaped glass chimneys flared bright, shedding a yellow-white glow. "Anna? My name's Toby. They said I'm to keep you company..."

A long exhalation sounded like, "Nooooo."

"Hello?" Toby reached for the bedcurtains. His hand shook and he berated himself. He was ten, maybe eleven, no puling baby! This was only a girl! A sickly bedridden girl, at that! Was he to let those Coppergate Street rumors get the better of him?

Firming his nerve, he drew back the drape and shone the lamplight in.

See? What a ninny he'd been to get worked up! It was just a girl, a girl near to his own age. Pale and thin... so very pale, so very thin... her arms atop the coverlet like white sticks... her face hollow, her lips colorless and dry with scabs... her hair the yellow-ivory shade of newsprint, framing limp around her shoulders, spread thin and brittle over the pillowslip...

Not until then did he think to wonder what she was sick with... the consumption? Worse?

His gaze shot to a nightstand, seeking clusters of medicine bottles, but found none. What sat there instead were a book, a waterglass, and a musical clockwork trinket box.

He returned his gaze to Anna and jumped to find her staring straight back at him. Her eyes alone about her did have color, a vivid shocking blue.

"Get out!" she said, her voice a weak whisper.

"It's all right... I'm Toby... they got me from the gearhouse, brought me to—"

"They got me from the orphanage."

"But Mr. Donlin told me—"

Despite her frailty, Anna struggled to sit up. "You have to go! Now!"

"I won't do you any harm—"

She moved, hair falling away from her shoulders, arms twisting to grip the coverlet. Toby's words trailed to nothingness as he saw that her eyes weren't the only color about her after all. On both sides of her neck festered furious crimson sores, the skin around them mottled purple-black. The undersides of her forearms showed flesh raw like meat gnawed by dogs, weeping clear reddish fluid.

"They brought *me* to keep their little boy company," Anna said. Her pallid, bony hand clutched his. Her blue eyes blazed, mad gasflames.

"What little boy?"

"He's dead. They've had me here weeks and weeks. You... you're next. Unless you get out now, while you can." She glanced up. Her expression twisted in dismay.

Toby also glanced up. He saw panes filled with deep twilight. A single star winked.

"Go!" she said. "Go, get out, go now!"

He thumped the lamp down on the nightstand, jostling the trinket box. Its winder began to revolve. The lid sprang open, revealing a painted ballroom where clockwork dancers glided and spun to sweet tinkling machinework music.

Toby considered banging on the locked door, shouting for Mr. Donlin, but Anna's vehement headshake changed his mind. He ran to the nearest window instead. But when he yanked open the drapes, he saw that the rickety, askew shutters from outside were only a guise, concealing additional shutters, and iron bars.

Break the glass and call for help? Would anyone hear from the street outside the garden wall, over the usual din of a city evening? The skylight? Could he reach it? If he dragged the furniture to pile, and climb?

Toby turned to Anna, but she had dropped back onto the pillow again. She lay still, with her head to the side, the gruesome sores on her neck stark and ugly in the lamplight.

He heard stealthy movement, a soft thunk, a faint click as of a key... not from the direction of the door. From... from elsewhere... close...

Above? On the roof?

No, that was foolishness.

From behind the patterned, textured wallpaper?

Surely that was also—

A split appeared on an unseen seam. Appeared, and widened into a gap as a section of the wall slid aside.

And someone came in.

Two someones.

Toby's hair, cropped short against infestations of lice though it was, did its best to stand on end like that of a hedgehog. He backed across the room until he bumped up against the far wall.

A lady and gentleman of means, Mr. Donlin had said.

This was not at all what Toby had imagined.

Not these grotesque, wizened things... greyish, gangly and hunched... naked and shriveled beneath thin cloaks... their spidery limbs too long, seeming extra-jointed... their nails sharp, rusty with stains of what could only be dried blood... hair in wisps and straggles... eyes pinprick hot-yellow embers sunk into dark sockets...

Those hot-yellow eyes fixed on him. They had black lips like dogs, black lips that peeled back in matching hideous, eager grins.

And their teeth...

"Such a fine, strong young man," the female said, her voice cold and eerie. She hissed what might have been a laugh.

"Ah-ah-ah," said the other, the male, in a chiding way. His voice was equally cold, equally eerie, like the grating of a resurrectionist's spade across a gravestone at midnight. He ticked a forefinger at her. "You lost the toss. You get the dregs of the last one."

"Stay away," Toby said. "Stay back!"

"He's feisssssty!" The female hissed her laugh again. "Oh, let me have a tasssste, jussst a tasssste, jussst a sssip!"

"Tomorrow night," the male told her. "Tomorrow night, we'll share."

"Come near me and—" And what, he didn't know. Toby cast around for something, anything. The lamp was near at hand, so he seized it up, brandished it. "I'll throw it, I'll break it, I'll burn you!"

The male smiled. It showed that mouthful of needles and points, curves and spikes. "Toby... Toby, Toby, Toby. Look at me, Toby."

Toby did. He couldn't stop himself.

As soon as he met the ember gaze, why, his fear and resistance drained away like ale from a cask when the stopper had been left out.

"Toby."

Had he thought the voice cold and grating? How silly! The voice was warm, kind, affectionate. Fatherly. Yes, fatherly. The look of him, too... not gaunt and strange, not at all... a handsome man, with backswept auburn hair, and a neat-trimmed beard like a fox's pelt... the very image of what Toby's own father might have been like, had he known his father... had his father been a gentleman of means...

From the corner of his eye, he also saw the woman... beautiful and regal... honey-gold tresses and a complexion of cream, a gown of silk... bending to the bed... gathering up Anna's limp hand... raising it to her lips... kissing the wrist... no, not kissing... not kissing but sinking her pearly teeth into the flesh... as if savoring a succulent, juicy piece of fruit...

Anna's eyelids fluttered once, showing a crescent of blue. Her head lolled. The woman, so very beautiful, gazed adoringly at Toby.

"You do not need this," the man said, removing the lamp from Toby's unresisting grasp and setting it aside.

"No, sir…"

"Aren't you a good boy?"

"Yes, sir…"

Fingertips caressed his cheek. Icy fingertips, a bit scratchy, a bit sharp. They slipped, trailing, down the side of Toby's neck. They lingered where his pulse throbbed fast.

"You'll behave, won't you, Toby?"

He nodded.

"You'll feed us well, and for a nice long while, won't you?"

He felt so very peculiar. Drunk sober and dreaming awake.

"This one's empty," the woman said. She tossed Anna's arm back onto the coverlet, indifferent as to how it fell. The fresh, gouged wounds puddled with a few last seeping scarlet drops. "I want more."

"You always want more." The man sighed, his breath chilly on Toby's face. Chilly and oddly earthen-smelling. Dank.

"A sip, one little sip." She wiped her lips on the back of her hand, and licked away the red smear.

"Finish her, then… unless you want to keep her as a pet. And let me drink first." He pulled at Toby's collar.

The woman lifted Anna's head, stroking the brittle hair. She gave a hard wrenching twist. The sound was that of a branch snapping.

It likewise snapped Toby the rest of the way back to awareness. He yelped, jerked away from the man's icy caress, and before he fully realized his own intentions had snatched up the lamp again.

"Toby—"

The word was barely out when Toby swung with all his strength. The lamp's brass base cracked across the man's jaw. Glass shattered. Sparks sprayed out, igniting the bedcurtains, setting them ablaze.

He saw the lady and gentleman of means then, saw them again as they truly were, the moment lost. They recoiled from the sudden heat. Toby burst past them and ran for the door. Locked! He beat on it with the lamp, yelling at the top of his lungs.

More glass shattered, a smashing hail scattering over the rug and floor, as a figure dropped through the broken skylight.

Toby, shocked as he was, still recognized her... the girl he'd glimpsed on the street, the tuppence girl... black ringlets, striped stockings... flounced petticoats, many-pocketed skirt... kidskin boots with rows of tiny glinting buckles... waist cincher with more glinting buckles... a capelet flaring around her shoulders to reveal some sort of small but bulky weapon secured in a harness across her back ... a leather and brass-fitted satchel slung on a strap from shoulder to hip... reflective lenses set into frames adorned with silver crosses, held in place by a sturdy strip of black vulcanized gum-elastica...

And a twelve-barrel repeater affixed to a wide brass-ringed belt.

She grabbed the handles and cranked. *Thp-thp-thp* the repeater went. With each *thp,* a narrow wooden dart shot out.

The first one missed, sticking in a bedpost. The second grazed greyish skin and scored a bloodless, smoking line. The third punched into wizened flesh.

Thp-thp-thp! Three more struck home. Eerie voices screeched. The girl's mouth was grim-set, not succumbing to their yellow-eyed stares. *Thp-thp-thp!* Gangly-limbed bodies thrashed. Blackish stuff like bile oozed from the female's impaled belly. A dart pierced the male's chest and acrid smoke rose up. He blundered against the bed, waving his arms, ripping the curtains from their hangers, burying himself in folds of burning cloth.

The girl pinned the struggling male with a boot, aimed the repeater, and—*thp!*—fired another dart. He shuddered and flopped.

The female rushed for the hidden doorway. Toby hurled the ruined lamp even as the girl fired again. *Thp!* and the dart plunged into the back of her knee… *clong!* and the lamp rang off her skull. The female pitched sideways, scrabbling as she fell, harrowing gouges from the wallpaper on her way down.

The girl kicked her over and sank the last dart squarely between those hot-yellow eyes. *Thp!*

Then, but for the rising crackle of hungry flames, there was silence.

"Who… who are you?" Toby asked, awestruck.

She shook her black ringlets back from her face, pushed up the reflective goggles, and looked at him. "Chantal Noir," she said.

Toby's mouth fell open. "Not the paranormalist? The one what caught the Garretton Ghoul?"

"He was no ghoul. Just a lunatic with a clever killing device." She tore down the rest of the curtains, smothering them to a smolder before the dreaded fire spread. Her lips tightened at the sight of Anna. She let a sheet settle gently down over the dead child. "How many others in this house?"

"Ah… the Donlins, mister and missus…"

"Human? Or like them?"

"I… I don't… human, I think… ordinary enough…"

The machinery in his mind was all slipping gears and loose cogs. To be standing right here talking to the famous Chantal Noir? Paranormalist? Ghost-hunter? Catcher of the Garretton Ghoul, who, whether a ghoul or not had certainly cut a ghoulish swath through that neighborhood? Why, it had been in the papers! Even the boys who didn't know more than a few letters could gawk over the pictures, illustrations or actual photographics. The more learned ones were always glad to regale—or terrify—their fellows by reading aloud from the newsprints or penny dreadfuls, in the dark dormitories when they were supposed to be sleeping.

"Who else?" she asked.

"No one I saw or heard tell of."

"What about you? Did they bite you? Lift your chin. Push up your sleeves. Show me your throat, your wrists."

He hurried to do so. "Bite me? No, I only just came here—"

"And now you have to go."

Before he could ask where, or how, fast footsteps clodded in the hall. Keys jingled. Mr. Donlin bellowed through the door. "Master? Mistress?"

"Get back," Chantal Noir said. With one hand, she swept Toby behind her, while with the other she delved into one of her skirt's many pockets and came out with a snub-nosed clutch gun. No, not a gun, but a miniature lightning-cannon, its barrel ringed with concentric metal loops, a teslic coil where a hammer would have been.

The bolt threw. The tumblers went.

Chantal yanked down her goggles and took aim.

Mr. Donlin shouldered the door open. He coughed at the hazy smoke hanging in the air and gaped at the twisted husks, all that remained of the lady and gentleman of means.

"What is it?" came Mrs. Donlin's cry from the hall. "What is it, what's wrong, what has that wretched boy gone and done?"

"Are there more?" Chantal Noir asked Mr. Donlin, pointing the lightning cannon at his chest. Its teslic coil gave off a faint, flicking buzz.

His face contorted. His throat worked. "You... you killed them."

"Are?" she said, taking a step toward him with each word, "There? More?"

Mrs. Donlin, redder and sweatier than ever, stumbled to a halt in the doorway. Her nightdress showed that she, too, bore grisly ropes of pale scar tissue on both wrists and the sides of her neck. She shrieked when she beheld the scene, and seized her husband's arm as if to pull him back.

Zzznap! Toby flinched from a brilliant purple-white flash. He smelled a whiff of ozone. Electricity leapt across the room. Mr. Donlin gave a sudden violent jerk. He fell, wracked with convulsive spasms.

"Why you painted harlot!" Mrs. Donlin flew at Chantal Noir in a fury, surprising-fleet for a woman her size.

Another *Zzznap!* and there went Mrs. Donlin, on the floor, twitching all over, feet kicking so that her bedroom slippers came off.

Then, silence again.

Chantal drew a deep breath of a sort such that even a lad Toby's age had to appreciate what it did for her corseted bosom. "You saw no one else?"

He shook his head, making sure to raise his gaze until he saw himself, in distorted duplicate, caught in the rounded lenses of her goggles.

"What's your name?"

"Toby, mum."

She grimaced. "Don't call me 'mum,' and I won't call you 'boy,' do we have a deal? You're Toby, and I'm Chantal. Fair enough?"

He nodded.

"And her?" Chantal indicated the sheet-shrouded bed.

"Anna," Toby said. "She told me they got her from the orphanage the way they got me from the gearhouse. She told me I'd be next."

"As you would have been."

Matter-of-fact, she flipped the unconscious Donlins onto their bellies, manacling them wrists-and-ankles with spring-loaded extensible/retractable metallic cable. As a further measure, she hooked them together with a double-loop around the bedstead.

Toby stood, watching, not knowing what to do. Mr. Donlin had taken him from the gearhouse… Mrs. Donlin had fed him a better meal than any he could remember… but they'd brought him here to… to…

He looked at the bodies, or what was left of them. Ash, charcoal and blackened sticks—bones? the wooden darts? both?—amid heaps of still-smoking bedcurtains for the male. The female was a shrunken, dry-spongy thing in a stain of dark fluids. Her fingernails had snapped off in the wall she'd clawed at on her way down. Their heads looked like cracked crockery.

And their teeth…

Needles and points. Curves and spikes. Hideous ivory clusters. The female's were still clotted dark with Anna's blood, with shreds of Anna's skin and flesh stuck between them.

"They… they were…" Toby said.

"Vampires." Chantal straightened up from the Donlins, who groaned and burbled, eyelids sporadically fluttering.

"How did you—?"

"No time for that now. I have to search the rest of the house." She hung Mr. Donlin's keys from her belt. "Bad enough finding a pair. If they've spawned a nest…"

"A nest?" Toby remembered what the male had told the female just before she broke Anna's neck—*finish her then, unless you want to keep her as a pet*—and shuddered.

"Can I trust you?" she asked. "Will you help?"

"Help what? Go… go with you? In there?"

What lamplight shone into the black gap in the wall showed only a narrow corridor of slats, boards and beams. It was dusty in the lower corners and cobwebbed in the uppers, but the middle was clean from frequent use… from when they came in the night to feed on whatever boy or girl was kept prisoner in this room… prisoner to their hideous appetites… as Anna had been, as he would have been, as who-knew-how-many there'd been before them.

What could be at the end of that passage?

"No," Chantal said. "Not go with me, not in there. Too risky. If we found more, all they'd have to do is look you in the eye, and—"

He shuddered again. "Had enough of that, all right! Fair mesmerized me, he did!"

"Oh, vampires knew that trick long before Mesmer came along. That's where he got the idea."

"I didn't even think they were real, vampires that is. I thought they were stories!"

"You could go on thinking so, if you like. If you left here right now, told yourself none of this ever happened, soon it'd seem like nothing but a bad dream."

"Would it?"

"Unless you ended up raving in Hartsbrook, or turned gin sotted and were dead from drink by the time you were twenty."

Toby had seen gin sots in the gutters, made old far beyond their years, old and ragged, miserable even by the standards of a gearhouse boy. And Hartsbrook, the asylum, was the source of tales and rumors a hundredfold more frightening than anything he'd heard about Coppergate Street!

"What… what do you want me to do, then?"

"Do you know a tavern called the Watchman? On Rail's Crossing, near the church with the iron belfry?"

Toby nodded. He'd never been inside the tavern, of course, but he'd been by Rail's Crossing, he'd seen the church, he was sure he could find it.

"Go there," Chantal said. She held out what he first mistook for a coin, then saw was a shiny brass button embossed with a police crest. "Find Constable Pearce. Give him this, tell him I sent you, and bring him back here. Be quick about it."

Here, too, was a name Toby recognized from the newsprints and penny dreadfuls. The constable had gone up against the Black Stack Butcher, gunning down the madman despite having his own leg near lopped off by the Butcher's axe. These days, word was, he went about on a clockwork leg, and hadn't let it slow him one whit in pursuit of his duties.

"I will," he said, taking the button.

He went at a dash, down the stairs and through the house, wary in case something should lunge from nowhere and grab him. His mind jumped at every noise or shadow, until he was through the gate and out onto the street, where welcome light shone from lampposts. Gaslight here, stark electric further on.

The Watchman proved easy enough to identify, its sign sporting a comical painting of a stick-figure man all rods and gears, with a smiling oversized pocketwatch where his head should be. Inside, the tavern was warm to the point of sweltering, but it was quieter than some Toby had passed, and didn't stink quite as much of gin, tobacco and sweat.

"Here now, boyo, what do you think you're doing?" A thin, pock-faced man in a battered bowler stepped in front of Toby. His scowl was formidable. "This be a fine establishment for them what's looking to soothe away the day's labors with a spot of the medicinal. We won't have no grubby urchins nosing about thinking to dip fair-earned coins from a workingman's pocket."

"I'm here to see Constable Pearce," Toby said.

"And what's the constable want with the likes of you?"

"That's for me to tell him, isn't it?"

"Cheeky bugger, aren't you?"

"I have to see him straight away! It's urgent!"

"Let him over, Tom," said a man from a corner table.

"You know him, Constable?"

"No, but he's no urchin. Work-boy, by the look of him. Newly taken apprentice from a mill, or a factory, more likely."

He had a leather-bound ledger or journal open in front of him, papers spread from teatime to breakfast, and held a gadget that appeared to be an illuminated magnifier-clarifier with built-in timepiece and calculation engine.

"On your say-so, then." The pock-faced man allowed Toby to pass, but his gimlet stare promised any manner of abuses should Toby get up to mischief.

As for the constable, the photographics had given the impression of someone old, skinny, and frail. But the hair that had appeared white proved to be blond, and he was slim, not skinny, wiry rather than frail. And really, Toby reckoned, a run-in with the Black Stack Butcher would have left anybody looking well past their years, even without having a leg lopped off.

"Are you in some trouble, son?" Constable Pearce asked. He spoke not unkindly, his grey eyes intent but mild.

"I...I-I-I..." An instant's panic—what if he'd lost the button on his way here?—made him stutter. His left hand, clenched into a painfully-tight fist, uncurled with an effort. The brass button had to be pried up and unstuck from his palm, leaving a round police-crest imprint. "I'm to give you this, sir, and—"

The constable sighed, passed a hand over his brow, and plucked the button from Toby's fingers. "Where is she?"

The answer had barely left Toby's lips when Pearce swept up his papers and dumped them into a steel-fitted case set with complicated locks.

"Take me there," he said, tossing down the last gulp from his drink. He dropped money on the table, set his hat upon his head, and made quick strides for the door.

Surprising quick, those strides... he moved with the swift economy of a cat. The faintest whirr-and-grind of well-oiled machinery, the slightest hitch in his step, the barest suggestion of edge and angle through the fabric of his trouser-leg, only those gave any proof at all of the clockwork limb. He wore neat-polished black leather brogans, one on his real foot and one on whatever weight of metal served as the other, so that you couldn't even tell by looking at his feet.

In a trice, they were out of the tavern and on their way. Toby had to hurry to keep up, and he wasn't even burdened by a heavy steel-fitted case.

"Coppergate Street, you said."

"Yes, sir." Trotting alongside, Toby rattled off an explanation. It sounded mad to his own ears, mad as a badger, but the constable nary so much as batted an eye.

"Vampires." A tight, frustrated expulsion of breath blew through his teeth. "Damn it, Chantal..." he added, in a lower speaking-to-himself tone.

"Begging your pardon, sir... but how did you know all that about me? With just a single look?"

"The cropped hair and underfed appearance told me that you must be a work-boy," Pearce said. "Not scabby or raddled enough with sores to be a guttersnipe. Were you from a cloth mill, you'd have been wheezing, out of breath. A shoe mill, the tannery fumes would make you red-eyed and rheumy. So, a factory. On closer inspection, by the scarring on your hands, I'd say a gearhouse."

Toby uttered an amazed bleat.

"Scrubbed clean, though, and put into fresh clothes, could only mean you'd been taken on elsewhere, but so recently that your change of trade hadn't yet had its chance to make a telltale mark. This morning?"

"This afternoon," Toby said.

"You got at least one good meal in your belly before the manure collided with the oscillator, I'm guessing."

"Stew and bread! How——?"

"Gravy on your shirtfront. Is this the house?"

"This one, yes."

Constable Pearce set down his case just inside the front door. He pulled the clerk's help from his pocket, and switched on the illuminator. White light shone forth, dazzling in the darkness. Dust motes drifted through the fan-shaped beam as Pearce tilted it about the room.

In his other hand—and Toby hadn't even seen him reach for it —was a very businesslike pistol. The same one as had gunned down the Black Stacks Butcher? He wanted to ask, but this was hardly the time.

From upstairs came the sounds of thumping, struggling and cursing. The constable ascended in a series of fleet bounds. Toby scrambled up after him.

And here, again, the room. The room where Anna had died, where Toby would have been next. Tendrils of smoke still wafted lazily from charred bedcurtains, the peaceful shroud concealed poor Anna, the husks of the vampires lay where they'd fallen, and the Donlins were doing their level, if futile, best to free themselves.

At the sight of the constable, they quit fighting at their bonds. Mrs. Donlin lowered her face in defeat, while her husband began shouting how it was the boy what had done this, the boy, the boy was a killer—

"Save it for the magistrates," Constable Pearce told Mr. Donlin. He went for the opening in the wall, shining the illuminator ahead of him.

In its much better light, Toby saw that the narrow passageway ended in mortar-crumbling brick... the outer wall of an old chimney, where the rest of it was gone and a shaft lined with bolted iron rungs plunged like a black gullet toward the bowels of the house.

The constable leaned over. "Chantal?"

"Down here." Her voice came floating back as if from a great distance. "Arthur... it isn't pretty."

"It never is." Pearce tucked the clerk's help beneath his chin to begin the climb. "You might not want to see this, son," he said when Toby moved closer.

"I don't want to, but I have to," he said. "For... for her, for Anna... I have to see."

The rungs had the cold, dank feel and vague rusty smell old iron often got, a feel and a smell that would linger on the skin long after. But they held secure enough, letting Toby reach the bottom safely. Chimney brickwork became cellar stonework. Liquid made an irregular patter somewhere off unseen. Elsewhere, also unseen, things squeaked and scurried and scrabbled.

The ceiling was a long low arch, with raised alcoves to either side. Decrepit barrels and broken crates filled some of them.

Bones filled others.

So many. So small. So many and so small. White jackstraw piles of them. Curved ribs and rounded skulls. Some still with long tangled strands of hair clinging to them.

Rats crawled over the bone-mounds, searching for and squabbling over any last scraps of skin, sinew, or flesh.

"It's a charnel," Constable Pearce said.

At the far end of the tunnel, the arch widened out into a vaulted room. A lamp had been set on the floor, and its glow outlined two oblong shapes... ornate oak coffins with brass latches and rails... their lids raised, their linings tattered and stained. Around them were some straw pallets and thin blankets, strewn with gritty dirt. A peculiar warm mist hung in the air, a moist bitter vapor that lent an odd contrast to the cellar's chill.

The lampglow also outlined Chantal Noir. Her goggles rested around her neck on their vulcanized gum-elastica strap. Her expression was solemn, almost grim, lending her a stark, pale beauty.

She held the weapon that had been in the harness on her back. Wisps rose and drips fell from its barrel, which looked half like a whistle-vent and half like a firehose nozzle. The rest of it was all tubes and corrugated piping, and some sort of rounded copper kettle-canister.

"Is that a portable hydromatic auto-heat steam gun?" Toby asked, wide-eyed.

Chantal nodded. "And no ordinary steam, at that." She patted the canister, which, Toby saw, was engraved with crucifixes, saints' symbols, and letters that looked to him the sort what he saw on church stained glass windows.

At her feet were three sodden rags of cloth, clumped in puddles of dissolving foamy slime. Toby, as the realization sank in, took a grimacing step back.

The constable went to her and set a hand on her shoulder. She raised her dark gaze to him. "All those children..." A shudder twisted through her body. "If I'd known sooner, if I'd moved sooner..."

"You saved this one," he said, nodding toward Toby.

"There's that. But what becomes of him now?

Toby smothered a sigh. "Back to the gearhouse for me, most likely."

Which wasn't all bad, wasn't so bad. He'd had a good meal, hadn't he? And did he ever have some tale of adventure to tell to the other boys! If any of them believed a word of it. Met the famous Chantal Noir and Constable Pearce? Been menaced by vampires?

Pearce gave Toby a considering glance. "He's clever, he's brave, he's trustworthy."

"Yes, yes he is," said Chantal Noir.

Toby scuffed a foot, blushing.

"He knows gears and machines," Pearce said.

A slow smile lit her face, remaking stark, pale beauty into girlish excitement and delight. "Are you thinking what I think you're thinking, Arthur?"

"Felix did say he could use an apprentice."

"Who's Felix?" asked Toby, turning a puzzled frown from paranormalist to constable and back again.

"My brother," she said, giving a pat to the barrel of the steam gun. "He's an inventor, a bit peculiar, but brilliant. You'll like him."

And Toby broke into a huge, gleeful grin.

THE GARRETTON GHOUL

IN A DARK, COLD PLACE that stank of a slaughterhouse, Alan Harmons opened his eyes. His head throbbed like a rotted tooth. He ached all over.

Where the devil was he?

What the devil had he been up to?

Had he been hitting the gin? No stranger to that, of course, but he'd never in his life wakened with a hangover the likes of this.

Or in a place such as this. Where the devil *was* he?

What *was* that awful stench? Slaughterhouse, he'd thought, before his mind was all the way to consciousness, and a slaughterhouse reek it was… blood and shit, piss and meat, rot and death.

Alan knew the slaughterhouse, had worked there as a boy. Following in the footsteps of his father, uncles, brothers, and cousins. Before the advancements came, the mechanizations, getting more done in less time with a fraction of the manpower, so that most of the Harmons men found themselves out of a job.

He blinked but saw only blackness.

Was he blind?

Dear God, let him not be blind. Anything but that. His eyes, he needed his eyes and his hands. The rest of him, he could do without. Strike him deaf, cripple his legs, *geld* him even, but for the love of all the saints, leave him his eyes and his hands!

As he blinked again, he discovered—with inestimable relief—that he could see after all.

Then he wished he couldn't.

His relief turned to terror. He tried reasoning… then begging. As a shrill and hideously eager whine closed in, he tried screaming.

With the gnashing teeth, and the pain, and the sound of cracking bone, he realized he was going to die.

Moments later, Alan realized he was wrong about that.

It was too late.

Although still conscious, he was already dead.

A talented quicksketch could make a tidy sum in a good spot at Riverfront on a fine, sunny spring Saturday.

Jack Blint was, as it happened, a talented quicksketch.

He also had himself a prime spot staked out, there along the park promenade, just a stone's throw from the hurdy-gurdy gazebo on the greensward, where vendors sold hot snacks from steam-carts and cold drinks from ice-wagons.

Today, being a Saturday in spring but far from fine and sunny, Jack's pockets stayed as empty as his easel, and his mood was fouler than the weather.

In that, he was hardly alone. The chalkarts had long since given up, their colorful tools of the trade no use at all with the pavement gone to puddles. Only a single watercolorist remained, hunched under a tarpaulin shelter to slop at a painting of the river view, drear and bleak, a gloomy grey scene that no one would want to hang in their parlor. The Portnoy brothers, caricaturists both, sat shoulder to shoulder in their matching fisherman's slickers, passing a brown bottle between them as the rain dripped from their hoods.

The last few vendors looked to be packing it in, closing up the folding sides of their steam-carts. The mechanical wonder that was the hurdy-gurdy sat silent, its brass calliope pipes dulled, its dancing clockworks motionless and dispirited. At the stand where bicycles, pedal-craft and velocycles could be rented, the shutters were drawn over dark windows.

No nannies with their young charges picnicked on the grass. No university students gathered under the trees, discussing politics and philosophy. No well-to-do folk strolled the walkways, gentlemen in top hats and ladies with parasols, taking the fresh air. They were where the best money was to be had… what courting swain or new husband could be so heartless as to refuse the flattery of spending a few pence on a portrait of the lovely lady on his arm?

Times like this, Jack on occasion caught himself wishing he'd done like Charcoal Pete and others had done… given it up, gone off to try their fortunes elsewhere. Some went 'round to say their goodbyes, make their well-wishes to their fellows. Others, why, others just went away and never did come back. Left to find work, poor blokes. There were jobs aplenty to be had in the city, jobs that paid rain or shine, indoor jobs where a man could have a roof over his head. Honest labor at an honest wage.

Yes indeed, times like this when he felt fair soaked through from his cap to his boots, Jack Blint did have to admit the prospect had a certain appeal. But he always came to his right senses soon enough. He liked being his own man, answering to no one, having the freedom to come and go as he pleased. That surely was worth more than being cooped up in a factory or foundry long hours at a stretch.

Thunder rolled a slow rumble across the sky, as if a fleet of massive airships moved just above the low-lying clouds. What had been a steady downpour heavied into a sheeting torrent, chopping the slate-dark river's surface into white froth and lashing sodden leaves from the trees.

Jack Blint knew when he was beat. He'd be earning nothing toward his overdue rent today, let alone enough for a tavern meal, a pint or two of stout, and a length of the lace-edged ribbon he'd had his eye on as a surprise for pretty Molly Blossom.

In a trice, he had his kit collapsed and folded all together— easel, stool, the case of art supplies—into a compact barrow-cabinet with a single front central wheel. An expense it had been and that was for certain, but he'd never begrudged it. Over all, he draped and secured the sheet of oilcloth, he'd been sitting under, its corners twine-tied to a bough to make a crude tent. Jack had gotten quite adept at steering this arrangement even through the most bustling crowded streets, and it was a sight easier than bearing the bulk and weight on his shoulder.

The Portnoy brothers nodded at him. Jack nodded back. He flipped up his collar, tugged down the brim of his cap against the rain, and set out away from Riverfront.

The tree-lined greensward gave way almost at once to the city, to grimy brick walls with soot-stained stone cornices, to iron rails embedded in cobblestones with the cable-lines strung above, to chimneys spewing desultory smoke black against grey clouds, to mudwater coursing sluggish in the trash-filled gutters. The lamplighters had been to their task early on this day of premature darkness. Shopfront windows glowed a beckoning welcome. Telegraphy wires hummed and sputtered. A line of edison-bulbs flashed in unison, framing a signboard advertising a talkie-movie that promised explicit scenes of the perils and pleasures of Lost Worlds... which, as far as Jack could determine, consisted of scantily-clad native girls and great toothy lizards. Henry Duchamp's artwork, unless he missed his guess. No one could do menacing monsters like Henry.

The sidewalks jostled with hats, coats, hoopskirts and umbrellas. In the streets, horse-buggies and auto-buggies vied for advantage, cutting ahead of one another if a space opened, or even if it merely appeared likely to. Drivers shouted, laying heavy on their bells, shaking fists. When the shriek-blast of a trolley whistle split the din, they would have to make way of the tracks to let the trolley-car chug through, crammed to capacity and with passengers clinging to the side-bars. Traffic of all sorts was thickest at Ainsleigh Station, where several trolley lines, two elevated train lines, and a substreet line converged.

Jack kept an eye peeled as he passed the station, but could not spot Molly Blossom among the flower girls selling their bundled posies from baskets. He smothered a sigh. Seeing her sweet smile would have brightened his day, it would, but no luck.

He turned toward Garretton, a neighborhood of tall and narrow brownstones that were boarding-houses, rooming-houses and cheap-lodgings. A fairly little room could be had there for fairly little rent. The topmost ones, attics and garretts—hence the name—could be had for even less, and were most prized by artists, poets and playwrights. To languish starving in a garrett, awaiting discovery, fortune and fame, was but part of the dream.

A cold, drafty part of the dream, to be sure... Jack had such a room, so small that he could touch both walls if he stood in the center with his arms outstretched, barely space for a cot and a chair and a tiny table, with a slanted dormer window that rattled in the wind. Or, he had such a room provided he paid up his rent, already almost a week behind, and the landlady was an uncompromising sort.

If he could slip 'round the side and up the fire escape, he might avoid Mrs. Whitte until he had what she was owed.

So thinking, Jack ducked down an alley between his building

and the next one over. Some ragged lines of washing that hadn't been taken in before the storm hit hung soggy between windows. A rat tried to drag a scrap of melon rind into a drainpipe.

The fire escape was no easy thing to ascend even without having to wrestle his barrow-cabinet, but Jack decided it would be worth his while. He hunted about the alley in hopes of finding a stout piece of rope with which to fashion a rough strap.

As he stooped, sudden rushing movement came from behind. Something large and dark, which Jack half-glimpsed before a heaviness fell upon him, rough and coarse and wet. He choked on a vile, suffocating stench.

His senses swooned away, and then Jack Blint knew no more.

"It isn't like him, I tell you, isn't like him not at all!"

Eliza Whitte tried to muster some pity in her soul for the girl, but Lord help her, it was a difficulty. Here she'd been, just about to sit down to a nice pot of tea…"Isn't like any of them, is it? Until it is."

"Not Jack!"

They never did learn, did they? Not until they'd gone and got themselves in the thick of it with some no-account wastrel… thick in debt and thick in the belly, more often than not. Eliza swept Molly Blossom's figure with a practiced eye and decided that if such were the case this time, it was too soon to tell.

A shame, when here Molly had been of goodly enough reputation before being taken in by a charmer the likes of Jack Blint. No doubt he'd told her how she was the loveliest thing he'd ever seen, him with his sketches and his sweet-talk, and fair dazzled her romantic little head.

Oh, Eliza knew *that* tale well enough! Hadn't her own daughter fallen for the very same, letting a good marriage go to ruins over it?

And see where it had gotten her? A wealthy, well-spoken husband, but she'd gone and thrown it all away because of a handsome young painter. A fine way to show her gratitude to the widowed mother who'd scrimped and saved to keep a roof over their heads. Now, instead of easing off the cares of the world, a comfortable dowager welcomed into her son-in-law's home, Eliza remained stuck here working her old fingers to the bone, renting rooms to the very type who'd spoiled everything. While her Abigail was God-knew-where, never bothering to write home even once.

Artists. Artists and poets, what *was* a body to do? They were same one and all. Dreamers. Full of pretty words and pretty pictures.

"So he's run off, he has," Eliza said, flapping a wizened hand. "Owing me more than a week's back rent, the vagabond, and him not the first—"

"He wouldn't! Not without telling me, without so much as a goodbye!"

"Wake up, you goose. Your fancy-boy Jack, he's skipped out." Searching for some greener pastures or following some other flip of petticoat, she shouldn't wonder, but didn't add aloud. That would only set the girl off again, wailing and indignant.

Artists and poets, oh yes, with their big dreams... glad enough to take even the smallest attic rooms, paying more than such modest spaces were worth. When they *did* pay, that was. More often than not, they'd make grand promises based on hoped-for commissions from rich patrons, or offer her pieces of their work, swearing it'd be worth a fortune one day.

Lord knew, she had let herself be swayed by it enough times already. Had a cupboard full of the stuff, here in the suite of rooms that were her residence as well as this office from which she took care of what business there was to take care of. This despite her bitter experience and best intentions, which did only go to show

how persuasive their lies were.

"Something must have happened to him!" insisted Molly.

"What's this now? Something happened to who?"

At the interruption of the nasal, familiar voice, Eliza pinched the bridge of her nose and tried not to groan. "No one knocks where you're from, Mr. Rillings?"

"The door was ajar, so I thought fit to step on in," he said, doing so the rest of the way. A tall, thin man, Roger Rillings was, partial to brown suits and bowler hats. His was a long-nosed ferrety face sporting a gingery moustache. He touched the brim of the bowler. "Mrs. Whitte… and Miss Blossom, isn't it?"

"Something you require, Mr. Rillings?"

"Stopped by to pay my rent, is all, Mrs. Whitte," he said. "Sold another of those stories you said was pulp rubbish. But if this is a bad time—"

"Excuse me a moment," Eliza said to Molly, waving her aside. She fetched up her lodging ledger and set it on the counter as Roger swaggered up. "Not that horrid thing you read me, the one about premature burials?"

"That very one." He grinned over at the girl. "Roger Rillings at your service, miss. Writer, reporter—"

"Pulp rubbish and scandal sheets," said Eliza with a snort.

"And you, you're a friend of Jack Blint's, aren't you? Haven't seen him in a few days. I say, is that who you were talking about as I came in? Couldn't help but overhear."

"Couldn't help but listen at keyholes." Eliza turned the ledger to the correct page.

"He's missing," Molly said, looking glad to have a more sympathetic ear. "Not been seen by you or me or anyone since Saturday. When it rained so heavy? I talked with the Portnoy brothers, and they said as how he was at the park by the river like he is most days, only when the weather turned they saw him leave.

Can't find a soul who's seen him since, and I'm a'right worried about him."

"Have you checked his room?" he asked.

"*I* haven't." Here, the girl shot Eliza a baleful look. "She won't let me."

"You know the rules, Mr. Rillings. No lady visitors allowed. Besides, checked it myself, didn't I? Five flights up, with my bad hip, thinking he might be in there sleeping off a bad drunk. But he wasn't there at all."

"Did you find anything?"

"Not but what he had much to start with. Only some clothes that'd be barely worth the rag-man's bother."

"Hmm." He leaned an elbow on the counter as Eliza scratched the amounts into her ledger. "Remind me, now... Jack, doesn't he have that art-case, the one he rolls around with him?"

"Yes!" Molly said. "Yes, he does, that's him, that's my Jack!"

"*That* contraption!" Eliza shook her head. "Banging it up and down the stairs at all hours of the day or night. Telling me how I ought to have one of those newfangled lifts installed, or a dumbwaiter at the very least... as if I could afford that..."

"Was it in his room? The art-case?"

"Didn't I just say, nothing but some clothes? That case, he took it with him when he left, he took it with him practically everywhere."

"Well, but now, that's the odd bit," Roger said. "Because I'm sure I saw it, or one just like it, in the side alley on Sunday morning."

He felt a tingle at the nape of his neck whenever he was onto something, something with promise. Faint, but electrical, as if a wire-fine teslic coil were being held, or passed, humming, an inch from his skin.

Roger Rillings most definitely felt that onto-something tingle now.

Jack Blint had indeed gone missing. Must have done. Missing, and not of his own volition. That, Roger knew in his gut.

Molly, Jack's girl, insisted he never would have left without saying goodbye to her. On that score Roger held his tongue—she was a ripe little peach, to be sure, but men ran out on ripe little peaches all the time… usually when those ripe little peaches started in with the talk of wedding bells.

What stuck in his mind, though, was the art-case. Roger knew Jack; they'd tipped a few pints together. Jack was one of those to whom Roger went now and again when he had need of an illustration in a hurry. Lurid news stories—tragedies and crimes, the gorier the better—sold more papers when accompanied by a picture. Photographics were best, but the equipment was bulky, and expensive far beyond the means of a freelance like Roger… and the constables tended to not take kindly to anyone nosing about a murder scene with a camera and magnesium-flash. In those instances, an 'artistic rendering' would do, and Jack Blint was a clever hand at turning spoken description into drawing.

The same went for Roger's fictions, which were of the type that featured resurrectionists unearthing cadavers in the dead of night, mad surgeons performing ghastly transplants, weaponized automatons turning against their human masters, and grotesque man-beasts pursuing terrified damsels across misty moors. Jack was not quite as adept at those, but another of their circle of drinking-mates, Henry Duchamp, was. If anything, *too* good. Scary, his stuff was.

No, wherever he went and whatever he did, Jack Blint would not be a man to abandon his art… his livelihood and true love. That case was his prized possession. No way under the heavens would he have up and left it behind, not of his own free will. Not left it in an alley, to be found by a pack of urchins, the contents strewn ruined, the case itself put to use as a jolly-ride in which those grubby juveniles pushed each other at a run up and down the lane.

What set the nape of Roger's neck most to tingling, though, was how in the course of his askings-around, he came to the conclusion it wasn't only Jack who'd gone missing from Garretton of late. Several had, so it seemed, in these past weeks. Ducking out on their debts, with nary a word to their nearest and dearest... not to be seen nor heard from again... not turning up elsewhere secure with some good new job... but simply vanished, vanished without a trace.

"Flowers, sir? Flowers, miss? Posies and violets, fresh this very morning! Flowers for your lady, sir? Flowers, mum? Tulips, daffodils, snapdragons and daisies!"

The words ran themselves by rote, Molly no longer having to think about them as she stood at her usual corner with her basket on her arm. She'd been blessed with a voice that carried well above the babble and din of Ainsleigh Station. A high, sweet, clarion voice, neither shrewish nor piercing. Only when one of the great trains arrived or departed would she be drowned out.

One such readied to leave the station now, an elevated triple-train, with its luxurious glass-roofed high-cars far above the bustling streets, its mid-cars all packed benches and standing room behind round brass-fitted windows like the portholes on a sea-liner, and the forest of poles with handholds and footrails that made up the under-hang suspended beneath.

Molly loathed the under-hang. There, the poorest folk clung for dear life like monkeys on vines, at the mercy of the weather. The women made sure to tuck their skirts between their legs and press their knees tight, or else louts below would have a fine view of their petti-pants. Some crafty souls would carry on rope or chain ladders, affix them to the hangs, and lower them so that their friends could leap, catch on, and ride for free… a dangerous thrift that often led to injury not only for them but for the hapless passers-by below.

The whistle shrieked. The engine bellowed. A steamy downdraft blew newspapers giddy-whirl along the gutters, flapped at garments, made men clutch at their hats and ladies their bonnets. The train pulled away from the platform. The elevated tracks swayed under its massive, moving weight. Its shadow slid, folding and bending, along storefronts. A boy lost his grip on a madly-swinging rope ladder. He fell, flailing, and smacked into the cobblestones. People parted around him without a look.

"Flowers, fine and fresh flowers, get your flowers here!" Molly called. "Carnation for your lapel, sir? Flowers, pretty posies! Sprig of lavender? Yes, mum, thank you, mum!"

"Moll!" A voice even higher than her own cut through the crowd-noise to reach her ears. "Moll, come quick, come and see, you've got to come and see!"

She looked around, spotting her younger sister darting around a bevy of maids-of-work with parcel-laden shopping-carts. "Pansy? What in the world—?"

Yellow braids bouncing, dress and apron hiked to her knees so she could run, fleet little Pansy shot across the street and narrowly missed being run down by a horse-trolley. The driver shook his crop after her, yelling, but Pansy paid him no mind. Her face managed to be both ashen and flushed. Her eyes were wide, though whether with excitement or alarm, Molly couldn't guess.

"Moll! Molly! Molly, quick!" Pansy reached her, seized her by the sleeve, and tugged.

The vigorous jerk almost caused Molly to upend her basket, which would have spilled all her flowers to be trampled or stolen, not to mention the handful of coins she'd earned that day. She clutched it to her bosom and gave Pansy a glare as sharp as a slap. "Careful, you ninny! My flowers!"

"Bother and bugger the bloody buggering flowers!"

"Pansy Louise *Blossom!*" cried Molly.

"Forget them, I meant, forget them, you've got to come quick, now!"

"What is it? Is it Pa? An accident? Ma? The baby?"

Pansy shook her head so fast her braids whipped her cheeks. "It's bodies, Moll! The drill-borers what's been putting in the cablemain down Finchley Street, they found *bodies*! And they say, Moll, I heard someone say how one of them might be Jack!"

At that, Molly did forget the bloody buggering flowers. She flung her basket aside, coins and all. Forgot modesty as well, hiking her own dress and apron to the knee, showing her woolen stockings to anyone who cared to look, as she set off at a full run.

Her heart hammered in ways that had nothing to do with the exertion. It hammered like as if against cold iron, hammered with fear that Pansy might be right. Jack, her Jack, her dear charming Jack... dead? It couldn't be! Something must have happened to him, yes, something dire to make him disappear without a word, and leaving his precious case behind, but... but not this. He'd gotten in a brawl, ended up in hospital, maybe. Prison, even, wrongly accused. Crimped by a sailing-master or airshipman, force-impressed into the crew. Bad as any of those fates were, they could be come back from.

She ran, and Pansy ran hard at her heels, caring not a whit for the angry shouts of whoever they bumped or jostled. Soon they were home to Garretton, then turning onto Finchley Street. It was torn up in a long open trench, scaffolds set everywhere. They were putting in a cablemain, as Pansy had said. When it was finished, it'd bring the electric to Garretton—their mother went faint at the very hope of saving up for a clotheswash—but no more work would be done today, that much was obvious.

The drill-bore machines sat idle in their cradles. Workmen in digger-hats and dirty boots clustered together at the far end of the trench. Junior watch-officers had their hands full with trying to keep back the crush of the curious, the numbers of which swelled by the second as word spread. Those whose upper windows overlooked the trench leaned out to peer unobstructed into the trench. Some seemed to be charging money to let people clamber out on the eaves or slanting rooftops.

"Let me by!" Molly said, attempting to wend her way through the barricade of broad backs and bustles.

It was no use. She could have screamed with despairing rage, but just then a hand caught her by the shoulder. She turned her head to see that man, the reporter, in his brown suit and bowler hat.

"Is it true?" she asked, clawing at his arm. "Is it true, are there bodies, is it Jack?"

"This way," Roger Rillings said. He drove a path, pushing, shoving, ignoring the curses engendered by his actions. Somehow, he brought Molly to the sawhorses marking the edge of the trench.

He pointed, but she did not need him to. Bodies. A piled tangle of them, some still half-buried in the mound of loose earth to one side of the trench. Stiff limbs jutting at strange angles, clothes torn, skin filthy, faces twisted in the most hideous of grimaces.

No one seemed to know what to do. The only actions any of the workers still down there took was to wave away buzzing clouds of flies, and jab sticks at any rat bold enough to venture out for a sniff or a nibble.

Though... some rats... some rats already... already must

have… the gnawed tips of dead fingers… empty eye-sockets… shredded lips and bitten cheeks… and… their chests…

Molly screamed loud enough to hurt. Her hands wavered upward, whether to plead to God or pull out fistfuls of her own hair she had no idea. Then she went over the sawhorse in an ungainly lunge, skirt to her waist, a stocking snagging, a shoe falling off. The reporter reached out but she flung his arm aside.

The sawhorse tipped into the trench. Down Molly went with it, roll-sliding, scraping palms and elbows, getting grit in her teeth. She fetched up at the bottom with a bone-jarring thud. For a moment, she lay stunned, the sawhorse across her middle, blinking up at all the shocked looks.

"Christ's britches, get that girl out of there!" someone ordered.

Heaving the sawhorse aside, Molly scrambled to her feet and ran. More men reached out, workmen, dirt-caked boots and grimy hands. She fought her way past, tripped, lost the other shoe, recovered, ran on, stumbled, and fell on torn-stocking knees beside Jack.

Her Jack. Her poor, dear, dead Jack.

With his chest ripped open and a flyblown, bone-splintered, gaping red-black hole where his heart should have been.

Onto something, onto something indeed! The tingle at the nape of his neck had been right! Not that Roger had doubted it, but the story in all its gruesome detail soon exceeded even his expectations.

Five men dead, dead with expressions of incomparable pain and horror on what was left of their faces, dead with their ribs split and their hearts torn out!

Torn out… and nowhere to be found.

As if taken.

Or worse.

Devoured!

Oh, the morbid thrill! Oh, the horrified panic!

A murderer stalking their streets! No, more than a murderer. A maniac! A lunatic! A cannibal, some savage brute brought back from an expedition to darkest Africa! Or a beast, a wild animal escaped from captivity, with a blood-hunger for human flesh! Or worse yet even than any of those! A monster, a devil, something altogether inhuman and evil on the loose!

The papers went mad for more.

Roger Rillings was delighted to oblige. He investigated reports of neighbors acting suspicious, strange noises, sightings of mysterious figures, missing persons. He interviewed wives claiming their husbands stayed out until all hours of the night and came home shifty-eyed, unwilling to own up to where they'd been. Something as simple as a delayed train or forgotten appointment could stir an anxious frenzy.

The authorities were less than forthcoming, dismissing him with stern 'police business' nonsense. So, what precise information he lacked, he felt obliged to fill in on his own. Didn't he owe it to his readers? It set him up tidily, too, flush with cash, between what the papers paid and having eager listeners line up to buy him drinks in exchange for tidbits... if he embellished here and there, could he really be blamed? A man had to think of his career, his future.

Roger spoke with the friends and families of the dead men who'd been identified, their grief adding a nice personal element to the tragedy—though perhaps nothing would top the description of Molly Blossom wailing over the cold, mangled corpse of her sweetheart. Her now-heartless sweetheart, that was, and were there black-humored jokes about *that*! How when someone said, "eat your heart out," that wasn't *quite* what they had in mind...

Bit of a shame the girl ended up being carted off to Hartsbrook over it. Pretty little thing like her wouldn't fare so well in the asylum. He should check in on her there in a month or two. Be a nice follow-story, that.

But if anything stirred the pot most, it was the whisper of the uncanny. Official brush-offs and 'police business' dismissals aside, Roger picked up plenty of tidbits. For instance, public outcry and demand into investigating the possible supernatural aspects made them call in a paranormalist, as well as various scholars and members of the clergy, to ease the general panic.

Easing the general panic, however, did not sell quite as many papers.

Determined to leave even more of a mark, Roger coined the moniker of 'The Garretton Ghoul' for the killer. Within days it was common use all across the city. People were frightened to leave their homes after dark, lest they be the next victims. Parents wrung good behavior from recalcitrant children with the ominous warnings—don't pinch your sister, Johnny, or we'll put you out tonight and the Ghoul will have you!

Henry Duchamp did up some fine, spine-chilling sketches of a most wicked-foul creature for him, hunched and hairy like an ape, with a pushed-forward muzzle and the snaggled teeth of a rat. In one of the illustrations, it crouched over an eviscerated corpse, shreds of bloody meat hanging from its jaws. In another, a dinner party of bestial maniacs sat around a long table, in formal wear, with a gruesome repast laid out before them on fine china and white linen. Roger had written a fine series of articles to go with those ones, 'Feasts of Flesh' he called them.

He'd even been to Hartsbrook once already in the course of this, to interview three killers who'd dined on their unfortunate victims. One of them compared the taste to that of a rare pork roast, salivating as he said it. And Roger's detractors claimed he was a hack who never did his research? Take that!

This was going to make him famous, it was! Soon, he reckoned, there'd be letters being sent, letters to him and the papers as well as the police, claiming to be from the Ghoul. Hoaxes, pranks, and fakes, but they'd keep the interest running at high tide. Already, Roger'd been flooded with offers from the penny-dreadfuls about his unsold stories, and inquiries about novels!

So, it was with high spirits and a jaunty stride he headed home to the boarding-house late of an evening, whistling to himself. Henry Duchamp was to have a new batch of drawings ready, and Roger could hardly wait to see.

He struggled to wakefulness with a head that felt hammered full of railspikes, and his mouth tasting like the bottom of a boot.

When he made to sit up, he found he couldn't move.

Held down. Held fast. Pinned on some cold, hard surface. His shirt was opened, baring him collar to waist.

His neck creaked as he craned it, trying to see.

A dark shape loomed there, indistinct in the shadows.

Then, light.

A sudden, harsh, flinching glare of light.

"Mr. Rillings? Have you no consideration for the hour? My word!"

"Sorry to disturb you, Mrs. Whitte," he said, mustering his politest smile and hoping she didn't see fit to be offended at the whiskey on his breath. "You haven't happened to see Henry Duchamp tonight, have you?"

"That one?" The landlady, wrapped in her housecoat, with a bed-kerchief tied over her hair, sniffed. "Who's been making those awful pictures to go along with your awful stories?"

Roger nodded. "And which he was to show me the latest, but he doesn't seem to be at home. Did he leave anything for me, perchance? A parcel? A message?"

"Not with me, he hasn't."

"Oh…" Roger shrugged off a twinge of disappointment. He'd been looking forward to those new pieces. "Ah well. Tomorrow's soon enough."

"Unless you think that Ghoul of yours has got him." Eliza Whitte sneered a thin-lipped smile at Roger. "Him being an artist, and all, same as Jack Blint, and Charcoal Pete, and that Harmons fellow who painted the miniature portraits. Isn't that what your Ghoul goes after?"

"Coincidence and numbers," Roger said. "Artists are ten for a penny in Garretton; you can hardly swing a cat by the tail without clouting one upside the head."

"Which some of them could use," she muttered. "Disreputable scoundrels that they are."

Hadn't he had this same discussion with the chaps at the pub earlier? Yet, again, the whiskey compelled him to defend the subject further. "I noticed it, of course, noticed it probably before the police did. There's nothing to it. More artists here than anywhere else in the city. Odds are if you picked any given man at random off the street in Garretton, that's what he'd be. Not strange at all."

"No stranger than suggesting there's some sort of monster in our midst?" She gave him a dark, narrow-eyed look of reproach. "Some devil that goes about pulling men's hearts out by the roots and eating them like a boiled turnip?"

"I'll have you know, they're taking that possibility very seriously," Roger said, with a hint of pride. Taking it seriously because of him and his stories, they were! "Brought in a noted paranormalist to track the Ghoul down—"

"Some tart from over Little Paris way, is what I heard." Eliza huffed, folding her arms beneath her scant bosom. "Educated by the Church, they say, but if she's any kind of a nun then I'm an airship pilot!"

"But it does sell papers."

"Hmf. You and your scare-stories, putting everyone into a panic, taking in a tidy profit off their fear!"

"Pays my rent, doesn't it?" He grinned at her.

"There is that." She looked him up and down. "Better about it than most of these artist-types, you are, at least. And I daresay *you're* not seducing any foolish, impressionable young wives into breaking their husbands' hearts, like my Abigail."

"Ah, God in Heaven, not this again!" Roger groaned. "Your daughter ran off with that portraiter weeks ago. That's old news, Mrs. Whitte. Old news indeed."

Henry Duchamp strained at the buckled straps binding him to the cold metal table, but they held fast. "Let me loose from here, or I'll wring your neck for you, I will!"

No answer.

The lantern suspended above the table had a conical copper shade, directing its light down onto Henry in a bright spot-shine. Squint though he might, the most he could make out of his surroundings were shelves and what looked like work-benches.

An acrid, chemical-cleaner smell hung bitter in the air. It overpowered, but did not erase, an underlying odor of mingled root cellar, sweat, shit, piss, blood, rust, oil and rot.

The dark shadow-shape moved again. Henry caught a glimpse in the backsplash of light, a glimpse that told him little. He saw a waterproof slicker, not unlike the ones longshoremen favored. He saw heavy black vulcanized gloves. He saw a curved sheet of tint-glass, the kind welders wore, down inside the slicker's hood.

"You're the one they call the Ghoul! The one who killed Jack, and Alan, and those others!"

Again, and still, no answer.

The man—it was a man, of that Henry felt certain—moved to the edge of the table. The welder's mask caught a sheen of light, and what with that and the tint-glass, obscured any view of his features.

Gloved hands reached up. Up past the copper-shaded light, manipulating unseen levers, making unseen gears turn. Henry bucked and thrashed but the straps gave him not so much as an inch. Ankles, wrists, and a broad belt clamped across his waist as well... he was trapped, immobile... as whatever contraption this was descended toward him on hinged armatures.

Inside a stainless steel cylindrical barrel were rings of razor-edged metal teeth, three concentric circles of them. When the madman thumbed a switch, an engine whirred. Slowly at first, the bladed rings began to revolve, two clockwise and one widdershins. At the turn of a dial, they sped up, spinning faster and faster, making a glinting, flashing, silvery blur. They gave off a hideous, eager whine that rose in pitch as their speed increased.

"What... what's that?" Henry asked, stammering, sickly sure he already knew the answer. He'd not seen the bodies in person, but he'd heard the talk, and when a man spent his life doing art for the penny-dreadfuls and fright-show posters, he honed his imagination well.

The hooded head gave a satisfactory that'll-do nod. The Ghoul thumbed the switch again, turning off the engine. The revolving blades slowed from a blur to a gradual stop, poised there, toothy, waiting.

"No," Henry said. "Don't do this. You don't as got to do this. We can talk it over, can't we? I've done nothing to you."

The Ghoul lowered the barrel until its end rested against Henry's bared chest. He felt it, a cold circle with countless sharp pinpricks dimpling into his skin. Lifting his head, he could see it as well, indenting the flesh. The shining metal reflected a warped image of himself, distorted as any unflattering caricature the Portnoys had ever drawn.

"No!" Henry blubbered.

He nearly pissed himself with relief when the Ghoul lifted the device away.

But that was only to reposition it.

Over his heart. Directly over his heart, pressing down against that rapid beating.

Henry did piss himself, a warm yellow flood soaking his trousers.

The tint-glass mask leaned down. Henry saw just another warped reflection of his own terror-struck, wild-eyed face.

"Now it's your turn," the Ghoul whispered. "Now you'll know. One by one, you'll all know."

His black-gloved hand thumbed the switch.

The shrill, eager whine swallowed up Henry's desperate scream. The cold circle on his chest became a searing, slicing agony. Blood sprayed up in a dense red mist. The whine's tone changed, deepened, chugged, as the whirring steel teeth met bone. The red blood-mist thickened with flecks and chips that stung Henry's eyes, that spatted hot wet grit into his open, screaming mouth.

The spinning blades bored in deeper. The spraying mist became a dark upwelling.

Inside his chest—*inside* his *chest!*—the device made a cleaving, meaty sound. Henry felt it as much as heard it, and in what dim detached part of his head as hadn't already gone mad, didn't know which was worse, the hearing or the feeling. What next he heard and felt was the popping of gristle, like pulling apart a Christmas goose.

The device drew smoothly up. Henry had a hideous sensation of suction and burble. More blood rained onto him, spouting from the precise round hole, dripping from the plug of meat and bone stuck in the end of the machine's cylindrical barrel.

His exposed heart pulsed to the open air. Henry quivered from shock.

"She liked chilled mint fizzes," the Ghoul said, turning to the worktable. His voice was conversational. Nostalgic. Almost fond.

A whimper gurgled up from Henry's throat.

"I'd make them for her in the evenings. Frozen mint syrup, and gin, carbonated with a gazogene. I grew mint in a kitchen window greenhouse just so she could have a sprig of it, fresh, with each glass. Oh, she was beautiful."

The Ghoul turned back, holding a small but heavy-looking canister. He'd pushed up the tint-glass, revealing pleasant-enough features. Older. Lined. Respectable. Badger-grey tufted eyerows and muttonchops. A dead blankness in the eyes.

"I kept the syrup in one of these," he said. He unscrewed the canister's top. A chill wispy exhalation issued out. "Marvelous, what they can do these days, isn't it? Have you ever had your heart broken, you wretched whoreson of an artist?"

Henry, whimpering and gurgling, stared at him uncomprehendingly.

"You might not think it *can* break," said the Ghoul. "I thought so too, at first. After all, it's muscle, not porcelain. Muscle can be crushed, sliced, minced, any number of things… but not so readily *broken*, if you take my meaning." He tipped the canister.

A frost-smoking stream of liquid poured into Henry's gaping chest. Cold white clouds boiled up and over. A white numbing flash doused him from within. His breath locked.

"And yet, that is how I felt. As if my heart had been torn from my breast and shattered before my very eyes."

So saying, the Ghoul stuck his black-gloved hand into the hole. He yanked. With a brittle crackle, a fist-sized lump tore free. Rimestreaked red, like a handful of bloody ice, like a chunk of raw and frozen meat.

He showed it to Henry, then struck it against the edge of the table, smashing it to pieces.

"There, Abigail," Henry heard him say as the world faded to nothingness. "There's another one for you…"

UNFATHOMABLE

LOW CLOUDS HUNG DARK in a darker sky, the damp wind promising rain. The sea stretched calm, smooth as slate.

From the galley came laughter and jovial conversation, the clink of crockery as dishes passed hand to hand. They'd put in a fine day's fishing, pulling in one full net after another, and were in good cheer.

The captain would join them soon enough, but it was his custom to enjoy his before-supper pipe at the privacy of the rail, weather permitting. Lars Gunderson puffed contentedly on the carved meerschaum, exhaling streams of sweet-smelling smoke.

A pipe was a simple pleasure and a timeless one, if all but unfathomable to the younger members of his crew. In this day and age, with factory-made cigarettes pennies by the carton, Lars wondered if his was but one more dying fancy.

They did want it quicker and cheaper than anything, didn't they? Quicker, cheaper, bigger, faster, mechanized, automated, all these modern advances and newfangled gadgets… available next-to-immediately, manufactured, ordered from a catalog, delivered… it'd be the end of hard-learned skills, craftsmanship, experience, wisdom…

Would his ancestors have felt the same? Theirs had been a glorious age of exploration and plunder, bold warriors turning dragon-headed prows toward unknown horizons, nothing but oar and sail. To those bygone seafarers of old, even this humble fishing vessel would have been an amazement beyond their ken. Yet, compared to the immense steam-liners or the submersibles that churned the oceans with their turbines, the *Duck* was a relic, a laughable little tub.

A tub, she might be, and even laughable… round and fat-bottomed, pitch-sealed wooden planks, creaky, leaky… but she was his own, paid for free and clear, and she regularly turned him a profit while other captains stood neck-deep in debt.

He patted the rail, smiling around the pipestem gripped in his strong teeth. Yes, his *Duck* was a stout enough old dowager, faithful and true. The crewmen could—and did, Lord knew it—go on about how much more profit they'd see if she was given an overhaul, but it was their greed and their laziness talking.

A glow and a rumble from above caught his attention. He turned his gaze skyward, scowling. The steam-liners were bad enough but these air-ships, bloated whales of the heavens, beaming their spotlights down without so much as a by-your-leave…

But he had never seen lights such as this, and the noise was like no engine-screws he'd ever heard. Almost as soon as he realized this, the glow turned fearful-bright, and the rumble became a roar. Crewmen came rushing from the galley, some with mouths still full, even as Lars shouted for all-hands.

Something tore though the clouds, ripping them apart like threadbare cloth. It streaked down and across at an angle, plunging from the sky. The fierce light—it was yellow-blue, not green, in no way green, but yellow-blue—flared with terrible, dazzling flashpowder brilliance.

The men cried out, averting their faces, shielding their eyes.

Only Lars, still staring up, saw how through this long tattered rent in the cloud-cover it appeared the very night sky itself roiled. He glimpsed stars, stars he knew as well as any sailor, stars that should, even in so fleeting a glimpse, have been familiar in their patterns... but weren't. They hung distorted, discolored, as if viewed through a thick sheet of tint-glass.

Flaring, blinding, yellow-blue! That relentless headsplitting roar! Men screamed and scrambled and fell. Lars clung to the frame of the wheelhouse door, aware in an instant of absurdity that he'd lost his pipe.

The sheeting flame and arcing electricity was reminiscent of St. Elmo's Fire but at the same time uncannily *not* St. Elmo's Fire. Its reflection tracked a blurred smear on the water. The two, the source and its reflection, made a narrowing convergence...

Lars shouted again, unheard, and too late anyway. Even had there been anything they could do, there was no time.

It hit.

The source met its reflection, and both vanished in the sudden swallowing gulp of the sea, which went from slate-smooth and calm to a pond into which someone had hurled a boulder. A violent upheaval marked the point of impact, a bulge of dark water surging out in an expanding ring. A tremendous spout shot up from the center, a towering spire to rival any skyscraper, spraying salt foam.

The *Duck* dipped and tossed at the mercy of the ruthless forces. Lanterns swung in mad arcs. Charts and instruments flew about. Lars held fast, still shouting useless orders.

Drawn inexorably into the tidal pull, the tubby ship swept up the swell's steep curve. She tilted until her snub-nosed prow pointed at the ragged clouds and roiling stars. The catch in the holds shifted backward, a huge, wet, slapping weight.

Lars felt his feet lift from their purchase, a sickening sensation of floating that made his stomach roll. He saw a froth of whitecaps edging the curling top of the monstrous wave, looming high above the poor little *Duck*.

Then, down it came, the wall of water, a crashing tumult of doomsday.

Dockside was a city in its own right, a city of wharves and warehouses, shipyards and shipping offices, markets and canneries. A thick stink comprised of tar, oil, brine, and fish predominated. A dozen languages could be heard in as many strides… sailors, merchants, travelers and immigrants going about the business of daily life.

Constable Arthur Pearce attracted no small notice as he made his way toward Pier 23, some of it speculative as if to size him up for robbery despite a bearing that proclaimed him as a man of the law. His clothes were understated in their fine tailoring but by no means cheap or shabby, and the trunk he wheeled behind him was of good quality.

He was not of imposing height or brawn, and the slight stiffness of gait given to him by a clockwork-prosthetic leg disguised a natural litheness and speed. His blond hair, fair skin and keen grey eyes further added to the impression of him as an intelligent man, a learned one, but perhaps not the most formidable of opponents.

The truth of this, of course, often came as a most unwelcome surprise to anyone who meant him mischief.

However, this day, no one chose to take the chance, and he reached the end of the pier unchallenged. A glance at the magnificent gleaming bulk of the *Thetis* committed countless details to memory—the forward sweep of its prow, the brass hull-plates held by bolts big as a child's fist—but what most held his gaze was the shapely figure of a young woman in traveling frock and hat, watching other passengers jockeying for position to embark.

"Miss Noir," he said, stepping up behind her.

She turned, ebony-black ringlets framing an alabaster complexion. "Why, Constable Pearce! What ever are you doing here?"

"Looking for you, as it happens."

"I thought you were out of the country."

"I only just got back."

"And you've found me already."

"To be fair, I had help. Your brother told me what you were up to."

"Ah. Dear Felix. You had to see for yourself to believe it?"

"Not at all. I know you too well."

"I hope you haven't come to talk me out of it," she said.

"As I said, I know you too well."

"So does Mother, and that never stops her from trying."

"I suppose she would be more at ease if you had a steady, stay-at-home trade."

Her ruby lips quirked into a smile. "Like hers?"

"Touché," he said, clearing his throat.

"Besides, my trade treats me rather well. Look, I've even had cards done." She presented one to him.

"*Things Man Was Not Meant To Know? Send a Woman! Chantal Noir: Paranormalist—Troubleshooter—Adventuress.*" He raised his eyebrows. "Indeed?"

"Oh, hush!" Laughing, she made to reclaim the card, but he deftly held it out of her reach. "Arthur!"

"This one's for my records," he said, tucking it into his pocket. "If I should need to contact you."

"If you should need to contact me," she said, "you'll just ask Felix again."

"He might not be in."

"He never goes out." She nodded in the direction of the gangway, where porters from the *Thetis* struggled with a luggage while a well-dressed banker tapped his foot and made an ostentatious show of checking his gold-plated timepiece. "So, you heard about the incident?"

"Mysterious object lights up the sky for hundreds of miles around, slams into the North Atlantic? Expedition team dispatched to investigate? Absolutely. Wouldn't miss it."

She tipped her head. "It isn't a ferry crossing; you can't just purchase a ticket."

"No, but I can use my credentials and connections." He touched his hatbrim to her, then moved to hail a man in a peacoat who'd just stepped onto the *Thetis'* over-deck. "Captain Burnham? Arthur Pearce. I wired you this morning—"

"The constable, yes!" The captain, a barrel on bowed legs, bald and bare-headed with a badger's brush of beard to make up for it, had a gruff but jovial booming voice. "And a Pearce, right enough, the very image of old Gussy or I'll be dunked in it!"

"Old Gussy?" Chantal Noir inquired, amused.

"My grandfather," Arthur said. "Augustus Pearce. He was a mariner, and—"

"And I sailed with him, I did, when I was no more than a pip of a lad!" boomed Burnham. "Started me off as a powder monkey, taught me everything I know. Now here I am, captain of my own nautilus! Come aboard! Come right aboard!"

Right aboard, as it happened, wasn't feasible, but the porters went to work with a will and soon enough had the various passengers and their bags sorted. Arthur went to his stateroom to unpack, change clothes, and perform minor matters of maintenance on his clockwork leg.

The *Thetis* was no trans-oceanic luxury cruise vessel the likes of the *Star of Cairo* or the *Gibraltar Empress*; her quarters were by necessity much smaller, less grand than those seagoing pleasure palaces. They lacked balconies, and had brass-ringed unopenable portholes instead of panoramic sliding windows.

A series of megaphonic speaking tubes served each deck and the public areas of the *Thetis*. Announcements from the bridge, gramophone-recordings in dulcet female tones, broadcast from it. The messages welcomed the passengers aboard, instructed them on the uses of various amenities such as the light fixtures and en suite washcabinets, informed them where to locate the dining room and at what ship's-hours meals would be served, and so on.

From deep within the craft, a steady thrumming began as the propulsion turbines powered up. It intensified until Arthur's toiletries jittered and chittered together upon the vanity shelf beside the mirror.

"Ladies and gentlemen," came another announcement. "it would be our honor and privilege to invite you to the forward observatorium lounge, to best experience our departure."

Arthur tucked a clutch-shockgun into a holster at the small of his back. Not that he expected to need the weapon, but, better than being caught unprepared. Armed as well with a fresh ledger and a fountain pen, he let himself out into the narrow hall and saw Chantal Noir emerging from her own cabin.

She had changed from the traveling frock into more casual attire... too casual for some, perhaps, with knee-buckle knickerbockers in lieu of a skirt. Her ankle-boots and bodice were black with brass stays and fastenings. Around her slim throat was a cameo on a silk ribbon, and her ringlets were piled atop her head, affixed with a gearwheel comb in a way artfully designed to appear artless.

"You look more like a clerk than a constable," she said, not without approval.

He patted the leather-bound ledger. "As I'm here in no official capacity, I thought I might keep some notes."

"Are you ever anywhere in no official capacity?"

"Officially?"

She laughed and held out her arm. "If you'd be so kind as to escort me to the observatorium, Mr. Pearce?"

"Delighted."

The forward observatorium lounge was, by far, the most impressive feature of the *Thetis*. Its ceiling was a geodesic dome of metal lattice-frames and triangular glass windows treated with an exterior opacity sheen. Seen from outside, this dome resembled a multifaceted, semi-translucent gemstone above the brass prow. Seen from within, it soared up and overhead in an enclosing insectile-eye crystalline bubble, offering a panoramic view.

Currently, sunlight streamed in, and the air had a pleasant greenhouse warmth. Once the *Thetis* began to dive...

Chantal glanced at Arthur. He read the familiar mixture of anticipation, trepidation, and devil-may-care excitement in her dark eyes.

A single decorative pillar rose from the center of the floor to the topmost point of the dome, all ornate metalwork and tiny bulbs that were currently unlit but promised a spiraling spray of twinkling illumination later. Around the base of this pillar were curved tables, linen-draped, set with a champagne bruncheon buffet. Two white-jacketed stewards stood attentively nearby.

"I say!" said a youthful voice. "This is rather a something, isn't it?"

They turned. The new arrival, goggling upward, was a tall and lanky young man in crisp shirtfront, pressed trousers and brocade waistcoat. His face had an open, affable character. His brownish hair was combed sleek with pomade. An attempt to convey maturity by cultivation of a moustache was unconvincing at best.

"Is it safe, do you think?" he went on, with his neck craned. "The glass and all, that is, once we're under? Hate to be going along and *ckkkk*—" He etched a jagged cracking line in midair. "—before you know it we're knee-deep in sharks or the like. Or jellyfish. Ruddy awful blighters, jellyfish. They sting, don't you know."

"For one thing," someone else said from the doorway, "if the glass does give way while we're at any sort of a depth, sharks and jellyfish would be the least of your worries."

This arrival proved to be a woman, though her choice of attire —corduroy trousers, a chambray workshirt, and a loose over-vest bulging with pockets—was even more casual than Chantal's. Her age could have been anywhere from hard-worn forty to hale and hearty seventy. She had masses of wiry grey hair, a creased and sun-browned face, and the blunt-nailed, scar-fingered hands of a laborer.

"Oh, the chill, you mean?" asked the pomaded young man. "The what-do-you-call-it, hypothermia? Or are you talking about drowning?"

"Won't matter." The woman was short, stocky, not soft enough to be rotund, and walked with heavy, clomping strides. "You wouldn't live long enough to drown."

"Here, now, no call for that! Because I can swim. I may not be good at a whole lot else, but, I *can* swim."

She picked up a custard-filled puff pastry from a serving tray, and held it out. "The weight of the water, laddy-buck. Squish you in an instant, it would, just like… that!" And she clenched her fist around the pastry, custard squirting through her fingers.

"Would it?" he cried.

The woman ate the flattened pastry, licked custard from her hand, and wiped her palm on her trouser leg. "But it won't, not if I'm any judge. Take a closer look at those windows. Double-paned, and the space between them filled with… pressurized etheric gases, I'll warrant."

"You'd be right," Captain Burnham said, coming in. "Sound as a dollar-pound to three thousand fathoms, is my sweet *Thetis*!"

"Three thousand!" the young man exclaimed, agog all over again. "That must be quite a lot!"

Chantal, meanwhile, addressed the stocky woman. "Professor Edison? Edwina Edison? Of the university scientifics department?"

"No relation to the other Edison," the woman said, giving her a sticky handshake. "Are you a student?"

"I sat in on one of your Egyptology seminars last year. Chantal Noir—"

"Paranormalist. Well, we'll put your lot out of work soon enough, no offense."

"Out of work?" asked Arthur, suppressing a smile at Chantal's astonishment.

"Pff. The paranormal, the supernatural, myths, legends… only means we haven't figured the science, yet. And you are?"

"Arthur Pearce. Constable Pearce."

"Constable, is it? Going to arrest a meteorite, are you, constable?"

"Meteorite?" The young man, who had been listening to Burnham wax eloquent about the *Thetis'* engines, rejoined them now. "Is it? Well, that'll be a letdown to the aunties, I must say. They're half convinced it's Star Wormwood or some such, a sign, a herald of the apocalypse. Why I'm here, isn't it?"

"I don't believe we've met," said Arthur.

"Haven't we? So sorry. Wilmott. Reggie Wilmott. Sent by my aunties, don't you know. Devoted believers in the unfathomable, they are. Seances, little green men, all that rot."

"And they sent *you*?" Chantal asked. Arthur nudged her with an elbow.

Reggie waved a hand. "They don't travel so much these days, getting on in years as they are, long in the tooth and whatnot."

Professor Edison snorted and quaffed a glass of champagne.

"Always after me to make something of myself," he continued, rolling his eyes. "As if card games and racing yachts aren't enough to keep a chappie happy? But, if a body's got to have an adventure, might as well go in style, right-oh? Far better this than trudging through some god-forsaken jungle where there's mosquitoes big as barn owls." He leaned toward Arthur in a chummy man-to-man way. "Besides, gets me away from those dreadful dinner parties, you know the sort, where they sit you by some girl with a 'wonderful personality'?"

Other passengers had come in as the *Thetis* glided out to sea, waves lapping at the lowest edge of the observatorium glass. They left Dockside and the cityscape with its smokestacks and high bridges behind. The usual bruncheon rounds of mingling and introductions went on over tea and coffee, juices and champagnes, pastries, fruit salads and cold cuts.

Most were experts in various disciplines. One, Lord Smedley, was an energy baron, investing in everything from coal and steam to oil and electrics. His secretary was of the humorless and severe high-collared sort, her squint either due to suspicion or the extraordinary tightness of her hair bun. General Thomsfield was ex-military, square of shoulder, square of jaw. The dark-suited pair who kept to the fringes might as well have sported governmental insignia for lapel pins.

"— the paper you and your late husband presented, the one theorizing a passage to the center of the earth from Australia—" someone said to Professor Edison, who was piling sliced cheese and roast beef between pieces of buttered toast.

"Hubie and that damned red rock, rest his soul…"

A scholar with the haunted look of someone who spent far too much of his time in dank library archives wanted to discuss non-Euclidian architecture with Chantal. "Particularly as it pertains to churches, temples, and houses of worship…"

Reggie Wilmott, munching sugared dates, listened to the engineers arguing the feasibility of Verne's 'moon-gun' and lunar colonies. "Fancy that!" he remarked to the company at large. "The moon!"

A woodwind threnody resonated through the speaking-tubes, followed by the female voice. "We will now commence descent. All crew, dive stations, dive stations please."

The sound and feel of the turbines changed. The water that had been lapping along the lower edges of the panes climbed as the *Thetis* began to submerge. Waves broke against the front, parted, rushed over the glass in foamy frills and swirls. A loose streamer of kelp undulated past.

A hush fell over the assembled passengers. Arthur Pearce found himself standing beside Chantal Noir, or found her standing beside him, without quite knowing which of them had moved. Drinks and delicacies went forgotten as faces upturned to watch the sea rise to close over their heads.

If their view of the sunlit sky through the faceted dome had been as to looking out from the heart of a diamond before, the diamond first lost some of its clarity to occlusion and blur… then a tinge of color crept in… diamond to aquamarine… to blue topaz glimmering with rays of gold…

A discomfort in his ears proved easily allayed by stretching his jaws, as the earlier announcements had informed him. Arthur noticed others doing the same, even as they stood transfixed by the deepening jeweler's spectrum above them.

Next came the rich, rare hue of a Ceylon emerald, with the sun a liquid bright rippling starpoint distant in it. He felt a touch as Chantal leaned against him, and looked down to see her gazing raptly upward. The colors played in her eyes, tinted her fair skin. Although he had seen her in many strange, uncanny, and even terrible situations before, he had never seen her with such an expression of wonder, almost childlike in its purity.

Emerald to sapphire… and darker… midnight sapphire… and without realizing or intending to he had slipped an arm around Chantal, as her hand settled soft upon his chest.

The last hint of light lingered like a mirage, or lingered only in imagination that could not last… and then even that was gone. Gone, and the *Thetis* rode through inky blackness more complete than the darkest night.

Silence held.

It seemed no one even breathed, or as if no one else were even there.

Utter silence. Utter darkness.

Then, by the doing of some unseen crewman, the myriad of tiny bulbs set into the central pillar winked on. A ribbon-tube of greenish-blue neon gases outlined the room. As their vision adjusted, the shapes of their fellow passengers once again became discernible.

Arthur became keenly aware of the intimate closeness of their pose. Chantal, at the same moment, also discovered this. They stepped apart with quick grace, almost like dancers. If a blush tinged her cheek, he could not tell by this eerie lighting… which meant, to his relief, that neither could she tell the same of him.

Then the silence was broken. And it was of course broken by the exuberant voice of Reggie Wilmott.

"Spec-*tac*!" he cried, bursting into wild applause. "Bravo, what a show! That alone makes it *well* worth the price of admish, hey-what?"

Chantal Noir had to agree, it was indeed some show; she'd seen some odd things but never seen the like.

The show was, as Captain Burnham explained, why he started his voyages by day. The Atlantic was vast, but fairly empty. Even with the *Thetis'* exterior illuminaries on, there wasn't much to look at most of the time.

Oh, there'd be schools of fish now and then, he told them. Whales, particularly during their migrations. Sharks, yes. Jellyfish, yes, sometimes thousands of them drifting together in pallid quivering swarms.

But, he said, it wasn't until the real depths, toward the ocean floor, they'd behold sights the likes of which folk on land could scarcely imagine.

Mountain ranges that put the Himalayas to shame, and trenches so deep the Grand Canyon would look a mere sidewalk crack by comparison... vents of scalding water and undersea smokestacks billowing sooty gas-bubbles... swaying forests of tube-worms each twice the height of a man... balloonlike fish aglow with their own inner radiances... spider-crabs bigger than trolley cars, their spindly, elongated legs moving with a jointed precision the finest clockwork figures couldn't match...

"Sea serpents?" Reggie asked. "Giant squids, aren't there? Mermaids? Shipwrecks? Sunken cities, lost civilizations and whatnot?"

"We aren't here for any of those," Lord Smedley, the energy baron, replied in a curt tone. "Put together your own expeditions, if that's what you're after."

They'd all taken seats around a conference table. The polished tabletop was littered with charts, maps, diagrams, books, and papers.

Arthur Pearce sat next to Chantal. His presence here was a surprise, a not unpleasant one by any means, but that earlier moment had caught the both of them off-guard. He made notes in his precise hand as the various experts reiterated the known facts of the case—something had cut a fiery streak across the sky, plummeted into the sea, capsized a fishing boat, and sunk into the deep.

"So," said Lord Smedley. "An object of substantial size, apparently of non-terrestrial origin and composition—"

"A rock." That from General Thomsfield.

"A space rock," said an engineer.

Thomsfield and the taller of the dark-suited governmental types shared a "we'll see about *that*" glance, clinging to their pet theory that an enemy nation had launched the object, perhaps from one of Verne's 'moon-guns.'

Lord Smedley rapped his ring on the table's edge. "The initial sighting was reported by several ships, as well as a research station in Iceland, all of whom reported compasses and other pieces of equipment gone haywire. That indicates—"

"Suggests," said Professor Edison.

"Suggests," Smedley amended, sneering, "some form of energy field, perhaps electromagnetic in nature, perhaps teslic, gaseous—"

"Or arcane," said Gabriel Marlecroft, the pale scholar. "At the moment it appeared, many notable mystics were disturbed by visions, omens and premonitions."

"Seems dodgy, if you ask me," Reggie said. "You'd think, wouldn't you, that a premonition would come *before* an event. In the very word, isn't it?"

Smedley's secretary, whom Reggie had already spent a portion of the bruncheon trying unsuccessfully to chat up, aimed a scowl at him that would have withered anyone else. His response was an amiable, even daffy, grin.

"Are you saying it's a power source?" The speaker, a portly banker with imposing white muttonchops and a more imposing cigar, puffed an indulgent smoke ring. "Is that what this is about, Smedley? A potential new fuel? Harnessing it, patenting it, charging for it, making a fortune?"

"Another fortune," Arthur murmured to Chantal. "Which would make, how many? Six?"

"At least."

Smedley ignored the banker. "Miss Philips?" He nodded to his secretary. She brought over a map marked with several lines and circles. "After plotting and comparing the trajectories, we've determined these as the most likely locations—"

"Begging your pardon, your lordship," Captain Burnham said, his booming voice rolling through the room, "but there's someone you could do to hear from first."

A man in a cableknit sweater came in, ducking his head in the manner of someone familiar with the confined quarters of seagoing craft. He stood of medium height and build, his hair grey-shot and shaggy, his skin leathery, his cheeks grizzled with stubble.

But his eyes... Chantal quelled a shiver at the bleakness of the man's eyes. They were dull blue stones at the bottom of sunken hollows. Gabriel Marlecroft, across the table from her, lifted his chin in a sagacious nod.

"This is Captain Gunderson," Burnham went on. "His was the fishing boat as was there when it hit. He can give you the eyewitness of it all."

Gunderson took one of the remaining chairs. He tossed back enough spirits at a gulp to raise impressed eyebrows from Reggie. His bleak gaze roved around the table, without seeming to register much recognition of his audience. Then he finished the drink, and began talking. He told them what he'd seen, what he'd heard, what happened that night. He told them how a looming wall of water bore down on his poor little *Duck*.

His coarse, scarred fisherman's hands were folded on the table.

Chantal noticed how, as he spoke, the topmost clenched upon the bottommost until the knuckles went white from the strain.

"I thought sure we were done for," he said. "We'd be swamped, scuttled, dashed to pieces. But she weathered it, our *Duckie*, weathered that wave like it was no more than a ripple in a washbasin. I'd like to see any of these newfangled ironclads or brassyhulls do that!"

An engineer stirred, but only grunted as Professor Edison bumped his ribs.

"The men, my crew," said Gunderson, "we could hardly believe it. Not a soul lost... battered about some, scraped, bruised... everything not nailed down thrown about or washed overboard... but not a soul lost. The *Duck* brought us through."

"Huzzah for that!" said Reggie. "Good show!"

"As we went about making her secure, seeing to the wounded, salvaging what we could... the new lad, Jim, he leans over the side and yells how he can see it, the glow of it, how it's getting bigger, how it's coming back up."

"That's impossible," said the engineer who'd started to protest before.

"So we told Jim," Gunderson said. "He'd have none of it, though, until we went and had a look for ourselves. And damned if the sonofawhore wasn't right!" He spared an apologetic grimace for the sake of the ladies. "We all saw it, the glow, yellow fire burning under the water, impossible, aye, impossible as can be, but there it was, and rising fast. Huge. Ten times the size of a whale, if it was an inch, a bloody island in its own right, popping to the surface like a cork."

"Devilish exciting, don't you think, Miss Philips?" Reggie beamed at the secretary, but her squinting attention remained on Gunderson.

"I called for the men to hold on," he said. "It wasn't directly below us, off to our starboard side, but I knew the waves would have another go at swamping us. You could see how the water belled up, where the thing pushed the sea ahead of it. The waves did try, but our good *Duck* weathered them again. When all was calmed…"

He described how the enormous object had floated there, festooned with kelp, rivulets of sea water sluicing off it, hissing and steaming from its own heat.

"Rocks don't float," General Thomsfield said.

Professor Edison snorted. "Some do. Pumice, a type of volcanic rock—"

"Right-oh, I know just the stuff!" said Reggie. "Knew a bloke had a bit of it, carried it around in his pocket, looked like stone but floated pretty as you please. Won him a lot of bar bets, that trick."

"Was it porous?" At Gunderson's blank look, the professor elaborated. "Full of holes, like a sponge, or a piece of coral."

He nodded. "Aye, mum. That's just how it was. Still aglow in places with that yellowish flame, sputtering here and there with those bluish sparks."

"An energy field," Lord Smedley said, vindicated. "A power source."

"We'd none of us seen the like." Gunderson directed another bleak-eyed stare around the table. "What we should have done, having escaped death by a hair already, was gone and gotten ourselves well away. The men, though… young, most of them, and greedy… took it into their heads this could be a valuable find."

"Absolute cert," Reggie said. "Wasn't there some caliph or rajah, bought a falling star on auction at Harbury's? Paid a fortune for it!"

The term 'falling star' elicited winces from the scientists, but, Chantal knew, the rest was true enough. Whether the object contained precious metals, was of mineralogical interest, was an energy source as Smedley maintained, or was simply a curiosity that could be exhibited, the crew of the *Duck* had not been wrong.

"You went closer," she said. "Your men, they went... ashore? aboard? Whichever. They wanted a better look. And you let them go. You were so glad to be alive, so relieved, you told yourself what could be the harm? So, you let them go."

Gunderson hung his head. "More than that, miss. Worse than that. I sent them."

Lars allowed none of the crew to set foot upon it until it had cooled so that no more steam arose, eager though they were to explore and gather keepsakes as proof of their find.

He cautioned them to keep their distance from the spots that glowed, burned or sparked... and to use their wits in choosing where to lodge hooks and hammer pitons for the securing of the tow-lines.

It would be slow going and clumsy, but if they could haul it like a barge, bring it into port...

"So much as a hint of trouble," he told them, "and you're to hie yourselves back with all speed."

When he first heard the screams, he mistook them for whoops and cheers, jubilation. They'd found treasure... gold, jewels...

No.

Men gladdened by discovery did not make such sounds.

Lars rushed from the wheelhouse to the rail. He saw none of his crew, nor any of the lights they'd taken. The ship's lanterns showed only ropes and chains stretching across the gap, where rubber-ringed drums buffered the wooden hull from scraping.

His shouts went unanswered by anything but more screams, screams of pain, terror, agony and anguish.

And there was another sound, a grating rumble, a grinding

crack like the splitting of a mountainside. Waves heaved in a disturbed sloshing and slapping. Gritty fractures raced in jagged paths over the strange, rough stone. Shards and pebbles skittered down its slopes, bounced, rained into the sea and floated there the way breadcrumbs floated strewn on the surface of a lake.

He scrambled over the rail and leaped, landing badly. An ankle twisted. He spilled full-length, clothes tearing, abrasions stinging his skin.

No sooner had he regained his feet than a tremor beneath them sent him stumbling again. He pushed up and ran on, ran on toward voices shrieking for God, wailing for their mothers and sweethearts, pleading for help.

Ropes creaked and chains clanked, snapping taut. The entire island shook as if wracked from within by jolting blows.

The sea around the immensity of rock began to burble, to gurgle, to bubble and glug. Wet gusts like whalespouts coughed up, filling the air with spray.

It was taking on water, Lars understood. Taking on water, the way a barrel punched with holes would, and when enough of its hollow spaces filled…

Half the island dipped down while the other half tipped up, a horrible slow wallowing grandeur to the movement. Lars thought of an upended turtle struggling to right itself, or a fat old woman lolling and rolling her bulk as she tried to get out of a bath.

He scrabbled for purchase, hardly caring how his hands bled, how a fingernail ripped off at the quick and another splintered. No longer flat on the rugged ground, he clung to a slope, clambering up a steepening precipice.

A rope broke, the ends whipping through the air. Lars twisted his head around and saw that the rest of the lines held, held even as the rock they were affixed to dunked lower into the surf… dunked lower, pulling the fishing boat's prow down and down…

waves surging over the sides, flooding across the deck.

The slope was rapidly becoming a cliff… it would teeter at some inexplicable balancing point and then it would go over… slamming down atop him, crushing him into the sea…

"Then it all went black," Gunderson said. "I don't remember anything else."

The way he spoke, and, more, the way he fixed his gaze upon his hands as he did so, made Arthur Pearce conceal a frown.

"I must have been flung clear when I lost my grip," he continued. "When I came to, it was to find myself adrift, hanging onto a buffer-drum. No idea how I got there."

"And the object?" Lord Smedley asked.

"Your men?" asked the general. "Your ship?"

"Gone. Just gone. Some flotsam, nothing more. But, what you need to take into account what with your plotted trajectories as you're thinking where to begin your search, is how the current moved along that damnable rock half the night. It didn't sink where it struck, you see."

Two engineers and Professor Edison slapped their foreheads. There followed a flurry of the scientechnical—jargon, calculations, comparisons of charts and consultations of instruments, meteorological reports and tide-tables.

"I say, old salt," said Reggie, turning to the fisherman. "You did have a rough time of it, didn't you? I say! Lucky escape for you, pity about your crew of course. Must admit, I'm wild to hear how you survived, another boat come along and pluck you from the drink, hey-what?"

"Later." The professor shouldered the eager youth aside. "What was your approximate position, Captain?"

As the discussion raged on, those of them not immediately of useful contribution returned to the lounge area of the observatorium. Small cut-crystal gaslamps had been lit during their absence, adding a golden shimmer to the eerie ambiance.

If not for the constant thrum of the engines—a sensation almost more felt than heard—Arthur might have believed the *Thetis* was immobile, at complete rest. When he went to the glass and peered out, he could only barely discern, or imagined he could, undulant fluid motion in the unfathomable darkness beyond… beyond the doubled panes, and beyond the ghostly reflections of himself, the lounge, and his companions.

"What do you think he's not telling us?" Marlecroft asked.

"Good question." Chantal perched on the arm of a chair, idly swinging a foot, unmindful of both the disapproving glance her stocking-clad shapely calf earned from Miss Philips and the appreciative ones it earned from the others.

"He did seem to be somewhat less than fully forthcoming with his tale," said Arthur.

"You mean there's more to the story?" Reggie strolled over from the depleted buffet table, having scrounged up more sugared dates. "And that grump of a professor tossed us out on our ears before we got to the exciting conclusion?"

"The man said he could not remember," Miss Philips said. "Do you suspect he was insincere?"

"Perhaps his lack of memory is for a reason," Marlecroft said. "Something else must have happened. Perhaps he was made to forget."

"It *was* a traumatic experience," said Chantal.

"Not traumatic enough to explain the way he looked. You saw it too, I know you did."

"The way he looked?" Miss Philips fussed at her collar and adjusted her bun. "What has that to do with it?"

"His was the look of one who'd witnessed that which is far

outside our understanding," Marlecroft said. "Things man—"

"Is not meant to know?" finished Chantal. "That reminds me. My card."

The two of them settled in for a comfortable session of talking shop, or as comfortable as could be what with Reggie Wilmott's frequent interruptions and anecdotes. Miss Philips, after a final distrustful squint at them all, went to attend to Lord Smedley where he sat with the banker and general.

It proved the start of what was to become a routine over the next few days… although the very term 'days' was of dubious use with the sun absent from their lives and only the ship's clocks marking the passage of hours.

The *Thetis* cruised onward and downward, bringing occasional recurrences of discomfort to their ears. Apart from that, and the oppressive nature of being confined so far from the world they knew, the voyage went by tolerably enough, with meals and reading and games to occupy their waking time.

More conferences were held, more plans made, for when they located their objective. The engineers and machinists in particular were kept busy, preparing and readying their equipment, under the gruff but efficient supervision of Professor Edison.

They had brought along several kinds of submersible automations, each with its specific purpose. The narwhals, pint-sized aquatic cousins to the more familiar enormous mole-machines, sported thin brass drills to bore into the rock. The crabs, a nickname given a type of propeller-powered scuttler, would break off and scoop up samples.

And the deep sea was, as Captain Burnham had promised, not so empty after all. Bizarre denizens of these lightless waters visited the *Thetis*, drawn by her illuminaries like moths to a streetlamp.

Many were clear and gelatinous, graceful, fragile-looking, oddly beautiful, displaying their own glowing rainbow hues as they moved with the effortless flex of long hairlike filaments. Others were so grotesque as to be the stuff of nightmares, revolting of countenance, spidery of leg, obscene of tentacle, sporting oversized jaws bristling with spiny teeth.

"Think that one's taken a fancy to you, Miss Philips," Reggie said, as a particularly hideous monstrosity that could have been some unnatural mingling of fish, frog, and squat-bodied gargoyle fixed its bulging gaze on the woman.

The creature went so far as to follow her around the entire windowed dome. A pendulous bulb at the end of a long fleshy protuberance above its snout blinked firefly radiance, as if signaling by some strange code. It persisted until she ultimately left the observatorium, to Reggie's great amusement.

"To them, I wonder, do we look as odd?" asked Arthur. He took extensive notes, and even tried his hand at sketching.

"I'd expect so, if not odder," Chantal said. She had brought, at her brother's behest, a photofilmographoscope. Whether any of the images captured by its wide lens would be useful remained to be seen, but, she was diligent in her attempts.

By the time the nautilus reached the outermost edge of the recalculated target perimeter, they'd all become so accustomed to her smooth speed that the slowing of motion was perceptible, as were the gliding arcs as they commenced a sweeping search pattern.

The terrain was as astonishing as the captain had promised—jagged mountains, fuming volcanic pillars, expanses of kelp waving in the current like cornfields in a breeze. In the midst of a vast silty plain, they saw the colossal carcass of a whale sunk to the sea bed. Scavengers picked the bones clean of every last shred of meat.

A disquieting moment came when the *Thetis* passed over a trench where sheer cliff walls dropped away into a blackness so deep that the strongest spotlights dwindled into wan, pathetic needles. That chasm served to remind them of the miles of ocean already above… chilling in a way that had nothing to do with the temperature.

"Rather different from chasing down vampires and ghouls," Arthur remarked to Chantal, while they made their way back to their staterooms one evening after another sumptuous dinner.

"Not to mention murderers and escaped lunatics," she replied.

"The company's certainly preferable."

"Very much so." She glanced up at him through lowered lashes, twining one ebony ringlet around her fingers.

"Yes… very much so."

Before the conversation's flirtatious turn could lead them toward less-charted territory, a tone sounded and the recorded voice issued from the speaking tubes. "All passengers to the observatorium lounge, please, all passengers to the observatorium."

Lars Gunderson was not sleeping, no, for there'd been precious little sleep to be had for him since that fateful night… only lying there in his bunk, stiff as a board, fists clenched, staring at nothing.

He'd skipped dinner as well, having a lack of appetite for food and even less of an appetite for the endless chattering questions. A sympathetic steward had seen fit to provide him a bottle, which was enough to see him through.

At the announcement, he got up, the sour taste in his mouth one that couldn't be blamed on whiskey. Nor could the gurgle of nausea in his belly.

When he reached the room domed by the great bubble, he was greeted by a crowd of backs. Like urchins at a confectioner's window, he thought. Overgrown urchins. Some even had their faces pressed, their hands cupped, as they peered where Captain Burnham pointed.

Something in the distance shed a dim yellowish glow through the darkness. It waxed and waned. Irregular. Pulsating. Marked by sporadic sputters of electric blue. Soon the shape of the thing resolved, the rounded mass of it, resting on the ocean's floor with the sand disturbed by its impact having re-settled around it in a ring.

And there, near it, small, sad, the waterlogged wreckage of the *Duck*... still tethered by what lines had held... it had fallen over onto her, then dragged her down... down into these depths...

Along with his men, his crew...

They'd already been dead.

He remembered that now. Remembered their screams and how those screams had cut off, and how in his desperate scrambling climb he'd crested a rise and seen what happened to them... why they had screamed, and why they had stopped...

He remembered.

The rays from the illuminaries played over the object. Its grey, pocked, porous surface was encrusted with coarse ridges like barnacles where blue sparks sputtered, and embedded with lumpy yellow nodules that burned.

Several of the company started talking at once, the scientists in particular beside themselves with excitement. Lord Smedley went so far as to rub his palms together in a miser's avid greed.

"The hooks, the pitons, yes," he said. "They had the right idea, just insufficient power. We can affix towing cables—"

One of the engineers mulled it over. "If we use the scuts..."

"And bring it to the surface?" asked a scientist. "Be able to do much better experiments there."

"Mine it," Lord Smedley said. "Those yellow lumps must be like coal, sulfurous coal, and the ridgelike formations must be natural teslic batteries! Once we harness those energies…"

"Good grief, though!" exclaimed Reggie Wilmott. "Unsightly bugger, isn't it? Dare say I'd be miffed if I went to a museum and paid to have a gander at *that*!"

"It isn't meant to be pretty," Professor Edison told him.

"Yes, but is it meant to be so damnably ugly?"

It *was* ugly, Chantal decided, uglier by far than the ugliest of the aquatic denizens who'd inspected them through the glass. Ugly, and worse, somehow, in some way she couldn't define, than anything she'd encountered before.

Which was—

"Turn about."

Gunderson's hoarse words rasped across the babble without much effect. Only she, Gabriel, and Arthur looked at him. He pushed his way past Miss Philips—the secretary stood like one entranced—and seized Captain Burnham's shoulder.

"Turn about, I'm telling you, we have to turn about and we have to turn about *now*!" His voice splintered into a hectoring shout, and this time it did have an effect.

Arthur and General Thomsfield took a step toward the two captains as everyone else stepped away in a widening ring.

"Here, what's all this then?" Burnham glowered. He was shorter than Gunderson but broader, and clearly unused to having someone put their hands on him, let alone take him by *both* shoulders to give him a wild shake.

"We'll die, you fool! It wants us!"

"Well, *he's* gone daft," Reggie said. "Psychosis of the deep, hey-what?"

"It killed my crew, destroyed my ship, and it *wants* more of us to come, to come and die!" Flecks of spittle flew from Gunderson's raving lips to spatter Burnham's beard.

"Belay that guff, sailor!" Burnham swatted his arms aside.

"Careful—" began Arthur.

With a screech of sheer madness, Gunderson threw himself upon Burnham. His strength must have been that of sheer madness as well, for he plowed the heavier man backward. Burnham's head struck the glass, making a sickening crunch. A spreading blotch appeared on the pane. Several people cried out, expecting the dome to shatter in upon them with the full weight of the sea's fathoms, squishing them like custard pastries. Pandemonium erupted.

The captains slammed to the floor, Burnham dazed on the bottom, Gunderson frenzied on top. His weathered fisherman's hands clamped around Burnham's throat.

Chantal moved fast, but Arthur Pearce was closer and faster. There was a *zznap!* as a spark flashed, and a whiff of ozone filled the air. Gunderson's spine arched into a bow. He went rigid, then collapsed twitching in a heap. A thin spiral of smoke rose from a smoldering patch on his side.

She looked at Arthur, who'd produced a shockgun from seemingly nowhere, with the speed of a prestidigitator's trick. He looked at her, gave a slight shrug, and tucked it away again at the small of his back.

As they had not yet been imploded by oceanic pressure, the pandemonium subsided. Reggie Wilmott showed presence of mind to dump the rest of his drink on Gunderson's sweater before it could ignite.

The blotch on the glass proved to be blood; Burnham's bald scalp was split and gushing. The glass itself had held, and showed no cracks. A general exhalation of relief went up.

Professor Edison took charge of the captain, wadding a cloth to press against the wound. He directed a bleary, cross-eyed smile at her and called her "Janey my sweet muffin" before falling unconscious.

"The devil was that about?" someone asked.

"Psychosis of the deep, I told you." Reggie found a replacement drink. "Pity, really. Such a likeable chap otherwise."

Thomsfield slung Gunderson into a chair and bound him. "He said it killed his crew."

"Drowning, obviously, when it sank," a scientist said.

"He said it wanted more of us to come and die." Gabriel Marlecroft had gone more pallid than ever, something Chantal wouldn't have thought possible.

"This isn't more of your Elder Signs rubbish, I hope," Lord Smedley said.

"Look!" said Miss Philips.

They looked.

The *Thetis* continued a slow in-spiral circling in accordance with whatever automation Burnham had set her instruments to, and came around enough to show them a previously unseen side of the object resting on the seabed.

Here, its rocky roughness smoothed into a shallow bowl-valley, divided by a long crevice like a seam of fiery molten gold.

"What is that?" someone asked.

"Looks like a river."

"Volcanic?"

"Beautiful…"

Then the seam split, and widened. And widened. And gaped. Eldritch yellow spilled out in a wavering toxic glow.

"It's fracturing," Professor Edison said. "A geode—"

"It's a bomb!" said the military man.

"An egg!" Miss Philips clutched at her collar. "A seeding pod! It's hatching!"

"It's opening," said Gabriel Marlecroft. "A gateway."

The hitherto hush-hush government pair launched into a hysterical duet.

"An eye!"

"A mouth!"

"An eye within a mouth!"

"A mouth within an eye!"

Suspended in it like bugs in amber or chunks of meat in aspic, silhouetted against that terrible luminescence, were bodies... tattered clothes... portions of bodies... flesh sloughing from bone... dissolving... melting... half-digested... the remains of the *Duck's* unfortunate crew.

At the innermost core of the burning light throbbed a knot of gristly, glistening tissue held in a net of veins and tendons. An eye, yes, it *was* an eye, a glaring lidless eye surveying them with measureless malice.

"It sees us," someone said.

The pandemonium descended again with a vengeance, plunging the assembled people into a chaos of screaming, fainting, gibbering, and tearing at their own hair. Their voices clashed over one another, passengers and crew alike, but their messages were the same—pleas, prayers, God help them, they didn't want to die!

More seams split the object's rocky crust. The rest of it began to uncurl, scabrous grey plating sliding over itself like broken crockery pieces shifting in a sack. Sediment whirled up in a silty cloud not dense enough to obscure the horror as myriad stubby legs emerged from the underside of the thing's carapace.

It reminded Chantal of a toy her brother once had—a wind-up tin roly-poly, which would scurry along the floor until it bumped into something, then tuck into a ball and roll randomly until it bumped into something else.

How Felix had laughed at its antics!

As she, now, laughed... laughed but it was a shrieking kind of laughter, a bedlam kind of laughter...

She slapped herself across the face and pulled her wits together.

Nearby, huddled with his arms locked 'round his knees, rocking back and forth, Marlecroft whimpered the same syllables over and over again. "Urzoth… Urzoth…"

Chantal ran past him to Arthur Pearce. He held the shockgun again, having redrawn it more by reflex than intent, but it dangled at his side as he stared at the loathsome cyclopean orb.

Which crept-scuttled closer, stirring up more clouds of silt, on a path meant to intercept the slow but inexorable programmed course of the *Thetis*.

"Arthur." She grasped his sleeve.

He turned to her. "Chantal."

They looked at each other, and for the moment there was little else to say. Then Professor Edison gave them both a shove.

"Don't stand about!" she barked. "We've got to *do* something!"

The few of them who'd found a precarious balancing perch between panic and catatonia met up in a group at the rear of the observatorium.

"Dashed eager to hear how science will explain this," Reggie said, joining them with his usual cheerful grin. "Put the paranormalists out of work, didn't you say?" He jerked a casual thumb at the rocking, muttering Marlecroft. "Did a deuced number on that poor bloke. Blimey, but he's in a state, isn't he?"

"Only because he's read enough, and knows enough, to understand how much trouble we're in," Chantal said.

"Scholars, hey?" He laughed. "Has been a right adventure, though. Cheers, chappies and chippies. Couldn't ask for a better lot to meet my maker with."

"We've not given up hope yet," said Arthur, who glanced at the shockgun in his hand, tutted in self-reproach, and holstered it. "This craft must have some weaponry."

The *Thetis* did indeed have armaments and defenses, an engineer confirmed: deck-guns for surface use, sonic cannons, automotive torpedoes, an electroteslic gridwork through the hull. "If they'd do bugger all against the likes of that monster," he added.

"Worth a try," said General Thomsfield. "We'll throw everything we've got at it, and if we might as well be lobbing spitballs at a Class-Nine Behemoth, so be it! We'll ram it if we have to! At least we'll die fighting, damn it all!"

"The trench," said Chantal, thinking again of Felix's roly-poly and how it would sometimes get stuck. "If we could push it in…"

"But the captain's out cold," a steward said, "and with the crew a shambles… why, there's not a man-jack of us fit to pilot her!"

A leaden weight of silence fell over them.

"General, you were cavalry and artillery, not navy," Arthur said, neither asking nor guessing, merely stating it as fact. "Chantal? Any pertinent experience?"

"Jack… or Jill… of many trades, but, piloting a nautilus?" She shook her head.

"You, boy!" Professor Edison grabbed Reggie by the shirtfront. "Didn't you mention racing yachts?"

"Yes, quite, took first in a—"

"Good enough!" She hauled him toward the bridge.

"What-ho! I hardly think—"

"Then don't try to start now!"

Trailing the sunken *Duck* behind it like a dented can tied to a dog's tail, the creature approached its gleaming prey. A hard outer shell covered the beings within; they blundered about, disorganized as inhabitants of a disturbed hive.

The prey faltered in its motion, dipped, lurched, groaned as it tried to go in several directions at once. It surged forward, then banked too sharply and almost rolled.

The creature advanced, implacable.

The prey steadied. It came on, menacing, to threaten, to fight.

Projectiles pattered on the creature's chitinous carapace… annoyances. A down-curl, a tuck, shielded the eye. Waves of sound shrilled and vibrated, irritations, quivering the gelatinous inner tissues.

As the prey sought collision, the creature reared up, exposing not a vulnerable underbelly but multitudes of legs, a synchronous flex-rippling of them, and a line of puckered, pincered orifices.

The creature latched onto the prey, onto the spherical clear part of the shell where so many of the beings tempted with their helpless tender flesh. The legs clasped. The orifices extruded their stomach-sac polyps, questing, probing for weaknesses through which it they could slip and ooze to engulf the tiny morsels.

The prey surged forward again, but the creature held on, letting itself be moved, letting itself be carried along.

It would not be shaken loose. The prey would not escape. Soon, the polyps would find their entrance. Or the burning nodules would melt through the shell and make entrances.

The water changed. A chasm gaped below, cold and dark.

Sudden crackling energy lashed through the creature, sensations of pain and convulsive shock exploding along the ridges of its own biogalvanic organs.

It recoiled by instinct, legs releasing in a violent spasm, body snap-curling shut into a protective ball.

"I say! Reggie Wilmott saves the day! Who ever would have thought?" His previously pomade-sleek hair stuck up in hectic whorls, his face shined with sweat, and his eyes were very bright.

Arthur gave him a hearty clap on the back. "Let's not get ahead of ourselves. You still need to pilot us home."

"Right-oh!" Grinning, he took hold of the levers again. "Shall we see what the old girl can do, hey-what?"

As the others busied themselves about the bridge—it was spacious but hardly seemed so, packed as it was with a conglomeration of instruments and equipment—Chantal moved beside Arthur and rested her hand on his arm.

"Aren't you glad you came along?" she asked, smiling.

He covered her hand with his and smiled back. "As I said, I wouldn't have missed it."

The great nautilus turned, turbines whirring. Her prow angled toward the surface far above.

Behind the *Thetis*, tumbling slow and silent, the thing from out of space vanished into the trench's unfathomable black depths.

Perhaps forever.

Perhaps.

BRASSWORTH

I'T'S AT TIMES, don't you know, when I'm aboard an airscrew-driven factory, about to meet a captain of industry while pretending to be a peer of the realm, that even I have to stop and ask myself, "Reggie, old bean, how do you get into these predics?".

Not aloud, obviously, as that might've drawn me a look or two, and I earned plenty of those already, on a daily basis.

Besides, the answer's simplicity itself.

A chap's got to be matey, doesn't he? Got to rally round for the sake of his nearest and dearest, his good chums?

As Moggy reminded me continuously, we'd been to *school* together, dash it all! If that didn't bond a pair of blokes tighter than brothers, what did?

Moggy being Cyril Moglington, of course. He'd turned up at my flat in a right state— *him* being in a right state, that is, not the flat... though to set the cards on the table, the table itself would first have to be cleared, if not unburied. Even in his agitated state, Moggy checked at the door to goggle about with some surprise.

Conditions *chez* Reginald Wilmott had gone a smidge lax of late, I'd have to admit. I'd burned through not one but two valets recently, under circumstances that had well put me off the idea of hiring another. The results, sorry to say, were more than beginning to show.

The first fellow... well, far be it from me to fault a man for having a fondness for spirits. But a chap has to draw the line when the hired help indulges that fondness at the master's expense, let alone by nipping away at my private reserves. And to put the pip in the cherry on the iced-cream soda, attempting a cover-up with the watered-down was adding insult to injury. I mean to say! We Wilmotts being known for our discerning palates, he might as well have refilled the bottles with industrial gear-solvent.

As for the second, well, the less said about a bloke who'd been not quite discreet about my indiscretions, the better. It was one thing, to be sure, to share an amusing or titillating anecdote now and then with the boys at the club. Then, it's all chumminess and good fun, don't you know. Ladding about, as it were, hey-what? To have one's own trusted manservant spilling the proverbial beans about the neighborhood, well, that was rather another matter.

However, be that as it may and whatnot, my current dishevelment of domestic affairs took the rumble-seat of the runabout, while Moggy's crisis claimed the seat with the legroom.

My first thought was that he'd gone and gotten himself in the soup over some girl again. Turns out, of course, he had. Just not in the usual way, where he'd fall in love with a waitress or hat-check chippie, then want my help convincing his uncle to permit the engagement. Not to mention convincing said uncle, a notorious skinflint, to increase his allowance in accordance with the commensurate costs of married life.

No, this time, Moggy had actually gone and taken the whole-hog propositional plunge. His family was in no financial opposition, and for deuced good reason.

"Gertrude Plimsby?" I'd echoed, sure I misheard him. "Not...

Plimsby-Plimsby?"

"Do you know her?" Moggy had a worried look I recognized; there'd been occasions before when he'd done the head-over-heels for someone I'd been engaged to myself, though I'd thus far always managed to escape the matrimonial noose.

He and I were both relieved to put him off the hook. I'd never met the girl—and when I did, it was to discover she was the chirpy sort, a fluffy blonde dumpling of a creature with bright eyes and one of those voices that sounds sweet to start, then drives into your ears like needles. Not my type, not my type at all.

The name, though…

"Plimsby, as in, George Plimsby?" I said. "The industrial manufacturist? The one with that ruddy great flying brass behemoth circulating over Bristol, periodically blotting out the sun? 'Another Fine Plimsby Product,' and all that rot?"

Moggy nodded. "He's her father."

"Great Scott, Moggy!" One's mind, such as it was, couldn't help but reel at the implications.

"She's his only child, you see, and he dotes on her—"

"And he's letting her marry you?"

"Thank *you*, Reggie!"

"No, no, sorry, what I mean to say is—"

"Oh, no, I understand very well what you mean to say. And that's the problem, isn't it? He thinks I'm a gadfly, a dilettante, a lay-about and do-nothing who stays out half the night at the clubs and the other half at the casinos."

I gave him the raised eyebrows as politely as one could under the circs.

"Which may have been true enough before," he hastened, blushing, "but that was the old Cyril Moglington. I've turned over a new leaf now. A good woman, treasured beyond pearls, or what have you. He's given me a job."

"A *job*?" I cried, aghast at the very notion. "Not in a factory, surely!"

"An important managerial sales post within the company. That's why I need your help, Reggie."

"*My* help?" I'd fallen into a repeating habit, which my aunts said made me sound like a parrot, but what else was there to do?

"Let me explain…" he'd said.

Little was I to know his explanation would lead to my being in accidental possession of the sole prototype of a revolutionary new invention that did not, strictly speaking, belong to me…

It had seemed like a solid gold scheme at the time. I hadn't even given any thought as to whether or how I stood to profit from it, beyond the noble deed well done and pip-cheerio *bonhomie* for a chum and all.

By the time that thought crept in, as well as others about the actual plausibility of Moggy's plan, it was half-past too late.

Which was how I'd ended up what felt like miles over *terra firma*, pretending to be someone else.

Well, not instantly ended up, to be sure. There'd been various travel arrangements required, beginning with the good old GWR to trundle me from the gleaming lofty brow of the metrop to the hearty workingman's backbone that was Bristol.

It is, they say, where those genius engineering chappies Brunel and Jessop had gotten much of their start. Locks, docks, and floating harbours… railways, steamships, airships… more factories and manufactures than you could shake a fish at. Or is it shake a fist at? Either way.

But, for each genius engineering chap like Jessop or Brunel, and each genius business-and-commerce chap like George Plimsby, there must be thousands of the non-genius everyday laborer chappies. Which meant that, overall, it wasn't the prettiest of places, to be sure. Rough-handed, bustling, and sweaty. Still and all, it's what makes civilized life possible for the rest of us, hey what?

After the train, it was a chug-a-tug down the river and into the aforementioned floating harbour, which did not float *per se* but had something to do with locks and ships and whatnot. There's an immense concrete and steel spire out there, sunk through into the bedrock, or some such, with an inner revolving axle. Tethered to that by the thickest cable I've ever clapped the oculars to was George Plimsby's vast hovering monstrosity.

Don't get me wrong; I've nothing against flying. I've taken the odd whirl in a whirligig and done the trans-oceanic via airship before. Very different, the dirigibles, the soundproof cabins, the takeoff from a skytower mooring station and all. You're up in the clouds before you know what's what. Quiet, and smooth. Like a balloon, up up and away, a drink in your hand and not a care in the world.

Plimsby's factory is another kettle of gears. The size of a town in its own right, it's kept perpetually aloft by grinding airscrews and roaring propellers that would give tornadoes a run for their money. A liftavator ascends the spire to a rather gantrylike topmost platform. Then, a fellow finds himself climbing into a suspended gondola that carries him up along the angled cable on motorized pulleys.

We Wilmotts aren't usually bothered by heights, as a rule, but every rule does have its exceptions.

I do admit, the ride *was* spectac in the scenery department, if quite the white-knuckler. Scarier, somehow, than any of the airship trips I'd been on. More… real, in a way. The wind, for instance. Could have done with some enclosed windows on that gondola, rather than open-sided waist-high rails.

I could see everything, and in greater detail than was strictly soothing to the nerves. Smokestacks, chimneys, slanted rooftops, crowded streets, colleges and hospitals and churches packed in among manufactures, the occasional spot of green for a park or winding ribbon of a waterway... that famed suspension bridge across the Avon, that marvel of modern design, looking like something someone's kid brother might have knocked together with a builder's set for his toy automotives...

All in all, stunning view, squirrelly on the nerves. Not so distant and indistinct as to be meaningless, but vivid enough that a person could readily imagine—whether he wanted to or not—the fall if that cable let go. By the time the gondola reached the factory, my knees were shakier than Moggy's plan. I'd had ample occasion for first, second and third thoughts by then, not that any of them were sparking the bulbs.

Honestly, it *had* made some sort of sense when he laid it all out for me. I'd agreed, after all. I might have come up with something similar myself.

Plimsby had, you see, entrusted Moggy with securing new accounts. Moggy reasoned that he'd make a better impression on the old man if he could land some juicy prospects snap out of the gate.

Hence, this viscount fellow, who was quite interested in placing an advance order for the upcoming line of the latest model of the whatever-it-was. Him being of the aged-and-infirm variety, however, he wanted to send his son to make a personal inspection before anything was engraved in bronze, as they say.

The son, Lord Bramford, had a desperate terror of heights and an even more desperate terror of his father learning about it. He got Moggy aside in private and asked if someone else couldn't possibly go in his stead. A proxy, as it were, who could have a look about, take some notes, and so on. If, that is, a fellow could be found who bore a close enough resemblance, had the right manner, and could be counted on to play along.

Someone like, say, Reginald Wilmott.

Moggy'd get his account and approval to marry Gertrude, Bramford the Younger wouldn't have to make the dizzying ascent, the viscount and old Plimsby would be none the wiser. Everyone happy, victory all around, hey what, and pop the bubbly for the home team.

In the meanwhile, here I was, aboard this citadel of brass and steel as it droned its endless circuitous route above Bristol. I'd heard somewhere that Plimsby did this to avoid certain laws, taxes, and regulations... his factory not therefore technically being *within* city limits, and so forth... crafty, if a bit uncouth.

The noise of the machinery drowned out most shots at meaningful conversation, which suited me just as well. I was, remember, impersonating the son of the viscount of something-or-another.

As for the actual inspection, I daresay it went well enough. Not that I understood half of what I was seeing, but, I was a social-events veteran at nodding in the right places even when I had little inkling of the particulars. Words such as "amazing" and "dashed impressive" tumbled from my lips at appropriate intervals.

I also had Moggy and Gertrude—she was in on it, of course; the sweeter they look, the more devious they are—on hand to coach me as needed.

No doubt, the whole affair was helped along by the fact that George Plimsby, a man who'd made his fortune through hard labor and the sweat of his brow, was properly overwhelmed by titles and peerage. Not to mention a snappy suit. The state of my flat notwithstanding, few were on par with Reggie Wilmott when it came to putting on the ritz. If my jacket was a tad on the bold side — Moggy's eyes half-popped when he saw it— well, it had been very much the fashion at the shore this season, and easily excused as an eccentricity. Plimsby himself was dazzled to the bone, I dare say.

I won't say the old chap fell all *over* himself at meeting the purported son of a viscount, didn't kowtow or the like. Still, he knew what was what. Those Fine Plimsby Products were very much the rage among the *nouveau riche* and jazzy set, but it was slow going to convince the blue-bloods to embrace certain modern conveniences over tradition. Nominal patronage of a viscount would go a fair ways in that regard.

So, I went on the factory tour and made the duly admiring remarks. I even took a habits-and-preferences test, filling out a questionnaire done with a punch card and brass stylus, which was then fed into a device that made bulbs flash and tickertapes chatter. Very technical, don't you know, very STOTA, as they might say, state of the art.

By the end of the thing, a deal had been struck that must have been satisfactory all around. More than satisfactory, judging by the dazzled looks gleaming in more than a few pairs of eyes.

I shook hands with old Plimsby. He wrung mine with a fervent and calloused grip that almost put me in fear for the Wilmott digits.

"I'd be delighted, Lord Bramford, if you'd accept the gift of a prototype, with my compliments," he told me.

"Oh?" I let him have my best beaming smile and hoped he didn't catch on that I'd come through this entire afternoon with the barest notion of just what this newfangled product he'd been pushing even was. "Awfully good of you, old chap, but hardly—"

"In fact, I've already taken the liberty of having one calibrated to your individual settings."

"Have you?" With, of course, no idea what he meant, until I remembered the barrage of questions earlier.

"I don't often leave the factory, but, in your case, I'd be more than happy see to the delivery myself—"

"Daddy," chirped Gertrude, coming to my rescue at that point, "I'm sure Cyril can take care of that. You've so much to do."

"Hrm, well, yes…"

I stifled a gulp when it struck me he'd been scheming for an invitation to the lordly estate and abode, which might have been stretching the ruse a bit further than was strictly comfortable. Thanks to Gertrude and her timely interruption, I was able to escape before getting in any deeper.

Don't get me wrong; I live well. My flat is top-notch, under the clutter. But, being adequate to my needs, it lacks many of the amenities old Plimsby would be expecting. Whenever I find myself craving those, I can pop over to the ancestral rockpile for a fortnight or so. My aunts are regularly after me to move back on a more permanent basis, of course, claiming that my habits (deplorable) and my housekeeping (slovenly) will land me in hospital with some disease or another. I agree that fresh air is fine and well in its place, but after about ten or twelve days at a run, I've had as much peace-and-quiet country living as I can take for a while.

No, give me the steam-city, the bustling metrop any day.

I went home, did something of a slapdash wash-and-dress, and headed out for a night on the town with the warm knowledge of having helped a chum bolstering the spirits. Soon, I'd nearly forgotten all about the whole affair.

A few days later, Moggy turned up and brought Brassworth with him.

I was, I must admit, flabbergasted. Stunned on sight wouldn't be an exaggeration. How often do you open your door and find standing there a full-size automaton, in the likeness of a man, but made completely of metal?

Yes, completely! Even the clothes, a rather natty suit-looking getup, were metal… from the top of the bowler hat to the tips of the shine-polished shoes! A brass mask of facial features… impeccable wire hair… jointed-finger hands that would have done credit to a concert harpsichordist…

I mean to say!

"Hullo, Reggie," Moggy said. "Going to invite us in, or stand there and gawp?"

I invited them in. Manners must, and what else was I to do?

"Well," I said. When it seemed I had nothing more to add to it, I said it again. "Well."

"Well indeed," said Moggy. "This is Brassworth. Your new valet."

"My what?" Stunned, now I *did* gawp.

"Your new valet. Your gentleman's gentleman. Your manservant."

I directed the gawp toward the automaton, which had come into the flat without the sort of clanking, spring-sproinking and gear-grinding you might imagine. Instead, it moved with a sort of gliding stride so smooth I half wondered if there were wheels set into the bottoms of those shiny metal shoes.

Brassworth, having come in, doffed the hat—I thought it might attach by magnets—and held it watch-chain level in the best deferential fashion. I saw that the eyes were not metal, but a kind of tint-glass, smoked amber in color.

And they moved. Side to side in their sockets like ball-bearings, none of that straight-ahead fixed stare like a statue. The eyes bloody *moved*… they even blinked with mechanized regularity! The more I stared into them, the more I felt the uncanny sense of an intelligence staring back.

Moggy kept prattling on, and it gradually dawned on me what the whole 'Lord Bramsford' business had been about.

"Another Fine Plimsby Product?" I blurted.

"Dash it all, Reggie, weren't you paying *any* attention?"

"I remember some drivel to do with mod cons this and revolutionary advances in that… are you telling me that… that

Plimbsy… that he's making and marketing…"

"Yes!" cried Moggy, flinging up his hands as if I were the most hopeless dunce he'd ever met.

"What's he sent *me* one for, then?"

"I couldn't very well take Brassworth to Lord Bramford, now, could I? He's calibrated to *your* settings!"

"My… the punch card and the machine…?"

"Exactly!"

"Those questions about… what time I wake up, how I take my tea, where I buy my shirts…?"

"Now, you needn't worry about it," Moggy said, sounding glad I'd finally caught up to speed. "I've already spoken to Lord Bramford, and he's quite willing to order his own on the sly so that old Plimsby doesn't find out—"

"Moggy," I said, "you know I don't have a valet, I haven't had a valet in months!"

Which was a not un-sore subject, as Moggy also knew.

I had, as I've mentioned, gone through a couple of them lately. Indignantly, I reminded Moggy of those unfortunate incidents, to which his retort was that on the first charge, Brassworth wouldn't be pilfering the potables. As for the second, well, that just meant I'd have all the more reason to appreciate the Plimsby absolute confidentiality guarantee.

"I am," I declared, "despite what my aunts might think, perfectly capable of looking after myself, getting the old eggs-and-b together of a morning, and all that."

He gave me a look that I hardly appreciated. The eyebrows were, I daresay, hoisted at a rather dubious slant. After the favor I'd done him, I found it a rather unsympathetic response to say the least. The fact of the matter furthermore being that I could scarcely cook an egg to save my life, and as for the b, the less said about that the better… well, that was notwithstanding. Not the point, as it were.

We bantered it back and forth, the way chappies do, until a drink stopped seeming merely like something that would go down well and started seeming like something of a necessity. I was so glad for the tumbler sitting at my elbow that I'd picked it up and had a sip of the fortifying before three things occurred to me in quick succession.

One was that I'd already finished the drink I'd made for myself just before Moggy arrived. The second was that, during our bickering, the brass valet hadn't been standing in the foyer but was taking such an unobtrusive exploratory around the flat that I'd not even noticed.

The third was that this was a deuced *doozy* of a drink!

Truth be told, I may have gotten a bit careless of late with my mixology. A splash and a plunk and there you go, whatever on ice, over the teeth and past the gums and all that.

But, this, well, I won't say it's as if the world stopped on its axis or the like… but it did give me pause. I don't know when I've had a better! Perfect ratio, perfect temperature… and with a twist! I preferred the twist, just, lately it had grown to seem too much a bother.

There was even a slivered curl of lemon peel for garnish as a final finishing touch.

I lowered the glass and looked at Moggy. He looked back at me, rather smugly, I thought, and dipped a nod in the direction of the automaton.

"Brassworth?" The incredulity was also meant for Moggy, so it gave me quite a start when someone else replied.

"Yes, sir?"

I half jumped out of the old epidermis. The drink sloshed nearly to spilling, which would have been a crime, so I reduced the risk level with another tip to the lips. Then I boggled at that impassive metal face and those tint-glass eyes.

"I say!" I said. "You talk?"

"Yes, sir."

His—that, I think, was the moment I ceased thinking of Brassworth as an it and began thinking of him as a he—his voice was low and modulated, with a hollow-ish undertone, as if some miniature fellow spoke from inside a metal-lined chamber. It was a steady sort of voice, if you take my meaning, a soothing one, a trusted banker's voice, unflappable, an anchor in a storm, a rock in a crisis.

"I say!" I said again. I held up the semi-depleted tumbler. "And you made this?"

"I took the liberty, sir, whilst familiarizing myself with the layout of your residence, to note the location of the bar. As it is also sir's usual cocktail hour…" He let it do the need-say-no-more trail off, with a slight inclination of the head to the exact proper angle.

My own eyebrows shot ceilingward. This was actual talk, as well, not just rote yes-sir and no-sir responses.

"Well then!" Moggy slapped his thighs and got to his feet. "I'll be on my way. I can catch the next train if I step lively. Thanks again, Reggie. Means a lot to Gertrude and me, really it does."

But he couldn't and didn't mean to just leave it at that, did he? I tried to muster the vocal cords to say as much and found them still too flummoxed to speak.

While I boggled, Brassworth showed Moggy out as if he'd always done it, and then the two of us were on our own.

I boggled some more. Brassworth stood waiting with what seemed infinitely polite expectation.

"Well," I said at last, having by now lost count of how many times I'd said it. "Right-oh. Here we are."

"Indeed, sir."

I looked at him, rather nonplussed. He looked at me, rather

impassive.

"What, ah, what do you do?" I asked.

"I am designed for a full range of domestic service, sir, with particular emphasis in gentlemen's personal valetry."

"Bravo." I finished the drink and tipped the empty at him. "Superb, quite."

"Thank you, sir."

"So... ah..."

"If you would permit me, Mr. Wilmott—"

"Hang on," I said. "You know my name? None of this 'Lord Bramford' rubbish?"

"Mr. Moglington was so kind enough to enlighten me with certain corrections and amendments en route, sir."

"Jolly good. Carry on?"

"As I was saying, sir, if you would permit me, it is, I believe, your usual habit to go out of an evening?"

"It is indeed. To some club or another. The, ah, Westfallon tonight, I think."

"Very good, sir. Shall I lay out your attire?"

I considered this, and decided, what-ho, why the devil not? If he made a ghastly bungle of it, I'd simply make the necessary amendments myself.

Imagine, of course, my reaction upon entering the inner sanctum a while later to find it all set out with absolute precision! If my trousers had ever been steam-pressed to such a ruler's edge sharp crease... and my shirtfront, starched crisp but not so stiff as to be a chafing discomfort... the shine of the shoes... if I might not have chosen that specific cravat to go with that specific waistcoat, the combination once donned on the person proved a smash hit, getting me more flattery at the Westfallon than I'd had in many a night!

And a night it was, a night to remember! Provided I'd be in any state to remember it, that is, after possibly imbibing a few more than was normally advised, even for a fellow of my experience and blessed with the Wilmott iron constitution.

Celebratory rounds, don't you know. The Westfallon had installed a Clockey-Jockey Racetopia Speedway recently, one of those miniature slot-spring horse-tracks, and I could not place a wrong flutter if I tried. My winning streak had me with a bouncy girl on each arm wishing me luck, and chaps buying me drinks right and left… we were in a high and jovial mood all around.

It isn't the money so much as the thrill, don't you know… the whirr of gears, the flash of the shiny horses streaking about the oval, the little jockey figurines ratcheting up and down… almost as good as the genuine article, and without that whole messy matter of being outdoors with sun, flying dust, and real horses.

When I reeled in at the wee-small-hours, the flat was in such flawless order that I first wondered if I'd let myself into the wrong one and was about to have an unfortunate encounter with an irate neighbor upon doing the late and unannounced. A moment's further inspection showed that I had in fact come to the correct address.

It forced me to slightly re-think my earlier insistence that I may have merely been letting a few things slip by, here and there, the way a bachelor will. Not that I'd go so far as to agree with my aunts, what with words like 'slovenly' and 'deplorable,' but… the difference was striking, to say the least.

I found my bed turned down, the pillow plumped to perfection, even with a spritzing of some sort of scented herbal stuff from a misting humidifier. I went face-first into it and there I stayed until the peeling up of the eyelids next morning.

Would you believe, I hadn't been conscious for five minutes and Brassworth glided in with a breakfast tray? As if he'd just known. With the tea done to a T, as it were, and the toast as I like it best but am almost never able to get it.

"Brassworth, you are a wonder!"

"Thank you, sir."

Uncanny how, in less than a week, I could barely fathom how I'd ever gotten by without him.

Oh, now and then I'd have the uncomfortable twinge—a mechanical valet? what next?—or worry over what the aunts and the bluebloods would think. Tradition versus the mod cons, and all that.

It got put to the test soon enough, when those selfsame aunts paid a surprise call. They weren't usually much for the metrop, those two, but some auction or estate sale or the like had drawn them hither with the hopes of adding to their collections of curiosities. Naturally, it would hardly do for them to not look in on their favorite nephew, now, would it? To say a hearty hello-hello-hello and make sure he wasn't living in squalid debauchery, hey-what?

Squalid debauchery, they did not find. Instead, they were met at the door by the unctuous politeness of Brassworth. Shrink though I do from the thought of such dear but aged relations' unmentionables, I daresay he soon had them charmed to the very stocking-garters. They were full-on lavishing his praises by the time they cleared off after an admirable luncheon.

And, really, even the bluest of the bluebloods aren't so bunged up with tradition that they still use candles instead of gaslamps or teslic bulbs, are they? When you could travel by steam-engine, automotive, luxury liner or airship, who'd pick a lesser conveyance so dependent upon the weak and fallible flesh?

Why not, then, a mechanical valet?

It was the wave of the future, as they say! The coming thing, the household staff of tomorrow, be the envy of your friends, the pinnacle of innovation... and I was at the very cutting-edge forefront!

So, it came as a rather nasty shock some weeks later when the entire Plimsby company took a drastic nosedive.

I don't mean literally; the airscrew-propelled factory didn't crash and burn in a spectacular fireball of smoking metal, debris and destruction, tragic losses of life, or whatnot. Oh, it was devastating enough, make no mistake... damages into the millions, jobs lost, fortunes ransacked...

Anyone who knows me will tell you that Reggie Wilmott is a stand-up fellow when it comes to his chums, but he's never been one with much of a head for business, and I'd be the first to agree. I won't even pretend to understand the ins and outs of what happened.

What I do understand is that it all went toes-up, and Moggy took it in the neck.

Something to do with those laws and regulations old Plimsby had been trying to avoid catching up with him in a big way... something to do with corporate rivalry and proprietary information... threats of lawsuits from domestic service agencies... orders canceled, investors jumping ship, stocks plummeting... the new line of automated house-help scrubbed...

Was it *all* Moggy's fault?

Dashed if I know. It didn't seem likely even he could have wreaked that much havoc in so short a time. Regardless, the Cyril Moglington who shuffled into my flat one evening and flopped onto my sofa, heaving the most dispirited sigh I'd ever heard, certainly seemed to think it was. He didn't even notice the drastic changes about the place, or spare a single complimentary word.

"My life is over, Reggie," he said. He looked it, too... unshaven, hair a fright, clothes so rumpled he must have slept in them.

"There now, old bean! It can't be as bad as all that, can it?"

"Gertrude gave me the boot."

"No!"

"Yes! The only girl I've ever loved, my light, my angel, my sweet sugar dumpling, and she pulled the beating heart from my chest and stomped upon it!"

I rang for Brassworth to bring us a drink. Not that I needed to ring; he must have been lurking just the other side of the door, awaiting the summons. He slid in with that unobtrusive manner of his, tray in hand, decanter at the ready.

Moggy carried on for a while in the heart-stomping sweet sugar dumpling vein—women, don't you know—while making a fairly serious attempt at drowning the sorrows.

The real pinch came when he informed me, in an oh-just-by-the-way sort of footnote, that, what with these unfortunate circs being what they were, the whole arrangement with Brassworth was probably off.

"Off? What do you mean, off?" I asked, more than a trifle alarmed.

"Well, they won't be making any more, will they? Whole line's been shut down." He poured himself a generous knock. "There were only half a dozen other finished prototypes to start with, and the rest have already been deactivated."

"I say!" I said. I glanced at Brassworth. His metal features remained impassive as ever, but there was something in his manner I'd stake the house and lot hadn't been there before. "Deactivated?"

"Liquidated." Moggy regarded the tumbler of whiskey, snorted, and commenced to further liquidate himself.

"I say!" I said again, appalled.

"Scrapped." Moggy downed another gulp. "Melted to slag."

"Show some respect for the dead, man!"

"The dead?" He reeled, blinking at me. "Reggie, they're machines. Lish… lishsten… listen to yourself."

"Machines!" I looked back at Brassworth. "What's your take on this?"

"While it *is* a technically accurate description, sir," he said, "I do find it a rather mournful, even dismaying turn of events."

"Dismaying? Downright ghoulish, if you ask me."

"To be sure," Moggy said, or slurred, listing to starboard as he was by then, "since yours was a gift, there's no contract to be revoked... but the guarantee, and the continooa... continuee..."

"Continuance, sir?" supplied Brassworth.

"Continuance, yes, that's it," Moggy said. "The continuance of terms. Scrubbed. No terms, no contract, no guarantee."

"And he'll be deactivated? Not to mention... liquidated?"

"Weren't you the one going on about how you didn't need a valet?"

"Well, pff, bah, yes, I might have said, but... dash it all, Moggy!"

"Don't blame me!"

"Was I?"

"You might as well," he said, slouching with a sulky cross of the arms. "Everyone else is. My uncle... Gertrude..." He did another of the heaving dispirited sighs and stared into the depths of his glass as if hoping to read the future in there instead of in tea leaves. "I'm only the messenger, after all, just a message-boy, probably get my allowance cut into the bargain..."

I found myself with a marked lack of commiseration for my old school chum, and turned to Brassworth with a doleful but brave buck-up-laddy kind of stiff-upper-lip, the best I could muster. Words utterly failed me. Dashed if I didn't find myself choking up, even going a bit misty around the corners.

The very notion left me staggered. To say I'd become accustomed to him was an understatement that put all other understatements to the pale.

"I do trust my service has been satisfactory, sir?" Brassworth inquired.

"Ra-*ther*!" I said. We shook hands, his brass-fingered grip firm and cool. "But this can't just be it, can it? Got to be something that can be done!"

I wasn't sure what, if anything, I had in mind by that remark, however fervently heartfelt. That he go on the lam, or whatever it was that people were always doing in adventure novels, was laughable. A life-size brass automaton would be anything but inconspic, don't you know.

"As my initial placement was in the form of a complimentary gift, it *could* perhaps be argued that I am no longer, technically, Plimsby property. However—"

Moggy scoffed, loudly. "Like to see you tell old Plimsby that!"

"Very well, Mr. Moglington. Shall I see to the travel arrangements?"

"How's that again?" I asked. "Travel arrangements? Where to?"

"To Bristol, of course, sir."

I was glad to see that Moggy also had a baffled look, though in his case being well on the way to pickled also had something to do with it.

"What, you mean, go back? Turn yourself in, as they say? Firing squad and all that?"

"I would hardly expect a firing squad," said Brassworth with a mildness that I could barely wrap the bean around.

"No, dismantled and melted, more likely," Moggy said.

I shot him a look, finding this remark far less than helpful, not to mention considerably lacking in tact. He ignored me, going for another drink. I directed the look to rest once more on Brassworth's tint-glass eyes.

"You've got something percolating, haven't you?" I asked.

"Sir?"

"I can hear the wheels turning in that head of yours!"

"Do pardon me, sir." He began to raise a hand to that head of his with what seemed like contrite consternation.

"Not literally," I said, giving a roll of the orbs in their sockets. "You've thought of something. You've got a plan."

"I may indeed, sir."

Moggy scoffed again. Even more loudly.

"One which," Brassworth continued, "may possibly stand a chance of restoring the company's good fortune. Not to mention perhaps even affecting a reunion between Mr. Moglington and Miss Plimsby, if all goes well."

At that, sozzled or not, Moggy was off the couch like it was spring-loaded. "Gertrude?" he cried. "My little sugar-dumpling?"

Then, as might be imagined, there was nothing for it but to go with all due speed. I hadn't seen Moggy so motivated since our school field days when there were prizes in the offing.

We caught a steam-trolley from my flat to the station. Brassworth proved a smash sen-sashe on the GWR to Bristol; the news had been all over the papers, wired, and wireless, for weeks now, and to see the sole surviving Fine Plimsby Product up close was an uncommon treat for our fellow passengers.

The trip went by for me in something of a blur, not only the blur of the countryside as the train sped along but a blur of anxious conversational babblings from Moggy such that I could barely get a thought in edgewise, let alone a word.   The one prospect that did snag in my mental net long enough to worry me was in regards to old George Plimsby and whether or not he remained under the impression that I was Lord Bramford. But, in the greater scheme of things, it seemed far down the list.

Brassworth maintained his impassive silence as the chug-a-tug carried us out into the harbour. We rode the liftavator up the spire to the platform, and although I'd reconciled in my brain the fact of another gondola ride, my innards remained far from sanguine, if that's the word I want.

Plimsby's behemoth continued its airborne circuits above Bristol, though once we'd disembarked the gondola, it seemed more a flying metal ghost town than the busy factory I'd seen before. The workers had been laid off, the great machines shut down except for the airscrews and propellers, and the clashing industrial din I remembered no longer drowned out the howl and whistle of the wind.

The man himself was in residence, and his daughter, but other flesh-and-blood beings were few. Gertrude Plimsby's welcome was almost warm enough to flash-freeze Moggy where he stood; the liquid N would have been a sauna by comparison.

I confess that, as the preliminaries got underway, the role of one R. Wilmott was to loiter off to a side with an ingratiating smile. Brassworth did the talking.

And was he smooth? I should say! Purest refined oil and honey! He opened with the stuff about having technically been gifted and therefore no longer Plimsby property.

"One might therefore extrapolate that this would render me something of a free agent. An autonomous automaton, if you will."

To which the old man blustered something about costs of materials and manufacturing, losses to be recouped, being sued by the domestic services unions for a threat to their livelihood, scandalous public doo-dah about human rights, and so on. The company was, he maintained, in more than enough trouble without having 'free agent' automatons on the loose.

Brassworth countered with a suggestion that made Plimsby's ears prick up, or would have if he'd possessed the kind of ears that could prick up. His were, as it happened, the ears typical of an elder party of his sort, complete with tufts of the grey and bristly.

But I believe they would have pricked if they could.

It was the habits-and-preferences questionnaire that Brassworth mentioned, the one I recalled filling out with a punch card and stylus. Moggy had, with a big show of pomp and circumstance, fed it into the device with flashing bulbs and chattering tickertapes, which had ultimately spat out the specifs they'd used to calibrate Brassworth to my individual settings.

"It seems to me, Mr. Plimsby, sir," said Brassworth, "that such a technology would have valuable uses and applications in today's world. The domestic service agencies, for instance, would benefit greatly from the ability to match prospective employers and employees based on skills and needs. The same could be said for many businesses and industries."

Plimsby's jaw worked, but not much in the way of words came out. Moggy and I no doubt looked similar. Gertrude, meanwhile, had a gleam in her eyes like her clockey-jockey horse was three lengths ahead and gaining.

"Imagine the commercial uses," Brassworth said. "Advertisements, perhaps, tailored to the tastes of a particular market. One might even consider the social prospects of such a system. Being able to seek out new acquaintances based on established factors of personality and compatibility would reduce or even eliminate the difficulties inherent in forming relationships."

He continued, still smooth as oil and honey, by saying that he would be quite willing to assist with setting it all up, by way of renumerance for the aforementioned costs of his materials and manufacturing, in exchange for his emancipation.

"Mr. Moglington advised that I bring the matter directly to you, sir," he finished.

Gertrude Plimsby gazed at Moggy with the love-stars rekindling, or something along those lines. "Oh Cyril! Was this *your* idea?" she cried.

"I... ah..." Moggy managed an uncertain grin, and that was the last I saw of him for a while as the girl flung herself into his arms.

With this, it was *fait accompli* but for the nuts and bolts of it all. I soon found myself face to face with Brassworth.

"I jolly well knew you were hatching a scheme!" I said. "But, what happens now? You sign back up with old Plimsby?"

"Perhaps not, sir. I am only obliged to assist with seeing the new program become operational. I am otherwise on my own recognizance, as it were."

"Indeed," I said, trying not to let on I hadn't the foggiest what he meant.

"For independent hire or employ," Brassworth added. "Should anyone be so inclined as to make the offer."

The penny finally dropped and I caught on.

Must admit, I did feel a touch foolish, asking such a question. Not like a Wilmott to be in the supplicant's role, don't you know. To anyone, let alone a valet, let alone a mechanical valet. But, blast it all, there it was.

"So... Brassworth, ahem... don't, ah, suppose," I said, rubbing at the back of my neck, "you'd consider staying on? For a bit? On a trial basis? Probationary and all, right-oh?"

Brassworth's face, as I've mentioned, did not lend itself to much in the way of movement or expression. But, I swear, something in the tilt of his head almost seemed to suggest a smile.

"I would find it most amicable, sir."

I nearly could have whooped. Forget shaking his hand; I wanted to embrace him like a brother. I did neither, of course; certain proprieties must be maintained in these matters.

"Bra-*vo!*" I settled for clapping him on the shoulder, hard enough to sting my palm. "It's a deal!"

And that, as they say, was that.

THE ETHERIC DYNAMO

Miss Lavinia Wilmott, having called on her cousin at his stylish metropolitan flat unannounced, and at what he doubtless felt was an appalling hour, accepted his automatonic valet's offer of refreshment whilst she waited for the young master to clear himself of the fog of the previous evening's revelries.

Reggie tottered in, yawning and rumpled, a few moments later. He was an affable enough fellow of the amiable and gangling sort, for whom the night went well unto the wee-small-hours and morning was something better left until at least noon.

They settled the greetings, cordialities, and prelims, and then she put the purpose of her visit before him.

"I never thought I'd be saying this," Lavinia said, stirring her cup, "but I need a man."

Reggie blinked, more than a little nonplussed. "Bit of a departure for you, isn't it, Vinnie, old bean? Still," he went on, "glad to rally 'round. Looking for introductions? I know plenty of chaps from the Westfallon Club who'd be—"

"I was more thinking of you," she cut in.

At that, he blinked several times more. "Oh, now, I do say...

flattered though I am, of course, and all…well, we *are* cousins—"

"Don't be a dolt, Reggie."

"Rather can't help it," he said. "Afraid you've stunned me to the marrow."

"Well, compose yourself." Vinnie sipped the caffeinated revivifying, which was strong and perfectly brewed, sweetened to the precise degree she favored.

He scrubbed the heels of his hands up the sides of his face and dove into the breakfast plate Brassworth set before him.

She glanced approvingly around the flat. It was pin-neat with all the mod cons and a lush view of the park. Far nicer than the abode where she stashed the parasol and hung the bonnet when the day was done. But then, Reggie hailed from a branch of the Wilmott family tree more generously leafed in the green… if also perhaps more generously laden with nuts.

Not, of course, that Vinnie herself was in any position to throw the proverbial stones when it came to nuts, as it were. Glass houses and whatnot, don't you know. By the standards and to the despair of her immediate parents and sibs, she was very much the cuckoo's egg in the henhouse, though it had nothing to do with her personal life or matters pertaining thereto.

They ran Ashfields, a respectable but struggling chain of department stores begun by Lavinia's maternal great-grandfather. The Ashfields code touted tradition, old-fashioned service and value over newfangled consumerism. Ironically, Lavinia had neither interest in nor a head for such business…and when it came to the newfangled, well, of that she embraced with élan. Thankfully, sufficient brothers, sisters and assorted in-laws of a responsible stripe were more than willing to do their part, so her eccentricities were indulged within reason. Books, tutors, a university education and so on.

While it was assumed that she would mature and abandon

frivolity, she survived on a pittance of an allowance that permitted a workshop and cluttered little apartment above. If she couldn't afford a cook or housekeeper, she got by… and if in dire need of a decent meal, she could always catch the crosstown steam-trolley to impose on Cousin Reginald.

Who had, meanwhile, downed a few gulps of the steamed black fortifying from his own cup and gotten on the outside of half a plate of scrambled with ham. He swept crumbs from his lips and looked at her, rather more lucid-eyed.

"Now, Vinnie," he said. "What's all this then? What's this about, you needing a man? Since you obviously can't mean for the…ah… typical…how does that even work, by the way?"

She elevated a stern eyebrow. "Reggie."

"Indeed. Sorry. Quite." He cleared his throat. "So, then. How could I, of all people, possibly be of assistance?"

"I need you to come down to Huntlyshire this week-end," she said.

"Way out there in the country? That far from the bustling metrop?"

"Yes."

"Health and fresh air? Exercise?" He looked positively afright.

"You don't have to exercise."

"Ah, but it's inevitable. With not much else to do, it's only a matter of time, isn't it, before someone suggests a nice stroll, or boating, or a ride. When I say ride, it's always horses, or bicycles, never a velocipede or motored scooter, now, is it?"

"There'll be lots to do. The Four-Counties Science Fair and Exposition is being held there on Saturday."

"And that's a plus? Eggheads and inventors trying to blow things up?"

"With substantial monetary awards, and a tenured professorship at Huntley College on the line," she said, taking no offense.

"Eggheads and inventors trying to blow things up for prizes, then."

"You mustn't bring Brassworth, though," Vinnie added as Reggie's valet glided in with a hot carafe. "He'd outshine all the other exhibits. No offense, Brassworth."

"None taken, Miss Wilmott," Brassworth replied, the polished metal mask of his face as impassive as ever. "More coffee?"

"Please." As the automaton poured and added sugar, she returned her attention to her cousin. "Some of the greatest minds of the age will be attending."

"All the less reason to have *me* bunging about the place," Reggie said. "Isn't that Clive Chapman bloke supposed to be there? The absent-minded recluse? Presenting that new what's-it of his, the… what was it again?"

"Etheric Dynamo, sir."

"Yes, that. Knew it was something to do with dynamos." Frowning, Reggie looked down at his plate as if it were an escape route from the conversation. "Do we have any of that sweet-orange marmalade left, Brassworth?

"I'll bring it at once, Mr. Wilmott, sir," Brassworth said, heading back to the flat's kitchen

"I've entered the judging under a false name," Vinnie said.

Reggie had been buttering a scone and paused now mid-butter. His gaze took in her earnest expression. His jaw did not drop, *per se*, but it did make something of a slow descent toward the collarbones. "Oh, you didn't."

She twisted her napkin into a frustrated linen rope. "I *had* to. You have no idea how difficult it is for a woman to be taken seriously in this new age—"

"Hardly seems cricket." Reggie set down scone and butterknife, then held up both hands palms-outward. "Furthermore, I suspect what you are asking of me. And the answer is a decisive no."

"But, Reggie!"

"Firmly in the negative. For one, I've met old Lord Huntley, and, to put it mildly, he's not a fan. What if he recognized me, going under your pseudonym?"

"But—"

"For another, even if he didn't recognize me straightaway, well, you can't possibly expect *me* to impersonate a genius inventor."

"Not at all. I expect you to impersonate, if that, a wastrel layabout."

He blinked yet again, relaxed, and beamed an amiable grin. "Oh, well, then, ra-*ther*. In that case, you've come to the right chappie." Picking up scone and knife, he resumed a thorough buttering. "What about old Huntley, though? Won't it croggle your scheme if he knows who I am?"

"Do you know his daughter?"

"Josephine? I should say. Was in love with her once…for about twenty minutes."

"Were you?"

"Oh yes. Probably would have popped the question in another hour or so, but she was already engaged to Donald Milkins, and I'd come to my senses by the time she gave Donny the big heave-ho."

"Then all the more reason for you to come."

"But I haven't seen hide nor hair of the girl in months."

"That doesn't matter."

"And her father thinks I should be put in a home for the terminally dilettante," he said, crumbs falling from his mouth.

"Better and better."

"Besides, isn't she tying the matrimonial noose around some other poor sap's neck soon? I'm sure I saw it in the society pages. Franklin somebody, wasn't it? Or was it somebody Franklin? Or Francis?"

"Never mind any of that," Vinnie said. She'd no sooner begun to make the motions of standing than Brassworth was there, smooth and unctuous and utterly professional, to draw back her chair. "You just be on the ten o'clock to Huntleyshire on Friday. I'll meet you at the station in the village."

"Hang on; I haven't agreed to this."

"You said you were glad to rally 'round and be of assistance."

"I also said I wasn't about to impersonate anyone, imaginary or otherwise."

"Which I'm not asking, am I?"

"Well…"

"You *will* be there," she said. "You'll help me, I know you will."

"With what, exactly?"

"I'll explain later."

"And what if I don't turn up?" Reggie belatedly scrambled to his feet, seeming only now to notice she'd risen.

"You'd never leave me in the lurch like that."

"I might. This entire conversation's given me an uneasy feeling in the pit of my stomach."

She pursed her lips. "Or perhaps you're just hung-over."

He affected a wounded puppy-dog's pout. "Ouch, cuz. To the quick."

"I hate to have to do this, Reginald, but if you won't help me, I'll not hesitate at taking drastic measures."

At that, he gave her an apprehensive look.

"You do remember Tom Terper, don't you?" she asked.

"Terper the Burper? That fat little git who used to follow us around those summers at the lake? Good heavens. What a pest. Last I'd heard, he married that ghastly American and moved off to Nebraska or some such territory. But what's he got to do with anything?"

"He and that ghastly American have two sets of twin boys now," Vinnie said. "He's bringing the whole lot of them over for a visit.

Naturally, if he had your address, I'm sure he'd love to look you up."

His eyes widened and his face paled. "You wouldn't."

"After all, I know how you do adore children."

"Podgy brats with sticky fingers and screeching voices?"

"You could show them the sights of the city. Make a day of it. Have them in for lunch. Why, I expect they'd gladly stay with you, save the cost of a hotel."

Reggie shook a finger at her. "That is a low and devious threat, cousin of mine."

Vinnie spread her hands and shrugged. "But, if you weren't going to be at home next week, there'd be no point my even mentioning it, would there?"

"The ten o'clock to Huntleyshire, you say? This Friday?"

"You *are* a treasure. I knew I could count on you."

"Right-oh," he said, and heaved a sigh.

Simultaneous preparation for the Four-Counties Scientific Fair and Exposition and the impending nuptials of Josephine Huntley to Mr. Stanley Alvin—or was it Lord Clifton's son, Herbert?—had Huntleyshire in a tizzy, the big house and the village alike.

With so much to be done, on such a schedule, the juggling of logistics made for a precarious, teetering state of affairs. A single hitch, delay or setback in any department could bring the whole works crashing down.

At the fair-grounds, there were exhibit halls to be set up, refreshment tents, vendor's stalls, display booths, rides and games and crafts for the kiddies. There were programs to be printed, arrangements made for the judges, ribbons, certificates, prizes. There was wiring to be tested for the electric and telephonic, piping for steam and hydraulic and thermodynamic. Deliveries arrived requiring special handling, refrigerated storage, security. Volunteers had to be organized.

As for the wedding, it was a matter of cakes, caterers, crises and confusion. The dressmaker and the florist nearly came to blows over color schemes. The ring-bearer caught measles, breaking out in itchy polka-dots. Not one but *two* socially important names had somehow been left off the guest list, the lapse not noticed until almost too late. Slipshod repairs to the church roof shingles, discovered during a brief rain, prompted fears of a leak.

Last-minute messages flooded in for both events—requests, demands, panicked emergencies. Such-and-such refused to be situated near so-and-so, special accommodations *must* be made for this or that, if X wasn't taken care of right this very instant or Y couldn't be managed to the smallest detail, it'd all fall to utter ruin.

Nearly everyone was frazzled to a fare-thee-well. Rumor had it that both Lord Huntley and his brother, the dean of Huntley College, were to the point of tearing out their own hair. Only bride-to-be Josephine, daughter of one and niece of the other, maintained a serene aplomb.

Hers was a peach sorbet kind of beauty, cool and sweet and refreshing. It was no wonder she had won the hearts of so many admirers, and been engaged so often that her own father could no longer keep track of which suitor she'd settled upon. Regarding some, the old lord had withheld his consent on grounds of money or prospects, family or respectability. Others had failed to hold Josephine's interest, or found out the hard way that peach sorbet could turn to lemon ice without warning.

She met Lavinia and Reggie at the carriage-yard gate when they pulled up Friday afternoon, looking more peach-sorbet than ever in a light summery tea-dress of airy layers that fluttered becomingly at sleeves and hem. A wide-brimmed straw hat adorned with ribbons perched at a jaunty angle atop her coiffed curls, shading her dimpled cheeks.

The motor chugged to a rest with one final gusty exhalation of steam. Vinnie, having borrowed one of the horselesses to fetch Reggie from the station, plucked off her driving goggles and untied her head-scarf. Reggie, for his part, pushed his goggles up onto his brow, sprang from the passenger seat, doffed his cap, and bowed with exaggerated formality.

"Hullo, hullo, hullo," he said. "Josephine Huntley, as I live and breathe. You look well."

"Dearest Reggie! So good of you to come." Smiling a gracious perfect-pearl smile, she swept over to clasp his hands and put air-kisses by the corners of his mouth.

"I understand congratulations are in order. Got you the requisite fondue pot, but it's been held up at the engravers, so, might be a day or two late."

"Psssh." Josephine gestured a wave as airy as her frock. "No trouble with the horseless, Vinnie?"

"It hiccuped a bit on the hill," Vinnie said, patting her hair into place as she climbed down, "but, other than that, no, no trouble at all."

"Oh, good." Josephine pressed her hand with great affection. They exchanged a private glance, brief but very warm.

"Quite the double production you've got going on around here," Reggie said, rocking on his heels as he inspected the surroundings. "Vin brought us around the long way past the fair-grounds, and I saw the servants setting up a pavilion out in the garden. For the reception, I take it?"

"Yes, a champagne buffet, I thought. I'll have someone bring in your bags. Let's go in. You must be thirsty."

"When am I not?"

Josephine laughed gaily, folding one arm through Reggie's and the other through Vinnie's to lead them up to the house. "I do hope you find your room suitable," she said. "We're packed to the rafters with relatives and guests, but I did what I could. You're just down the hall from Vin."

"We Wilmotts can rough it when necessary," he assured her.

"He once," Vinnie said in a confidential tone, "went transcontinental in a shared-occupancy Pullman rather than a private."

"With the bath at the end of the car, rather than *en suite*?" asked Josephine, miming great shock.

"I know," said Vinnie, wide-eyed. "Rooming with, might I add, a complete stranger."

"Reggie, you poor thing. How ever did you endure?"

He puffed out his chest. "Like I said, we Wilmotts can rough it. We're made of strong stuff, don't you know."

"So I gather."

"Tell me, though," Reggie said, "because Vinnie here won't spill the beans, who's the condemned? I mean, the lost soul? I mean, the lucky bridegroom?"

"Same old Reggie, haven't changed in the least, have you?"

"Despite the best efforts of many to improve or make something of me. So, who is it? Stanners? Herbie Clifton? Old Donny Milkins? Anybody I know?"

Josephine made with the airy wave again. "We'll see who turns up."

"I say, that's rather on the *lassez-faire* side for a girl's big day, isn't it?"

"You know how it is with weddings," Vinnie said. "As long as everything else is absolutely perfect to the bride's exact specifications, from the dress and bouquet to the cake and the band, the rest is practically interchangeable."

"And everything else *is* absolutely perfect to the bride's exact specifications," Josephine said. "Well, except for little Brucie coming down with the spots, but I hadn't really wanted him as ring-bearer anyway. I'd only agreed to placate Great-Aunt Ida. Now, with him out of the way, I can go back to my original plan."

"Which is?" asked Reggie, sounding braced for the worst.

"Buttercup, my dog."

"Your dog?"

"I'll fix the ring pillow to her collar."

"Hmm," he said, and opted with conversational suavity to change the subject. "So, how long have you two known each other? I had no idea you'd become such close chums."

"Oh, quite a while now," said Josephine. "We met at a seminar hosted by the Delaney Institute."

"That women's hospital?"

"Feminine Wellness and Well-Being," Vinnie said. "It was a seminar on—"

He raised a hand. "Say no more. *Please*, cuz, for pity's sake, say no more."

"Men." Josephine rolled her eyes at Vinnie. "They can be *so* squeamish, can't they?"

"Squeamish? No, no-no-no! Just... preserving the integrity of the feminine mystique, hey-what?"

They'd reached the house by then, parted ways long enough to freshen up and sponge off the road-dust, then regrouped in the east salon where French doors overlooked a terrace with trellises and dainty climbing roses. Reggie lit up like a cinema marquee when he saw the well-stocked bar fitted with a multi-setting ice dispensary, a gazogene for making carbonated fizzes, racks of colored syrups in different flavors, and shelves aglitter with bottles of all the finest in sustaining elixirs. He fell to with an enthusiasm that wouldn't have been misplaced in a budding young genius given his first chemistry set, mixing up cocktails made-to-order for the three of them.

"Right, so," he said, once they had sipped to their satisfaction. "Here I am… so, why *am* I here?"

Barometrical predictions held true despite grim predictions of rain, gloom and doom over pints in the village pub the night before. It was an indicator of the inevitable triumph of science over superstition, something also lost on those who'd been downing the pints and making the predictions.

The sun rose bright as a new-minted coin in a brisk blue sky, with just enough breeze and occasional drifting of cumulonimbal formations as to counter any excess of heat. Light dappled on the lake, meadow grass and leafy boughs swayed, birds chirped, the scene was as picturesque as any photo-imagist could have hoped, and on first look, all was right with the world.

"Welcome," said the Dean of Huntley College to the assembled crowd, a megaphonic nicely amplifying his stentorian lecture-hall voice. "Welcome to the Four-Counties Scientific Fair and Exposition!"

Cheers arose. Many of a rather restrained tenor, of course, as these were, after all and for the most part, learned men and women of education and reserve… or those aspiring to be. The more raucous whooping and waving of arms was left to the youthful exuberants, schoolboys, and those simple country folk who knew only that this meant a rare entertainment.

"I should like to take this moment," the dean went on, "to offer praise and thanks to the man whose generosity has made this event possible… my own good brother, Lord Archibald Huntley!"

Applause and more cheers greeted this, albeit somewhat dutiful. Lord Huntley, standing near the podium, inclined his head. His smile looked not a little frayed around the edges, the tension of the previous weeks of preparation having taken their toll.

When, at dinner, he'd been presented with his latest houseguest, a furrow of concern—"Wilmott? Reginald Wilmott? I remember you; what in the world are *you* doing here?"—had shortly given way to a look akin to that of an ox struck amidship the eye sockets with a ball-peen hammer. This, of course, had been due to his daughter's giggling reply.

"Oh, Daddy," Josephine had said, in a such-a-kidder-you-are tone. "Surely you can't have forgotten that Reggie and I are engaged."

Reggie jumped in his chair. "I say now—"

Lavinia kicked his ankle under the table, shooting him a look. When he'd asked why he was here, Josephine had most artfully demurred, changing the subject to racing yachts, and said subject never had gotten changed back.

The stricken Lord Huntley noticed none of this. He gaped, goggle-eyed, at his precious daughter. "Engaged? To *him?*"

"Well, of course. Who else?"

"But I thought… but, Josephine, my lamb… I thought you were engaged to Clarence Stoddard."

At that, she'd put on a hurt expression. "That was *weeks* ago. Honestly, don't you pay *any* attention to what's going on on my life?"

And so on, issuing tears to be dabbed at with the handkerchief, until the lord had been falling all over himself in bumbling apologies, which failed to mollify Josephine's dramatics.

"I suppose, next, you'll have forgotten that I'm to be *married* in a few days," she'd wailed, and had to rush from the dining room to compose herself.

"I haven't forgotten," he called after her, then looked around the table at the other guests, most of whom were in attendance for that very reason. "I haven't!"

"There, there, old man," Reggie had said, rising gamely to the occasion of the ruse despite his dearth of detail in understanding. "Girls, don't you know. They can get emotional. Especially when weddings are involved. Turns the best of them high-strung, I shouldn't wonder."

"To *you?*" He bleated the words, turning the goggle-eyed gape upon Reggie. "She agreed to marry *you?*"

Gulping, Reggie managed a weak but daffy grin. "Bit of a surprise to me, too, but, cheerio, there you are and what can you do?"

A day later, Lord Huntley, still, clearly, had not fully recovered from the news. He now raised a beatific but shaky hand to the crowd. "Thank you, one and all, thank you," he said.

The dutiful applause trailed off, prompting Dean Huntley to carry on with the opening ceremonies. He introduced the judges and other dignitaries of the scientific community, the main sponsors, and the key participants.

"It is with particular pleasure," he said, "that I'm honored to announce our guest speaker, that most distinguished, if elusive—" here, a general knowing chuckle arose from the assembly, "—innovators, forward-thinkers, and geniuses of our time… Mr. Clive Chapman."

Now the applause was louder, and eager. Heads turned this way and that. Necks craned. People stretched on tip-toe to peer over their neighbors. An abashed courier-boy scurried onto the stage, spoke in rushed whispers, and handed over a telegram.

Dean Huntley took it as well as might be expected, under the circs. In an only slightly pained manner, he folded the missive, tucked it away in his pocket, and addressed them again.

"Elusive, didn't I just say? As it happens, Mr. Chapman has been unavoidably detained—"

A collective moan of disappointment went up. The dean managed to quell it.

"—but assures us he *will* be arriving as soon as humanly possible and apologizes profusely for the delay. In the meanwhile, he has requested that we carry on without him, including the exhibit of his Etheric Dynamo."

The crowd remained let-down. Still, what choice had they then but to stiff-upper-lip and move on? This, they did, though not without some further sighs and mutterings.

"Now, without further ado," Dean Huntley said at last, "I declare this Fair and Exposition underway!"

With the most rousing cheer yet, the crowd commenced filing through the token little wooden fence-gate that had barred the lane between the rows of halls, stalls and tents.

Moving with the tidal current, several comments on the subject of the elusive Clive Chapman were to be overheard... smug remarks from those who claimed to be on quite close personal terms with the man... anecdotes about chance encounters at restaurants or on trains... a talk he evidently gave at someone's sister's friend's son's school last year... the darts tournament he'd won, though, tragically, the man telling the story had been out of town and missed it himself, but had it on the *best* authority from eye-witnesses...

And so on.

Lavinia, Reggie and Josephine wandered the fair-grounds together, taking in the sights. Everywhere were wonders to behold. Among them:

An indoor greenhouse system, with solarcandescent bulbs and piped irrigation, that would function even underground, available in sizes suitable for growing anything from a windowbox herb garden on up to a complete orchard, with no natural sunlight or rain needed.

A wireless vision telegrapher.

Bicycles equipped with folding ornithopter wings or velocipedes with motor-driven airscrews, for when street traffic was too congested.

Opium-extract chewing gum in a variety of flavors.

A proposed orbital capsule with chemical atmospheric filtration and liquid recycling capable of sustaining three astronauts for up to thirty days, launched by inertial galvanized elastics with canister-fueled propulsion jets to allow for maneuvering.

Steam-powered leaping boots that rivaled the feats of that American Olympic medalist James Connolly.

A portable personal player piano that strapped to the forearm, spring-wound by the simple act of walking, with multiple and easily interchangeable music cylinders and hollow-wire ear cups attached to a convenient headband.

The latest in emergency collapsible aquatic inflatables, from life jackets that could be worn beneath normal clothing without unfashionable lines or bulk to multi-person life rafts guaranteed to weather even the worst storms at sea.

There were gadgets for the home, clockwork toys for children, patent medicines, mesmer-ray treatments that claimed to be able to cure everything from insomnia to addiction, electronic pet-training collars and the shoe-polish-o-matic.

How about samples of modern packaged and convenience foods? The most popular was a stuffed pastry sealed in an aluminium-alloy envelope with a magnesium strip, so that when the strip was pulled, the burning magnesium instantly cooked the pastry to a piping-hot temperature... fruit filling, cheese, and ground meat varieties were all available.

The crowds found interactive amusement with an analytical encyclopaedia difference engine said to be able to answer any factual question with incredible accuracy, a stenographic typewriter that transcribed spoken words into printed text, phrenological and graphological personality evaluations, and a magnifying tracer-printer that would turn the impression of fingerprints into a valuable keepsake on acid-etched foil ribbon...

"I say," said Reggie, when they paused at the refreshment tent for flash-frozen chocolate custards.

"You say what, exactly?" asked Vinnie.

"I don't know," he said. "I just... I say. All this is a bit, well, astonishing. Who would imagine. Hardly the first time I've been wrong, is it, cuz?"

Poor Reggie. Vinnie had no idea what her cousin imagined.

"Shall I reference the list?"

"No need for that. But, here now, you told me you'd entered something for the judging, when's that?"

"We'll get there in due course. There's so much to see."

"Isn't it wonderful, though? Like having our own World's Fair," Josephine said, rejoining them after making the quick rounds to mingle. "We should make an annual occasion of it. Really put Huntleyshire on the map!"

"Are you sure your father could take the strain? Poor old chap looked like he was stretched to the breaking. And, on a similar matter, what's all this about us being engaged? No one told me that was part of any plan."

She batted her lashes at him and did a pretty pout. "Why, Reggie, are you saying you don't *want* to marry me?"

"Ah... I... er... that's a dashed trick question, isn't it? One of those what-do-you-call-its, where there's no safe answer!"

"Well," said Vinnie to Josephine, finishing her custard, "you'll have to marry *someone*. After all, you've already got the dress."

"And the cake! Oh, the cake, such a cake, it's a work of art!"

"Not to mention the flowers."

"Or the guests! Some of them have come quite a long way. They're expecting a good show. Wouldn't do to send them away empty-handed, now, would it?"

Reggie tugged at his collar. "But, sooner or later, you'll have to deliver the goods, produce a fellow who'll stand there at the altar and pony up the old I-do… and I don't mind telling you, a lot of chaps, that gives them right the cold feet all over, say-what?"

"It will, I'm sure, work out one way or another." Josephine stood, drawing Reggie and Vinnie to their feet as well, each by a hand. "Come along. I daresay by now the initial crush of the crowd will have died down and we can get into the Dynamo exhibit without need of a shoehorn."

Without need of a shoehorn?

Such was not quite the case, but the press of personages had decreased enough to allow them to gain ready admittance. They made their way to the rope-and-post barricade a few feet from the edge of the platform upon which the Etheric Dynamo was displayed in a containment dome made from layers of pressurized ethereal-absorbic glass.

The Dynamo itself, not much larger than a serving platter, hung suspended on a haze of energized and ionized particles at the center of a gyroscopic gimbal. The gimbal's brass rings flicked off bright glints as they swiveled, rotated and spun, each on its own axis. No stage spots or overheads were needed, because the luminiferous ether emitted from the spinning Dynamo itself provided a fluctuating white-gold radiance. At regular intervals, that radiance would first dim appreciably, then flare outward in concentric spheres like expanding soap-bubbles of dusty liquid light.

These, as they came into contact with and passed through various objects arrayed around the Dynamo—a vacuum-chamber, labeled balloons of different gases, a block of ice, a tank of water, a billow of steam from a valve, a clear canister of quicksilver, a chunk of talc, a slab of stone, a steel sheet, a cross-section of tree trunk, a smoked ham, a fishbowl with goldfish swimming about in it, a birdcage with finches flitting likewise—rippled in patterns consistent with the densities of said objects.

Easels held panels of diagrams, blackboards of formulae and equations, and photostatic duplications of Clive Chapman's notes and correspondence with colleagues. In the inventor's continued absence, a closemouthed German assistant named *Herr* Gloeckner presided over the device. He gave it his utmost focus of attention, much to the disgruntlement of those trying to ply him with questions and pry from him answers, most of which had less to do with the Dynamo and more to do with Chapman himself.

The boldest among the spectators could, if they wished, take turns stepping through a special portal done in the style of an airlock. This would gain them admittance to the containment dome, within the Dynamo's field of effect, to personally experience the sensation of the etheric waves transversing their own bodies. Most were not so bold, despite the lack of distress evidenced by the fish and finches. The few who dared reported, upon emerging, that it was a singularly unique sensation, most extraordinary.

"What-ho, what-ho," Reggie cried, delighted. "I'm game!"

"Oh, I like that," Josephine remarked sidelong to Vinnie. "Cold feet at the prospect of walking down the aisle, he says, but give him a chance at the ether and he's on it at a shot."

"We Wilmotts have a strong adventuresome streak," he said. "I'll have to tell you about my little sub-Atlantic nautilus excursion some time."

"Don't get him going," Vinnie said.

"Tut-tut, cuz."

The ladies found a good vantage as Reggie took his place in the queue. "He really is adorable, isn't he?" murmured Josephine. "The right woman could no doubt make something of him."

"No doubt." Though, of course, there was in Vinnie's mind plenty of doubt; without Brassworth, her dear cousin was next-to-hopeless, and needed not so much a wife as a full-time nanny or governess.

"Cheerful disposition and a good sense of humor." Josephine swept him with a well-practiced eye, smiling. "And attractive enough, if you like that sort."

"I suppose." Which, in fairness, he was, and the Wilmott men had a tendency to age into a distinguished silver.

"He wouldn't be one of those stuffy, penny-pinching husbands with a stern eye on the children."

"He doesn't care for children." Vinnie could imagine Reggie as older but otherwise unchanged, but found she could not wrap her head around the notion of him as anybody's father. Perhaps because it would require his own growing up.

"Pff, they all say that until it's their own."

They watched as Reggie, after an amiable if one-sided conversation with the taciturn *Herr* Gloeckner, entered the dome. He rocked heel-toe-heel, grinning eagerly. The Dynamo's emissions dimmed, then flared. The rippling etheric energy coursed outward in its white-gold luminescent spheres. It washed over him and he chortled like a boy being tickled by a favorite nanny.

"That," he said upon rejoining them, "was really rather a something! Can dashed well *feel* it, moving through you, the ether. Like being a spectre, half-insubstantial, hey-what? You girls should try it!"

"Best to save any odd scientific experiments until after the wedding."

"It's harmless," Vinnie said. "There aren't any dangerous side-effects at all."

"See there? Vin's got the chops, she'll give it a go."

"Not just now, I think. Besides, I've worked with etheric waves before," Vinnie said.

Linking arms again, they continued touring the fair-grounds. As afternoon bent on toward evening, the volunteers at the refreshment tent began serving up sausage rolls on a stick, steamed dumplings, iron-pressed sandwiches, flavored iced teas, and piping-hot salt-and-pepper potato crisps. Sugar-driven children, faces sticky with candy floss and sno-cone syrup, whirred about like hummingbirds—noisy, chaotic hummingbirds.

Eventually, as it always does, twilight followed afternoon. The sun set in a bed of rose and gold. The sky's hue deepened to a paisley of pink, blue and lavender, sprinkled with the sequins of glimmering stars. Gaslamps and strings of tiny edisonian bulbs lit up the lanes. Moths flitted. A breeze sighed across the lake.

From the stage with the podium, the megaphonically amplified voice of Dean Huntley rang out to announce that it was time for the judges' results and prize-giving. Everyone flocked over to that area, where the esteemed judges sat behind a long table draped with white linen. There were the requisite several moments of jostling and jockeying until the crowd settled, then the ceremony could proceed.

The dean, assisted by the two Huntleyville Grammar School students who'd come in top of their class, distributed ribbons, framed certificates, stamped bronze plaques, and the envelopes containing signed checques. Name after name was called. Distinguished scientists, fussy academics and madcap-looking inventors filed up to accept.

When it seemed things were nearing the close, Reggie leaned over to Vinnie. "Well, dash it all, cuz, looks as though you got the wrong end of the stick. Can't believe these stuffed shirts snubbed you. Ruddy rude, if you ask me. But, remind me again, what was it you'd put in for judging? We did see it, didn't we? Or was it a paper?"

"Shh, Reggie dear," Josephine said.

Dean Huntley gestured for attentive silence. "And, First Place—with its commensurate award of one thousand dollar-pounds and a tenured Professorship of the Sciences at our own Huntley College—goes to, unsurprisingly, I'm sure, Mr. Clive Chapman, for his Etheric Dynamo."

Buzzing with excitement and anticipation, the crowd all once again began craning their necks, standing on tip-toe, and trying to catch a glimpse of the genius, that most elusive and reclusive. People murmured. Had he arrived? Had anyone seen him yet? He was here, wasn't he? Someone said he'd been at the lecture on lunar landers, sitting in the back row. Hadn't someone matching his description brought that lost little girl to the children's tent? Someone else said they'd shared a cigarette out behind the psychokinetic resonance exhibit. He *was* here, he *must* be!

But, the celebrated man of the hour did not appear. The dean's brow darkened. Lord Huntley pursed his wrinkled lips as if he'd bitten into something sour. The overall prevailing mood began to turn, stormy weather hoving into view on the otherwise blameless horizon.

Josephine squeezed Vinnie's hands, then released them. "Go," she whispered, giving a nudge.

The epiphany struck Cousin Reginald a ringing clout atop the noggin. He made a sound not unlike a terrier with a biscuit lodged halfway down its gullet and just about staggered on his feet.

Vinnie worked her way through the press of bodies, reached the steps at the side of the stage, and ascended toward the podium. Another stirring of curious murmurs passed among the assembled. Their stares made her terribly self-conscious, aware of the conspicuous spectacle she must be presenting... petite thing that she was, the spray of freckles across her upturned nose making her look even younger than her true age... brown hair in a shingled bob... ankle-skirt and buttoned shirtwaist, simple shoes... but she kept her head high and her spine straight as she approached the dean.

It suddenly rather all seemed a most dreadful mistake. What in the world had she been thinking? They would laugh her out of the place, at best, if not a good old-fashioned tarring and feathering, followed by the proverbial running out of town on a rail. Forget being welcomed to work in the field; she'd be lucky to so much as get a job as a stenotypist!

To think, such a scheme had ever seemed clever when she and Josephine first devised it...

"Miss... Wilmott, isn't it? What is the meaning of this?" the dean asked.

A palm to her shirtwaist in hopes of quelling the frantic race of her heart, she cast a stricken look over the baffled and whispering crowd. She saw that Reggie had recovered enough to flash her an encouraging double-thumb's-up, but, of course, dear Reggie was no stranger to making an ass of himself in public. In fact, he'd grown not only accustomed to but deuced good at it over the years. While she, Lavinia, had dedicated her life until now to avoiding just this sort of scene or scrutiny.

Desperate strings of plausible excuses and lies tangled on her tongue. She would tell them she was Chapman's secretary, she would claim to have received a last-minute wireless from him, something, anything to get her out of this predicament.

"Dean Huntley... Lord Huntley... distinguished doctors and professors... ladies and gentlemen..." Her voice shook. She faltered. Then her gaze found that of Josephine, unwavering, full of faith. Vinnie drew a deep breath and lifted her chin. "No more pretence. I am Clive Chapman."

This, of course, caused considerable uproar and outcry for the next good half-hour or more. A barrage of questions—very nearly an inquisition or interrogation—came at her from all sides. Shouts and indignation tried to overtop each other. Proof was demanded. Insistences that it was a prank were proclaimed.

But, once all the evidence had been thoroughly examined—documents, signatures subjected to graphological comparison, microscopic analysis of fingerprints, testimonials, the sworn statement of *Herr* Gloeckner —they had to agree, there could be no doubt. Miss Lavinia Wilmott, and the mysterious Clive Chapman, were one and the same. Clive Chapman, in fact, did not actually exist. Never had.

Howls of mortification and embarrassment arose from those who'd claimed to be acquaintances. This was followed almost instantly by backpedaling excuses along the lines of "so I'd been told, at any rate" and "I never should have taken so-and-so's word for it" and the like. Some eyed Vinnie with outrage, for daring to perpetrate such a deception. A degree of disgruntled resentment was voiced by many of the male parties present, but she was met with overwhelming support from the members of the feminine minority.

In short, it was, as the chuffed-to-bursting Reggie later said, "quite the sen-*sache!*"

Reggie was, however, rather less chuffed the next morning. Lavinia found him in the breakfast room, poking without much appetite at the choices laid out on the sideboard.

"You look a bit pasty about the gills," she said. "Hung-over?"

He looked insulted. "I was only up until just past midnight, I hope you know. That's an early, and sedate, night for me."

"True, I imagine there's a marked difference in styles of and tolerance for wild revelries between your Westfallon Club chums and the typical attendee of the Four-Counties Scientific Fair and

Exposition."

"You've no idea."

"Then what is it that's gotten you off your feed?" she asked, spooning fruit salad into a dish.

"Have you forgotten what's on the agenda for today? Two hours from now, I have to be in topper, spats and boutonniere, and on my way to the blasted church!"

"I have to wear a gown."

"But, barring some miraculous stay of execution, I'll be honeymooning with the new Mrs. Wilmott before I know what hit me! Thanks to *you*, might I add."

"Me?"

"Oh, don't turn the innocent eye and go 'me?' at *me*, cuz. You never mentioned this was part of your scheme. Come to think of it, you never told me what your scheme actually *was*. Yet, here I am, about to be ritually sacrificed, a lamb to the slaughter, a lamb in topper and spats!"

"Reggie, calm down."

"Calm down?" He quaffed a tumbler of orange juice as if wishing it were something stronger. "Calm down, she says. I'm sure that's just what they told them at Versailles, as they marched them to the guillotine."

"You don't have to marry Jo," she said.

"Oh, right, and what am I to do? Leg it? Ditch her at the altar? What kind of decent gentleman could do such a thing and still meet his own eyes in the shaving mirror?" He heaved a sigh clear from the toes. "No, there's nothing for it. What was it that Greek fellow said? Brassworth would have it in a snap. Something about fate and reckoning, and knowing when your number's up."

"If you're thinking of Demosthenes," Vinnie said, "that was because Philip of Macedonia was about to sack Athens."

"Was it?"

"Yes, and he was trying to encourage his countrymen not to sit there and take it."

"He wasn't suggesting they accept the inevitable and surrender?"

"Not at all."

"I must be thinking of some other Greek fellow, then." He glanced at the clock and heaved another from-the-toes sigh. "Best get to it, I suppose."

Shaking her head, she finished her fruit salad and returned to her own room, there to don the gown and do the hair, with the help of a housemaid loaned to her by Josephine.

The quaint little church in the village was packed with flowers and well-dressed wedding guests. Ladies rustled in the lace-trimmed, with elegant gloves and feather-bedecked hats. Men milled about in their morning coats and striped trousers. Several of the young bachelors, including Clarence Stafford, Francis Tutt, and Herbert Clifton, also wore uncertain expressions, and kept making anxious inquiries of one another.

Vinnie saw Reggie come in, peer about, go over to them, and join in the making of anxious inquiries. Then he made his way over to where she was sitting, and dropped beside her on the pew with a slow exhalation.

"Are you all right?" she asked him.

"Ran into old Huntley outside," he said. "Figured I should say a few words of buck-up-old-man to the future father-in-law, but before I could get a word out, he had me in such a handshake I thought he'd oscillate himself to pieces, going on about how *sorry* he was it hadn't worked out for Jo and me, *such* a shame, but no hard feelings, he hoped."

"You mean your engagement is off?"

"Evidently, she broke it to him in the car. Thank heavens for those miraculous stays of execution! I don't mind telling you, cuz, the persp was greatly dewing the Wilmott brow. Now, I do doubt old Huntley was the most sincere in how sorry he was and such a shame and all; I've a notion he would have liked to dance a jig. Whoever's for the chop, he's just glad as the dickens it's not me."

"That makes two of you, I think."

He mopped the dewy brow with his handkerchief. "Weight off the shoulders. Marvelous. Of course, I asked some of those other blokes and we're all in the dark about who it is, but, gift horses, hey-what?"

"Absolutely."

"And, dare I say, Vin, you look positively smashing."

"Thank you."

"Don't often see you dressed to the nines."

"Well, it is a special occasion."

"That it is."

A signal given, the congregation took their places. There was a pause, an expectant hush, and then the organist struck up the familiar notes. The church doors opened. In came the flower girl, strewing petals from a basket. In came Buttercup the dog, velvet ring-pillow tied to her collar. In came Lord Huntley, walking his daughter down the aisle.

The universal oohs and ahhs went up at the sight of the radiant bride, bouquet clasped, eyes shining, veil floating about her like a soft cloud.

Halfway to the altar, Lord Huntley faltered with a mis-step. He stared. Confusion creased the seamed old features. The other guests, whose attentions had been fixed upon Josephine, followed his gaze.

Altar... candles... flower girl, holding onto the dog's collar as Buttercup wagged her tail... vicar in vestments... but, where a nattily-attired groom should have been waiting, there was a vacancy.

This, needless to say, caused a bit of a stir.

"We'll just have to cancel the wedding," Lord Huntley said, at length.

"Oh, Daddy," Josephine said. "How could you? We're already here, in the very church. Everything's paid for and arranged. You can't expect me to walk away and forget the whole thing. I'd be devastated."

"But, Josephine, my dear, you can't get married without... well... somebody *to* marry..."

She laughed musically.

At that, Vinnie noticed Cousin Reginald and the other bachelors who'd been on engagement roulette ducking their heads and averting their faces. They looked like schoolboys trying to avoid being called on by the headmaster.

Josephine smiled, extending a hand. "Lavinia?"

Vinnie stood. "Yes, Josephine?"

Stunned gapes filled the little village church. Poor old Lord Huntley's mouth flopped about so that if he'd had false teeth, they surely would have fallen out.

A sudden broad, beaming grin suffused Reggie's countenance. "Why, you sly devils," he whispered. "This is part of your scheme. You had it planned from the start."

She winked at him, then made her way up the aisle to join Josephine by the altar.

The father of the bride managed to stammer a few words to the effect that this was rather irregular and unexpected, to which Jo gave another of her musical laughs.

"You said it yourself, Daddy... I have to marry *somebody*..."

"W-Why... well, yes, but..."

"You did also say that whoever I married should have money or a respectable career. What could be more respectable than a tenured professorship at our own Huntley College?"

"I-I admit, I did say that—"

"*And* that I should marry for love."

"Yes, but—" He pulled at his lapels.

Josephine nodded as if her father had just stated that the Union Jack had stripes. "There you have it. I love Lavinia, and she loves me."

The vicar, who'd been told weeks in advance and therefore was one of the few not to react with shock, gave a benign nod.

"Gerald?" Lord Huntley turned imploringly to his brother for advice.

Dean Huntley shrugged. "She was intelligent enough to devise the Etheric Dynamo—"

"*And* clever enough to pull off that whole Clive Chapman business," Reggie added. "Kept the wool over everyone's eyes for how long? Bloody brilliant, if you ask me."

Lord Huntley turned the imploring to Vinnie next. "You… you love my daughter, Miss Wilmott?"

"Yes." Vinnie folded her hand into Josephine's. "I love her."

"You'll take good care of her and make her happy?"

"As best I can."

To be sure, there would be the matter of last names to consider, not to mention any eventual hopes the distinguished elder might have for grandchildren, but all that could be dealt with in due course. There were always options. Hadn't the seminar at the Delaney Institute, where she and Jo first met, covered that very topic?

"Don't think of it as losing a daughter, old man," said Reggie. "Think of it as gaining, well, another daughter."

"This is what you want?" Lord Huntley asked Josephine.

"It is, Daddy." She squeezed Vinnie's hand. "It is."

"All right, then. Carry on." He let the dean guide him to the front pew, where he sank in a dazed manner into his seat.

As the crowd settled into an expectant hush, and as the vicar prepared to begin, Josephine leaned over to whisper into Lavinia's ear.

"You see?" she said. "Just as I told you."

"Oh, of course," said Vinnie. "All it took was creating an entire false persona, not to mention the invention of the decade, and convincing your father to simultaneously host a science fair *and* a wedding. Easy as pie."

THE MODERN WOMAN

"DR. MERVIN?" I steered my crinoline and bustle a weaving path through the other noonday diners. "Dr. Clarence Mervin?"

The shabby little café was well off the beaten track of usual university haunts or museum gathering spots. Finding this man here instead, given the reception he'd recently received in those august scholarly quarters, was therefore no great surprise.

He glanced up, shoulders making a furtive twitch as if in anticipation of a blow, either of the verbal or physical varieties. The fact of it being a feminine voice thus addressing him did nothing to assuage this, nor did the sight of me, that voice's owner.

"Yes?" he asked in a tone so hesitant it bordered on the quavering.

I am not, for the record, of imposing stature or build. I've been described in terms like 'angular' and 'severe.' Or, to put it another way, in terms of an hourglass, I'm more a grandfather clock. Tall, straight, and wooden. Even the tightest-laced whalebone corset can only do so much with so little.

That said, it saves me a fortune at the dressmaker's. I have no need for frills and fancies. A simple tweed skirt and cape-jacket over a prim blouse, high-button shoes, and a cap with only a token bit of feather did the trick as far as I was concerned. I wore the hair—an unremarkable shade of brown—drawn back, caught at the nape in a netted snood.

Given the temperate nature of the day, I was not even carrying a parasol or umbrella with which I might have suddenly beset him a barrage about the head and ears. I had only my clutch-bag, held at the waist in walking-gloved hands.

I suppose that the very elements contributing to my lack of threatening physical appearance may have lent themselves well enough to the threat of a verbal tirade. On first acquaintance—indeed, often on second, third, or fiftieth acquaintance—I seemed to convey something of a stern headmistress or humorless governess note. The thin lips, pressed together in what was often taken for a disapproving scowl... the sharp eyes behind the spectacles... the posture... I tended to give the impression of being on the verge of cutting loose with a tongue of ice and acid, wielded with rapier-like efficiency.

This was not, as it happens, unwarranted when the situation called.

Since this situation, however, did not call, I mustered the thin lips into a smile. "I am Dr. Genevieve Delaney of the Delaney Institute for Feminine Wellness and Well-Being. I was privileged to attend your presentation, 'The Revival of Primitive Man' at the recent Scientific Discoveries Symposium. Might I join you?"

Had he been doing more than merely picking at the toast-crust, I daresay he might have suffered an asphyxiational mishap. I'm not sure which element of my speech was the primary cause, or if it was a combination thereof, but the results left him boggling at me, gulping, mouth working like that of a landed trout.

He started to stand, struck the table's underside with his thighs, clattered the crockery, dropped his napkin and nearly upended his chair.

I took this as permission to join him, seating myself opposite. I set my clutch on the table and folded my hands atop it.

Clarence Mervin sank back down. He blinked.

He, too, was far from imposing. The physiognomy was boyish, of a round-cheeked variety, the skin that fair sort made for going the most florid shades of red. The hair was sparse, sandy, and in need of barbering. The eyes were owlish, wide and of a watery blue disposition.

Judging by the way his clothes hung on the frame, he'd once been well-padded if not trending toward stout. For all that, when I'd first spotted him, it was to find him brooding over a meager repast of tea with toast, plucking at the crusts in a manner that could only be described as 'desultory.'

Speaking of his clothes, not only were they ill-fitting, but several seasons out of style even amongst the staid, stuffy, and even stagnant social circle to which he nominally belonged. This defect in tailoring, combined with the aforementioned meager repast, convinced me of what I had hitherto only—but with good reason —suspected. The man was, as they say, barely keeping body and soul together. Broke. In the dire straits chin-deep and rising.

I therefore offered to buy him lunch.

Part of it was, I must admit, to observe the anguish of his inner struggle. Men, you know. As if it wasn't bad enough, the very idea that some strange woman should march up unannounced and introduce herself, that she should then also be the one to foot the bill? A female doctor, no less?

But, pride doesn't put much food on the table, and after a moment's agonizing, Dr. Mervin accepted. The next bit of time was taken up with the rituals of signaling the waitress, ordering the edibles, having the teapot replenished and glasses brought of iced lemon-water, and the arrival of a basket of only barely stale rolls with jam.

"You… you attended my presentation?" he ventured.

"I did," I said. "It was most fascinating."

The owlish eyes peered at me with searching suspicion. He then swiftly scanned the café, perhaps expecting to see a host of sniggering professors and curators looking on to see how well the prank was going over.

"We'll get someone to approach him," these conspirators might have plotted to one another. "Someone earnest, very sincere. A woman, perhaps? Yes, a woman, that would be an excellent touch. Really let him make an ass of himself!"

They had, of course, soundly denounced him. All but laughed him from the podium, or driven him from it with a barrage of rotten vegetables—which were, for precisely these sorts of reasons and occasions, banned from the Symposium floor.

It was a disgrace! they'd cried. A discredit to higher education, to the university, to his peers! An insult to the entire fields of paleontology, archaeology, anthropology, evolutionary studies and the humanitarian sciences!

Not that they'd quite been howling for his blood, but, honestly, they may as well have been. Instead of having his work rewarded with prestige, tenure, a comfortable funding grant, and his name immortalized in the hallowed halls alongside those of the giants, he'd been ousted. Accused of attempting to perpetrate a hoax. Given the bum's rush.

I didn't doubt they would have tarred and feathered him, if they'd had the supplies handy. Right when he'd been expecting triumph and acclaim, to boot. That had to make it an all the more bitter pill to swallow.

"…most fascinating?" he echoed when the owlish gaze returned to me.

"And a shame you weren't allowed to finish," I said. "I very much wanted to hear the rest, not to mention have the opportunity for follow-up questions."

"Ah," he said. He fiddled with his cuffs. He slathered jam on a roll and devoured it in three bites.

By the time our meals arrived, I'd managed to convince him of my bona fides and that I was not part of some scheme to mock, expose or ridicule him. The way he fell to, all but wolfing his food, lent credence to my notion that he'd been on a diet restricted by frugal necessity.

"What does he eat?" I asked. "Your Primitive Man? I would guess that our modern fare, heavily salted and sugared as it is, has made for a rather drastic change."

"Absolutely," said Mervin, wiping his chin with a napkin. "He won't touch tinned or processed meats. Got to be fresh. He prefers beef or pork to fish and fowl, though in a pinch he'll suffer the latter. What he likes most is calf's liver, if you can believe that."

"It makes a certain amount of sense, given a hunter-gatherer lifestyle."

Mervin nodded. "Same for greens and vegetables. Fresh, fresh, fresh. Won't touch the tinned of that, either. Except when it comes to fruit. Funny you mentioned sugar; he will guzzle as much in the way of canned peaches or apple-sauce as I can lay my hands on. Salt, too. Never seen the like! I've wondered if I oughtn't get a salt lick to hang on the wall!"

"I shudder to think of your grocer's bill," I said.

He groaned. "I'd never understood my parents complaining about my brothers and I eating them out of house and home until this."

"What about candy, pastries, other sweets?"

At that, he shook his head. "Less so. At first, yes. Stuffed himself. Gorged, even. The same for cheese and butterfat; he ate an entire brick of lard once!"

My nose, I must admit, wrinkled. I began to regret opening the conversation in this direction before we'd finished our own lunch.

Now that he'd gotten going, however, Mervin kept right on.

"Fortunately," he said, then caught himself with a scoff. "Fortunately? I say that now, but at the time it was another matter. Regardless. Fortunately, it made him sicker than I've ever seen. Thought he was going to die of it. Both ends and—"

I held up a hand and tipped my head toward the neighboring tables. "Doctor."

"Oh. Yes. Sorry. Suffice, he hasn't touched the stuff since."

"Alcohol?"

A grimace wracked his features. "Those spirits which turn the most civilized of men into beasts? That's how I got tossed out of the cottage I'd been renting. The brute half tore the place to pieces, and when my landlady came by to complain, he…"

A crimson flush flooded his face. He coughed, and cleared his throat. I think he'd forgotten for a moment he was conversing with a member of the so-called fair and gentle sex.

My eyebrows climbed. "Did he knock her over the head with a club and drag her off by the hair?"

"Dashed if he mightn't have tried, if I hadn't been there!"

"How ever did you dissuade him?"

"A shock prod."

"You use a shock prod on him?"

"Not anymore," he hastened to assure me. "Only at the start. In the early stages, don't you know, as a training tool, an aid to learning."

"An aid to learning," I repeated.

"It's no different from a schoolmaster with a birch switch."

"Or a horse-drover with a goad."

"No harm was done!"

"What about modern pharmaceuticals?" I asked. "Drugs?

Laudanum, say, or a tincture of opiates?"

Mervin hesitated. The flush, which had faded, resurged. I held the thin line of my lips against an impulse to smirk at his discomfiture. Would he tell me?

Stammering, mumbling, and stumbling over his words, he did try. He told me that most patent medicines had little to no, or adverse, effect. And that opiates, well, that opiates did not send the specimen on a destructive rampage as the alcohol had done, but... well, had inspired other... cravings... not unlike those in the manner of which the landlady had nearly been accosted... so it had become necessary to... well...

It occurred to me that this mortified fellow had never once before so much as even hired a girl for himself, let alone for something like this. I had to press the lips more firmly against the smirk that so very much wanted to surface.

Little would he have any reason to suspect that I'd already interviewed both the landlady and the girl in question. But he'd understand, in due time.

Meanwhile, and perhaps eager to move on to other matters, he mentioned that there'd been hardly any further need at all for the shock goad, once they'd gotten communication sorted.

"So you've taught him to speak?"

He shrugged, jabbing an asparagus spear. "His mandibular and laryngeal structure aren't suited for complex utterances. He understands well enough, provided a clarity and slowness of enunciation, but full speech? No. Some simple words. The rest is gestures... we've devised a fairly sophisticated sign language."

"Interesting," I said.

"I'd been going to demonstrate at the Symposium, but, as you saw, they didn't give me the opportunity." He jabbed another asparagus and bit it in half with a savage snap of the teeth. "I barely got through the accounting of the expedition and discovery, let alone the revival or anything further."

I nodded, well recalling the uproar.

Having by then warmed to his subject, Mervin went on more expansively. I was familiar with the articles he'd had published—in somewhat sub-optimal scientific journals, it must be admitted—detailing his earlier work at the *Vallée des Arbres Pétrifiés*, near the Franco-German border. But I chose not to inform him of that at this time, and let him continue unabated.

The region had long been of scientific interest, of course, initially to geologists and vulcanologists. The petrified forest there was unlike others of its kind, the stony trees curiously porous and even hollowed. The prevailing theories maintained that a volcanic eruption, earthquake or meteoric impact had released a pocket of superthermal subterranean gases. This produced such a blast of intense heat that the moisture within the trunks and branches had been flash-boiled away, even as the harder wood became calcified and ceramicized, instantly baked like pottery in a kiln.

When signs of neolithic settlements were uncovered in the vast warren of limestone caverns beneath the petrified forest, archaeologists and anthropologists also flocked to the valley. Cave paintings, ancient midden piles, flint-knapped tools and evidence of ritualized burials tantalized those excited by the 1856 discoveries in what was now more properly known as Neandertal.

Those such as Doctor Clarence Mervin. He'd begun his research in the caverns, then shifted to a site further down the valley. There, on what had once been a riverbank, were the buried remains of a prehistoric hunting camp, as well as the remains of prehistoric hunters.

His theory, expressed in his papers—a condensed version of which he related now to me as we finished our lunch—was that the event responsible for the petrification of the forest had not just boiled away the tree-sap and resins, but vaporized them into a dense airborne cloud. This cloud, according to Mervin, sank back to earth, settling over the hunting camp on the riverbank in a manner similar to the pyroclastic flow of ash and mud that had famously engulfed the ancient city of Pompeii.

"Under normal conditions," he said, having by then ordered a ham slice and scoop of egg-salad on lettuce to supplement the gluttonous meal he'd already dispatched, "the process by which resin or tree-sap solidifies into what we know as amber requires millions of years. However, the presence of gaseous molecules, mineral dust and other substances—combined with a marked drop in local temperatures, as borne out by the botanical and sedimentary records of the time—"

"Indeed," I said. "It cooled and condensed far more rapidly, with the result that the hunters at the camp became encased in amber... or, this amber-like hardened resin... much as insects have been."

"Precisely. And, as in Pompeii, it happened so quickly, so thoroughly, that they were caught in place, locked in that final, fatal moment. All of them except one, that is. Were you able to see the slide-projection photographs before they jeered me from the podium?"

"I was. The one specimen preserved perfectly intact. With, as you soon observed, gas bubbles and air pockets trapped in the resin with him. Inducing... what was it that the test samples suggested?" I knew, of course, but many men preen and enjoy being able to show off their learnedness, and this one was no different.

"A chemical anesthesia capable of inducing a state of torporific catalepsy." As expected, he did preen. "It's been linked to cases of premature burial, as I'm sure you've heard."

"Oh, yes," I said. Safety coffins had been all the rage when I was a child; family lore had it that a great-uncle had been buried alive. Even now, in these days of enlightenment, modern medicine and embalming, people fear that fate. Poe's famous but sensationalistic popular tales had only added to the lingering dread. And no wonder... the prospect of falling into a cataleptic trance, only to waken in the grave... that could send a shiver up the steeliest spine.

The thought of Poe led me also to recall another of his stories, the one in which a hapless sailor brought some ape or another back from foreign shores. It had escaped, and, whilst attempting to imitate the habits of its master, committed murders. I thought of mentioning this to Mervin, but decided he would see no humor in the comparison.

He went on to relate how he had, upon determining this one particular specimen to be intact and perfectly preserved, speculated at the amazing scientific possibilities should it prove to actually be alive, or revivable. Through a careful series of experiments, he'd devised a way to remove the resinous prison without causing damage, and invigorate the long-dormant tissues in the process.

"The answer, obviously, was electricity," he said, in a tone that gave me reason to second-guess the decision of pandering to his ego and offering him the opportunity to preen. "We get the very word from ēlektron, the Greek word for amber, by virtue of how when rubbed with fur, it acquires a charge."

"I'm quite familiar with the principles and applications of electricity, thank you, Doctor," I said. Mildly enough, but the rebuke brought him up short. Chagrin flickered briefly in his eyes. When he continued, it was with a rather less patronizing manner.

The upshot of it all was that he'd succeeded. Against all odds and reason, he'd done it. He'd revived a living example of Primitive Man.

It should have been the find of the century, sure to leave the world awestruck. He'd be more famous than Darwin, who may have devised evolutionary theory, but here was proof in the actual, breathing flesh!

Think of what could be learned! A window to mankind's own past! If such a creature could be tamed, socialized, communicated with—!

Fine and well, as far as it went, but as Mervin had since become very aware, all those lofty plans and dreams fell apart when one was denounced as a fraud.

Farewell, fame and fortune. Farewell, hopes and dreams.

A fraud, they'd said. A hoax. Taking some miserable, deformed wretch… what did he suffer from? A bone disease? Or was his grotesque appearance faked as well? Gum-rubber prosthetics and glued-on hair? Was it madness? Retardation? All an act? A sham?

The nerve! The gall! For Clarence Mervin to think he could make fools of them in such a manner? They were esteemed professors, scientists, the learned men and great minds of science! They were nobody's laughing-stock to be tricked with anything as blatantly ludicrous as this!

I, having been on the receiving end of no small amount of disdain for my profession myself—*a woman? a doctor? the very idea!*—was not altogether without empathy for his plight. He'd put everything he had into this. His savings, his reputation, his career, everything. What did he have to show for it? A smashed-up cottage, an angry landlady, a mountain of bills and debts, a houseguest of voracious and costly appetites…

No, I was not altogether without empathy for him. But, by the same token, it did mean he'd be more inclined to accept my offer.

"And now…" He raised his hands and let them drop, one to either side of his emptied plate. A hopeless bark of a laugh escaped him. "I might as well buy a striped suit, join the circus, and take him on the road as a sideshow attraction!"

"I think I can offer you a far more preferable alternative, Doctor Mervin."

He looked at me, not without skepticism. "How so?"

"My purpose in seeking you out today was not solely my own," I said. "I represent a small group of influential personages—wealthy, respected, influential personages—with a considerable interest in certain aspects of the physical sciences and humanities. An educational society, of sorts."

The man perked up visibly, though a shadow of the skepticism remained. I suppose he was wondering again if this were all some prank sprung on him by his erstwhile peers.

"Do go on, Doctor Delaney," he said. "This... educational society you mention...?"

"...is conducting one of their meetings tomorrow evening," I said, sliding him one of the Chesterton's gilt-embossed cards across the table. I'd already written the time on the back. "I do know it's woefully short notice, and for that I cannot apologize enough, but I ran across some difficulties locating you—"

"Yes, well, never mind that." He flapped my apology away with a hasty wave and snatched up the card. His owlish eyes widened further as he recognized the noted judge's address, smack amidst the city's very best neighborhood. "A meeting? Tomorrow, you say?"

"They would be most gratified if you and your—does he have a name, by the way?"

"The nearest I've been able to pronounce it is Jayok," Mervin said, sounding for a moment like he'd caught a bone in his throat. "We've agreed, for convenience's sake, to call him Jacob."

I inclined my head in gracious acknowledgment. "If you and Jacob, then, might be available to—"

"Absolutely!"

"Because it *is* such short notice, naturally, a substantial financial compensation would also be in order. The society would insist. An educated professional deserves something for his—or her—time.

Provided, of course, the prospect doesn't insult you."

"No insult at all!" he assured me, with enthusiasm so ill-concealed he could barely keep from bouncing in his seat. "I mean yes, obviously, I'd be delighted for the opportunity to present my discovery, but it would be rude to decline a well-intentioned token of appreciation."

"I'm glad we see eye to eye on this, Doctor." I smiled.

He looked at the card again, running a fingertip over the lettering that read Chesterton House. "Are you a friend of the Chesterton family, Doctor Delaney?"

"Mrs. Chesterton and many of the ladies of her acquaintance are faithful, unfailingly generous patrons of my own work."

"Ah. Patients? At the… what was it again? Institute of…?"

"Feminine Wellness and Well-Being," I told him. "For the treatment of maladies such as hysteria, and other female afflictions."

His expression changed to one with which I'm very familiar. I see it all the time on the faces of the husbands who set out to inquire about just what these treatments entail and why they should cost so much. Within seconds of my beginning to explain, they inevitably decide they emphatically do *not* want to know the particulars. Desperate to escape before I can say anything more, they cannot write the cheques fast enough. Ignorance, they tell themselves, is not just bliss. In some matters, it's a bargain at any price. Even the esteemed Judge Chesterton had harumphed and gone purple.

Clarence Mervin clearly had no further curiosity on the matter. He pocketed the card, beaming like a boy at Christmas. "So… tomorrow evening?"

"Yes. Shall I bring a motorcoach by your cottage? Perhaps at, say, six-thirty?"

"A motorcoach?"

I honestly thought the man might swoon. He collected himself as I settled the luncheon tab. We walked out together, exchanged farewells and pleasantries, and then he went on his way with a spring in his step.

As for me, I caught a cross-town trolley, dispatched a wireless to inform Mrs. Chesterton that everything had been arranged, and returned to the Institute at a brisk pace. Ensconced in my office again, I brought down the large leather-bound journal filled with news clippings, sketches, photos, mimeographs of academic papers, and page after page of my own notes.

Primitive Man.

Those stuffy old fools had laughed Mervin out of the Symposium. Mocked him, discredited him, barred him from the university. They could hardly have been more offended had someone presented them with half a monkey stitched to half a flounder and claimed it was a mermaid.

I slept well, passed the following day tending to rounds and appointments, and dressed for the meeting in slate-blue with black trim. No jewelry, minimal cosmetics, the sole nod toward finery being a lace snood to hold the hair rather than the usual netted ones.

The motorcoach arrived promptly on time, and rolled up outside the front garden gate of Doctor Mervin's rented cottage with five minutes to spare. I surmised by furtive curtain-movement that Mervin himself had been waiting, anxious, lest it all prove to be a ruse.

He emerged in what must have been his good suit—which no doubt had been a good suit, once—and in the company of another figure of far different description. Even at a distance, and concealed as he was in a large over-coat and broad-brimmed hat, there was something about him so strange, so altogether uncanny, that the instincts could not help but respond.

The driver, who'd stepped out to open the back door, shifted from foot to foot as they approached. I saw him toss me one quick glance, as if concerned for my safety, but he had been paid well enough to keep to his own business.

"Doctor Mervin," I said.

"Doctor Delaney."

"And this must be Jacob."

They sat opposite me. The driver closed the door, returned to his upper cabin, and started the engine with a chugging rumble and a back-fire that Jacob did not seem to care for.

I studied him with avid attention. Beneath the coat and hat, he wore baggy wool trousers and a cotton shirt. They did not fit him well. Not in the same way that Mervin's clothes didn't, but in a way that suggested tailoring to Jacob's frame would require an expert. These oversized factory-mades were the best Mervin had been able to afford.

He was barrel-chested and slightly slump-shouldered, broad through the torso, hunched of posture. His thick arms looked disproportionate in length to his stocky body, his legs shorter and somewhat bandied or bowed. He had wide hands, the backs hairy, with wisps of it also sprouting also between the base and first knuckle of each stubby finger. Some uneven success had been managed in the manicuring of the strong, yellowed nails.

"Doc-tor," he said. His voice was a rough bass-baritone, the word glottal, as if uttered through a mouthful of gravel.

His head, though… his face… there most of all was where the differences were the most striking. The skull was larger, low-set on a squat neck, the back of it forming a bulge of heavy bone beneath coarse dark-brown hair. Instead of a high and clear forehead, his brow sloped into a prominent and bristly supraorbital ridge overhanging his eyes. His prognathous jaw was immense, like a steam-shovel, the lower pushing forth into a hint of an underbite.

Between bristly eyebrows and wiry beard was a flattish nose. His skin was not quite leathery, but sun-weathered and swarthy-complected.

While I studied him, Jacob in turn studied me. His eyes, overhung though they were, gleamed with definite intelligence. They had the color and clarity of strong black coffee, and as much of an effect on the nerves.

And this, the scientific community had scorned as a hoax?

Mervin, who'd brought his presentation case, prattled on with worried questions as to whether there would be a slide-show projector available and how much lecture time should he expect to have and what level of education might his audience have, would he need to simplify it for the benefit of their understanding?

I reassured him—he'd soon find out for himself just what the meeting's actual agenda entailed—and continued studying the Primitive Man as the motorcoach carried us through the city. Only a few months ago, he'd been in an entombed cataleptic state, dug up and transported, and revived. Unknowing that tens of thousands of years had gone by.

In his mind, he'd been hunting with his tribesmates. Making camp on that riverbank, feeling the earth lurch and shake, seeing the sky change hues. Had they marveled? Had they quailed in terror of angry spirits or gods? Had they tried to flee? Or had there been no time?

Then, oblivion… until waking to a world so alien to him that it might as well have been another world altogether. A world in which Man mastered Nature rather than exist alongside it. A world of cities, rather than wilderness. A world of machines, technology, and invention.

Amazing, really, that he hadn't simply snapped and gone mad. How would any of us have fared, were the situation somehow reversed? Here he was, riding in a motorcoach through a noisy, crowded landscape of monoliths and pollution... but, aside from the occasional clench of a fist or jaw, or narrowing of eye, he was calm.

Had Mervin, I wondered, given any thought to the possible consequences of his actions? The sudden reappearance of Primitive Man in modern society... the effects it would have upon both?

I doubted it. His hurt surprise at the Symposium, and at the barrage of furious letters he'd gotten from scientists and clergymen, were signs of that.

The motorcoach turned in at the gate of Chesterton House, proceeding up the drive. It was a stately place, dripping with wealth and privilege to excess. We disembarked as a footman paid the driver. Moments later, we were shown in.

Doctor Mervin seemed torn between intimidation and envious yearning as he took in the lavish décor. I noticed Jacob's head lift, nostrils flaring, scenting the air.

No butler came forth to greet us. The great house was hushed. I took the lead. "The salon is downstairs," I said. "That is where Mrs. Chesterton does her entertaining, meetings, and social events."

Mervin's nervousness rose with each step we descended. By the time we reached the lower hall, he, too, sniffed at the air.

"What is that?" he asked. "It smells like smoke."

"Opium," I replied, and pushed open the salon's double doors.

Hazy tendrils of it wafted, intoxicating ribbons and fumes. The room, dim-lit by lamps and heavily curtained, was furnished with luxurious cushions, chaises and lounge-chairs.

And here waited Mrs. Chesterton with her guests. Well-to-do society ladies all, the wives of lawyers and bankers, doctors, politicians... they reclined around the room in languid relaxation.

Mrs. Chesterton herself swayed toward us. "Genevieve," she

purred at me, "you are a veritable angel."

Had we been out at some proper function, the judge's wife would have been attired to the very pinnacle of fashion, shaped by crinoline hoops and corset and bustle, confined in stiff satin and brocade. It rocked poor Clarence Mervin back on his heels to behold her ample curves unfettered, voluptuous flesh loose beneath a sheer silken chemise.

The other ladies were in similar dishabille of chemises, cami-knickers, robes and draped sheets. The scene entire was not unlike a painting by one of the old masters, depicting nymphs at some banquet or bacchanal. They regarded us—or, to be fair, they regarded *Jacob*—with half-lidded eyes. Tongues slipped wetly over parted lips.

The Primitive Man, for his part, drew so deep a breath of the smoke-rich air that his chest strained his shirt to the buttons' very limit. What I'd been told by the girl that Mervin had hired, which had been supported by Mervin himself, was confirmed as to the effects of opiates on his system.

"My goodness," said Mrs. Chesterton, removing Jacob's hat and tossing it idly away. "Aren't *you* a magnificent specimen!"

"Doctor Delaney...?" Mervin looked at me, his owlish gaze more confused than ever. "What is this? What's going on here? You said... a meeting... an educational society... with... with..."

I nodded. "...with a considerable interest in certain aspects of the physical sciences and humanities. Quite so. Particularly that which pertains to female sexuality. I believe I mentioned to you that my field involves treatments for hysteria and other such afflictions."

"But... yes, but..."

"This is our meeting," the wife of the city's police commissioner told him. "This is our educational society."

"Oh, yes," said the spinster sister of a captain of industry. "We've had Aboriginals, Plains Savages, Islanders, Orientals—"

Additional voices chimed in.

"Don't forget the albino!"

"And the midgets, oh, the midgets!"

"And Rex," a dowager railroad baron's widow said. "Dear old Rex. He was such a good boy."

"We even had a Shetland pony, once," the commissioner's wife said. "That one was a bit much. Hardly anyone dared to give it a try."

"But *this*!" cooed the mayor's eldest daughter, a recent divorcee. "What a find!"

"I could hardly agree more," said Mrs. Chesterton. She favored Mervin with a decadent smile. "Doctor, you are to be congratulated. He's perfect. Thank you ever so much." She tucked a folded cheque into his breast pocket, then patted it. "*Ever* so much!"

Mervin just gaped. He once again reminded me of a landed fish. I took him by the elbow and steered him from the room, before the opium fumes could addle him too much. He didn't have my tolerance for them, I was sure.

Jacob, meanwhile, had reached understanding long before his stunned and scandalized discoverer. His reaction as the ladies flocked dreamily toward him was what might have been expected.

At the far end of the downstairs hall was a small drawing room. It was there I led Mervin. I got him to a chair, then poured him a hefty knock of brandy. He downed it at a gulp. His watery blue eyes watering all the more, he blinked up at me.

"Educational society…" he said in a feeble whimper.

"More of a libertine debauchery society, to be true." I refilled his brandy and poured one for myself.

"They…" He realized he was still holding his presentation case, and let it fall to the carpet with a brittle kind of laugh. He'd be giving no lectures, showing no slides, not here, not tonight.

"They're…"

I chose my own chair and sat. I sipped. I shrugged. "Roman noblewomen used to enjoy the company of champion gladiators. In the sultan's harem, bored wives and concubines had the services of their eunuchs."

"Well, perhaps, but…"

"It is much the same for women in this modern day and age, Doctor Mervin. Neglectful husbands, scolding churchmen, physicians who insist that it's all in their minds… craving release is improper, they're told, and unladylike. They're pent-up, frustrated, dissatisfied. So, they seek other options."

"They go to you."

"They come to me."

In the brief silence that followed, we could hear from behind the salon's closed doors the sounds of grunts, moans, squeals and sighs. All seemed to be going rather well.

"There is," I said after a while, "one more matter I'd like to discuss with you. The Institute, my Institute, could use someone of your specialized knowledge and expertise."

Face creased with bafflement, he only looked at me.

"Besides my office here in the city," I explained, "the Institute maintains a very nice country estate, with a private boarding school. The staff are of the utmost discretion, and the pupils are… children of exceptional interest and breeding."

Comprehension went on eluding him. I leaned forward in my chair and tried yet again.

"As you are the foremost scholar on the revival of Primitive Man," I said, "perhaps you'd be willing to continue your research." I raised my tumbler of brandy to him, as if making a toast. "In the event that this evening's meeting… this evening's experiment, if you will… should bear fruit."

ROSIE RED-JACKET

"BOYS ARE THE HORRIDEST," someone said. "Aren't they just?"

Georgina, on the stone bench by the garden hedge, started so that she almost dropped her book. She caught it against her lap and looked around.

Here was the yard, grassy lawns and flower-beds and tree-shaded paths sloping up toward Drewbury Hall, where her uncle's family lived. Where she, too, now lived, because she had no place else to go. The brick walls climbed green with ivy, the roof-slates were grey, and curtains stirred in open windows as the maids aired out the rooms.

The only person she saw was Partridge, the driver, out by the carriage-house. He crouched in front of the big brass-grilled snout of Uncle's gleaming auto-motor, polishing the luminaries with a soft rag. It couldn't have been him that she heard, because he was too far away, whistling as he worked.

And the voice had sounded much more like that of a child, a girl her own age.

Which would have been nice, but the only other girl for miles about was the coalman's daughter in the village. Mrs. Curtis, the housekeeper, insisted it simply wouldn't do for Miss Georgina to associate with the coal-scuttle girl. Such things weren't proper, and therefore, weren't done.

She was about to decide she'd imagined it when the someone spoke again.

"Don't you wish that they'd all get the speckles and die?"

The garden hedge rustled, shedding leaves, as the someone pushed through. Georgina saw with amazement that it *was* a girl, a girl her own age. Not the coalman's daughter, either, though her clothes weren't much better. Her paisley-print dress was faded, patched and shabby. Her feet were dirty, bare of both stockings and shoes. Her jacket, though, was fine and fancy, bright red with shiny buttons all in a row.

Georgina gaped. It was unladylike; Mrs. Curtis would have given her a stern look. But she gaped nonetheless. "Where did you come from?" she asked in a gasp.

"From here and there and everywhere," the girl said. "This side, that side, the up-side and down-side, the other side." She tossed her head and laughed. Her hair bounced. A few stray leaves were caught in it.

She had the most incredible hair, Georgina noted with envy. A moppet-mop, her mama might have called it. Curls all over, loose and springy, the effortless kind that did not need to be wrapped and pinned, and slept on so that it was like rocks in the pillow. Quite different from Georgina's own hair, thin and fine, straight as ironed flax.

Such a color it was, too, that hair! As red as her jacket, brilliant scarlet. While Georgina's was the kind of dullish-blonde Mrs. Curtis called 'wash-water.'

"I'm Georgina," she said, remembering her manners. "Georgina Drew. Who are you?"

"Rosie."

"Rosie who?"

"Rosie Red-Jacket." The girl laughed again. Rosy, as well, were her cheeks, and her pert-smiling lips, and the scatter of freckles across the bridge of her nose. Her eyes were as shiny as her jacket-buttons. "Were those your brothers that went riding velocipedalers off down the lane?"

"My cousins." Georgina closed her book and set it aside on the bench. A sort of anxious hope swelled in her heart at the prospect of a playmate.

Mrs. Curtis, she suspected, would not approve of some barefoot moppet-mop stranger in a shabby dress, no matter how splendid her jacket, but, for the moment, Georgina didn't care. It was hard to sit and read day after day, quiet as could be, a well-behaved young lady, when her cousins got to romp, and ride, and have fun with their friends in the village.

"Your cousins," Rosie said, in a musing sort of way, as if thinking this over. "So, the man with the funny moustache is not your papa?"

"My uncle. My papa was a soldier."

"What about your mama?"

"She pined away after Papa died," Georgina said.

Often, this was met with clucks and sympathy. But Rosie shrugged, said an unconcerned, "Oh," and added, "so, they sent you to live with your uncle and auntie?"

"Well, not so much my auntie." It verged on gossip, though it was hardly a secret that Caroline Drew cavalierly left her husband, home and boys to fend for themselves on a regular basis while she pursued a career as a famous opera singer. "My auntie's in New York right now, I think."

"Oh," said Rosie again, still unconcerned. She picked a daisy, examined it, and began plucking off the white petals one by one.

"What about your parents?" asked Georgina.

"My mama is a lady-in-waiting to the Faerie Queen, and my papa is a handsome courtier with silver buckles on his boots."

Georgina giggled despite herself. "No, really."

Rosie pursed her red lips, poked her red tongue between them, and made a noise that would have scandalized Mrs. Curtis. "Yes, really!"

"The Faerie Queen?" When the very book on the bench had for its cover a fanciful color-picture of pixies dancing in a ring to the music of a fieldmouse orchestra, and *'In the Court of the Faerie Queen and Other Tales'* in gilt-stamped lettering.

"The Queen, the Queen, the Queen of Between, the Queen of Underhill and Overmeade, east of the Sun and west of the Moon and north of the Stars and south of the Skies."

"You're a fairy, then?"

"Maybe." Rosie skipped around the slender trunk of a green willow tree, then cocked her head and grinned. "Or maybe I'm the devil's imp, a wicked, evil sprite!"

"Don't," said Georgina, uneasily, but still giggling.

"Oh, fine, all right." She flopped into the grass, elbows propped and chin on her hands, dirty heels kicking up. "What do you *do* all day? You looked bored half to a frazzle, sitting here with your dumb old book."

"It isn't dumb."

"I'll bet you a butterfly that those cousins of yours, *they* aren't sitting with books, bored to frazzles. I'll bet *they're* out having a grand time. Getting into plenty of mischief. Having plenty of fun."

"Well, but they're boys."

"Horrid, hateful boys who *abandon* you. And why?"

"Because I'm a girl."

"Doesn't that make you cross?"

"They're hardly going to have tea parties with me."

"Tea parties." Rosie made the rude noise again, flipped onto her back, rolled her head, and looked at Georgina upside-down. "Phooey and piffle and tra-la-la to tea parties. Why not play with them? Do what they do?"

"Because, I told you, I'm a *girl*! They wouldn't have me tagging along, even if I wanted to! And Mrs. Curtis—"

"Phooey and piffle and tra-la-la to Mrs. Curtis, too, the pinch-faced wretch!"

Alarmed, Georgina cast another quick glance around, sure that she'd find the housekeeper's grim figure looming out of the garden. But she only saw Partridge, leaning on a fence post, chatting to a laundry maid with a basket on her hip.

"What you should do," Rosie went on, "is go find them, your cousins and their friends."

"They won't—"

"Not like you are, no. Put on my jacket. It's magic. It'll disguise you as a boy so that they can't even recognize you." She sprang up, removed the bright red jacket with the shiny buttons, and held it out to Georgina.

"Magic, is it? Then how come it didn't disguise *you* as a boy?"

"Because I didn't say the magic words, silly."

"And even if I did go find them, what if Mrs. Curtis comes looking for me? She told me not to leave the garden."

"I'll sit here with your book and she'll think I'm you."

"You don't look anything like me."

"I'll use magic! Now, put on the jacket, do up the buttons, and say *snips, snails, puppy-dogs' tails*."

"This is a peculiar game," Georgina said, but she put on the jacket and did up the buttons. It was a perfect fit. "*Snips, snails, puppy-dogs' tails.*"

A dizzy swirl rushed over her and suddenly...

"I'm... I'm a boy!"

Her dress and stockings had become a shirt, socks, and knee-britches. Her shoes were boys' shoes. Her hair, instead of falling fine and straight past her shoulders, had gone short and messy. The ribbon that had held it back was now a jaunty tweed cap.

"I'm a boy," she said again, hearing how even her voice was different. She stared at Rosie, whose grin was wider than ever. "It really *is* magic!"

"I told you!" Wider than ever, yes, that grin of hers was. And not a little bit scary. The shine in her eyes made them look like lantern-panes. "Now, go find your cousins and their friends. Play with them as long as you like. Then just come back here, say *sugar, spice, everything nice*, and you'll be a girl again."

Georgina laughed loud with delight and turned toward the gate.

"One more thing," Rosie added. "There's a packet in the jacket pocket—packet-jacket-pocket!—with hard candies in. Lemon drops and cherry, in twists of waxed paper. Have as many as you want."

"I don't care for cherry candies, thank you," Georgina said, remembering her manners again. "They taste like medicine-syrup."

"Then give those ones to your cousins, and you can have the lemons. But don't say thank-yous that way and be all polite and ladylike. You're a boy now!"

And so she was! As a boy, why, she could run down the lane, she could whistle and whoop as loud as she wanted! Nobody tutted. Some even smiled, or called out a cheerful, "Halloo there, laddie!" as she dashed through the village.

She soon spied her cousins' velocipedalers tipped in a heap down on the riverbank under the trolley bridge. The cousins themselves—Robert, Tom, Edgar and Petey—were with a few other boys. Friends of theirs from school, she supposed.

How they shouted! How they laughed! How they rough-housed and wrestled, and splashed in the shallows, and ran races, and held mock sword-fights with sticks!

Then Edgar caught sight of the bright red jacket. He elbowed Robert. He pointed. Ruddy, muddy faces turned. They looked at her. For a moment, Georgina stood scared half to pieces.

"Oy!" cried Robert, raising a hand. "Want to play?"

"Yes, pl—" She coughed. "Yes!"

A spate of introductions followed. She almost slipped on hers, but stopped herself in time and told them that her name was George.

"We have a cousin named George-*eeeeee*-na!" Petey said in a sing-song way. "She's a g*iiiii*rl. Tom thinks she's pr*iiiii*tty!"

"Shut it!" Tom gave him a swat. The others laughed.

"*Is* she?" Georgina asked.

"No!" Tom had gone purple. "She's a right bland pudding!"

"Forget her," said Robert. "Come on, George. Let's play!"

"Let's!"

Such an afternoon it was! They hunted tadpoles, skipped stones, sailed twig-boats, climbed trees, and hit conkers. Two of the boys had pop-guns. Edgar had brought his yo-yo, and another had a paper kite. When they tired of that fun, those who didn't have velocipedalers balanced on the handlebars of those who did— terrifying, but exhilarating!—and they rode back into the village with clangy-bells jangling.

Georgina offered out the packet of hard candies. Instead of politely accepting a single one, her companions of course grabbed by the fistful. Waxed-paper wrappers flew like confetti. They stuffed their mouths until their cheeks bulged like chipmunks, the cherry ones turning their tongues a vivid red. It gave them great amusement when they made faces at one another.

In a brick alley, they shot marbles and aggies, pitched penny-coins, and a boy named Jack chalked bad words on the wall. They kicked a canvas ball around the market-square, trying to score it off the big bronze numerals of the steam-clock.

A better time, Georgina hadn't had since before the day the wireless came with the news about Papa's regiment. On that day, the life and heart had run right out of Mama like water from a cracked jug.

The steam-clock tolled the hour of five. The smaller boys, Petey among them, began to fuss and complain. They were tired, they said. Tired and hot, half-sweated from top to toes.

"Quit your whining," Robert told them when he'd had more than his fill. "We'll head for home in a while."

"I want a cold drink," Petey said. "And my dinner."

What he *needed* was a bath and a nap. But that, Georgina didn't say. She realized she'd best hurry quick if she was to return to Drewbury Hall before her cousins. She couldn't go with them, couldn't let herself be found out.

"I'd best go," she said. "Chores."

"Chores!" They all groaned.

Jack added, "Bother chores!" and spat into the gutter. Robert gave him an envious, admiring look. Georgina wondered what Uncle would say if he knew the kind of company his sons were keeping.

They said their goodbyes, agreeing it had been jolly grand all around and they'd have to do the same again soon. Maybe they'd go down to the trolley yard to throw rocks at rats, or see if they could get their hands on some snap-bangs and spark-fizzers, or even cherry-bombs.

Tired and hot and half-sweated from top to toes herself—it was vigorous work, boy-playing was!—Georgina could not afford to dawdle. She went at a run, then a trot, then a brisk walk, keeping a ready look to throw over her shoulder if she heard the clangy-bells of the velocipedalers approaching up the lane.

She cut through the woods and came out by the garden hedge,

pushing through its scratchy branches. The stone bench, where Rosie had said she would wait, stood there empty but for the book of fairy-tales.

"Rosie?"

There was no answer.

Rosie wouldn't have just gone away, would she have done? Even if she'd gotten bored to a frazzle with what she'd called a dumb old book. Had Mrs. Curtis come along and caught her, the housekeeper not fooled by whatever magic Rosie had used? If Rosie even had waited? Or had Mrs. Curtis come along and saw no one here at all? Just the book on the bench, which she'd scold Georgina for leaving behind?

But if that were the case, surely Mrs. Curtis wouldn't have left the book behind either. No, not her... she would have marched it right in to Uncle's study to show him what a forgetful and neglectful silly creature his niece was. An expensive book such as this, there just asking to be dew-soaked and ruined!

"*And* she went wandering off," she imagined the housekeeper saying. "When I *told* her to stay in the garden. This kind of disobedience simply cannot be permitted, Mr. Drew. I know you mean well by the child, but perhaps a girls' school would be a better place for her after all."

"Rosie?" Georgina tried again.

Yet still, there was no answer. Dusk's cool shadows had begun to stretch long across the yard. In Drewbury Hall's downstairs windows, the light of gas lamps glowed. The shapes of servants moved to and fro in the dining room, setting the table.

"*Sugar, spice, everything nice,*" Georgina said.

In a wink, she was a girl again. A tired, hot, half-sweated from top to toe girl, but a girl nonetheless. Her fine straight hair fell long down her shoulders, the cap turned back into a ribbon, the shirt and knee-britches and boy-shoes and socks became her own

CHRISTINE MORGAN

familiar clothes.

She undid the shiny buttons, took off the red jacket, and then did not quite know what she should do with it. Certainly, she couldn't very well take it to her room, where her cousins might see and recognize it as belonging to their new chum, George.

With Rosie continuing nowhere to be seen, she settled for folding it carefully and placing it upon the bench. Then she picked up the book of fairy-tales and walked up to the house.

Braced as she'd been to be scolded, to land in trouble for leaving the book lying about in the garden and be called upon to answer for her absence, she raised her head and went inside.

"Oh," said Mrs. Curtis upon seeing her, as if she'd entirely forgotten Georgina altogether. "Yes. You. There you are. Dinner at seven sharp."

It was, in a strange way, almost disappointing. She washed and dressed, brushed her hair, and arrived at the dining room promptly upon Cook striking the bell. Tidy, proper, and ladylike, she sat without squirming or fidgeting. A good little girl. Seen but not heard.

Uncle and his guests came in. They'd been out shooting clay pigeons, testing his new wind-up launcher, and it had put them in lively high spirits. None of them paid the first bit of attention to Georgina.

The boys were late to their chairs, clothes hastily changed, having splashed their faces but with dirt behind their ears and their hair needing combed. Petey continued to fuss and complain, whining when reminded to sit up straight. Tom and Edgar only picked at their food, declaring that nothing tasted any good. Robert had sunk into a surly mood, which wasn't mollified even when his father said he could go out shooting with the adults tomorrow.

But nobody went shooting the next day. By morning, all four of her cousins lingered in bed, feeling poorly. Their throats hurt, they said. The sides of their necks were swollen and sore. Their faces were flushed. They were itchy and hot.

Mrs. Curtis consulted her mercury-stick and pronounced them feverish. Partridge was sent to fetch the doctor. It was some while before they returned. Uncle paced the whole time, wondering aloud if he should try to get a wireless to his wife in New York, or if he should wait. She would not want to be dragged from the stage and limelights without good reason.

The doctor came in with his black bag and examined the boys. He had them each in turn open their mouths, stick out his tongue and say, "Aahhh."

Their tongues were still as vividly red as if they'd been eating cherry candies. Georgina hid a giggle, but then she saw the doctor's grim look. He had Mrs. Curtis lift their night-shirts. A rash of tiny red bumps spotted all up and down their backs.

"It's the scarlet fever," the doctor said. "I've seen several other cases of it already today; that's why I couldn't be here directly as you called. Half the children in the village seem to be coming down sick."

"Scarlet fever, dear God," said Uncle, and rushed to dispatch that wireless.

His guests took their leave with rather unseemly haste, despite the doctor's attempts to reassure them that the disease was most dangerous to young children, and that many fine scientists were making excellent progress in the development of serums to reduce the mortality rate. Mrs. Curtis put the servants to frantic work changing linens and cleaning everything the boys might have touched.

Georgina, sent to the garden and told not to get in the way, went down toward the hedge. She saw at once that what she was looking for wasn't there. The jacket, with its row of shiny buttons, was not where she'd left it, neatly folded upon the stone bench.

Something else *was* there, though. Something pale, something crumpled and dew-damp. She picked it up and smoothed it flat.

It was a bag. A small packet of white paper, the kind that hard candies would go in. Lemon drops, and cherry. The very one that had been in the pocket of Rosie's red jacket.

The other girl's words echoed through Georgina's mind.

"Boys are the horridest, aren't they just?" Rosie had said.

Her words, and her grin... the grin that had been not a little scary...

"Don't you wish that they'd all get the speckles and die?"

OF THE UTMOST
DISCRETION

"While attentive to all, the footman should be obtrusive to none."—*Beeton's Book of Household Management*, 1861.

"IF YOU ASK ME," said the young man in smart livery, tipping back his chair to prop his heels on the table, "the doddering wreck, he's ruddy well past it. So far past it, in fact, he couldn't see 'it' from there if 'it' was a mile high and lit up with edison bulbs."

"Then it's just as good no one's asked you, isn't it?" the woman with the kerchief tied over her hair retorted. "And you shouldn't talk that way. It's disrespectful. Supposing someone should hear you?"

"Supposing someone should?" He shifted to get more comfortable and struck a flame to the end of a fresh cigarette. "There's no one to hear me but you and the kitchen maid, and *that* little dunce won't be running to tattle to old Bennings or Mrs. Harte." He raised his voice. "*Will* she, Alice?"

At a sink of steam and soapsuds, the girl hunched as if bracing for a blow. "B-b-b-beg p-p-p-p-pardon?"

"Leave her be," the woman said. "Back to scrubbing, Alice; pots won't clean themselves."

The young man smiled. "So, there we are. Unless you're planning on spilling the beans, Mrs. S?"

"I'm too good a cook with too much pride in me work to go about spilling beans, Rupert Landrey. Least of all yours. You couldn't pay me to touch your beans. Not with a spit-fork."

Rupert chuckled, sending a thin ribbon of smoke curling toward the kitchen ceiling. He was blond and fit, blue-eyed and handsome, and his manner told the world that he not only knew it but banked on it.

The cook was twice his age, three-quarters his height and half again his weight, round and red-faced in the hallmark of her profession. For all that, she didn't balk at snapping his ankles with a pantry-cloth as she bustled her way around the table to fetch the sugar tin from the cupboard.

"And get your feet down from there. Bad enough you're stinking up the place with those lung-gaspers."

"You're a cranky one since the doctor told you to quit." He drew another deep puff and exhaled the grey plume in her direction. "Used to be you'd burn through them like they'd be outlawed any day now."

"If you're not going to be helpful," she said, "the least you can do is stay out of me way."

"I am out of your way."

As she passed behind him, she shot the chair such a look—tilted on two legs as it was—that a casual observer might have suspected she wondered how much of a bump it would take to send it crashing over. And whether Rupert's head would smack the brick hearth-corner on his way down, which would no doubt make a frightful mess.

"Besides," he went on, experimenting at smoke-rings, "I'll have work enough to do once They roll on in. In the meantime, my dear Mrs. Sullivan, this is the last of our leisure and we should make the most of it."

"Leisure." She snorted. "Maybe a footman's got naught much to do when the family's away, but dashed if you still don't expect to eat, and that's work for me."

"Oh, listen to you complain, with the house all but empty."

"Mrs. Harte said the housemaids are arriving tomorrow, and the rest of the staff the day after that." She turned a bowl of dough onto the floured kneading-board. "Oh, and the new second footman some time today."

"Joy," said Rupert, rolling his eyes.

"Think you'd be glad of it, less for you to take on. You were a right whiner when Freddie gave his notice. You never liked him and don't pretend otherwise."

"I'm not. I never did like him. Funny-looking fish-faced git. He knew his duties, I'll give him that much. He'd fold a napkin and black a boot like nobody's business. Waiting at table, though? Gah. What a no-hoper."

"He couldn't've been that bad," Mrs. Sullivan said. "If he'd spilled or clashed the cutlery, I'd've heard about that."

"No, no." He waved an idle hand, the cigarette between his knuckles shedding a fine drift of ashes. "Fine at that, too, but did you ever see him serving?"

"'Course not. How would I? Go in the dining room, during meals? Me? Fancy!"

"Take it from me, then. When it came to being unobtrusive, he was anything but. There he'd be, dishing up soup, listening to Their talk—"

"Oh, and like you don't? How often have you gone with one of Their surefire tips to the horse-track?"

"Let me finish. Listening's one thing. That's different. Can't very well shut off our ears, can we? Using what you hear, well, a man must as a man must. What you *don't* do is let on about it. You don't react, you don't show the slightest expression, and you certainly bloody well don't laugh at Their jokes!"

Mrs. Sullivan winced. "He did that, did he? And with *his* laugh? Blimey."

"Worse even than that, Mrs. S. I recall a particular evening, His Lordship'd had a few of the fortifying beforehand, don't you know. Well, there His Lordship is, telling a ripe one about a couple of Frenchmen, and what does Freddie do? Jumps in just at the good bit and finishes it for him!"

"No! What did His Lordship do?"

"As I said, he'd had a few; he thought it was funnier than a fart in church. Her Ladyship, on the other hand... I'm surprised Freddie wasn't chucked straight out the door then and there. More proof that old Bennings is well past it. For that matter, I'm surprised they still keep *him* on."

"There's such a thing as loyalty, you know," Mrs. Sullivan said. "He's been butler here fifty years or more, Mr. Bennings has. Since His Lordship was a tot."

"All the more reason he should retire already! Be put out to pasture. Or out of his misery." He added this last in a mutter, which the cook, bringing down crockery, did not seem to catch.

"Woadcastle wouldn't be the same without him," she said.

"He's going deaf, forgetful, and shaky, and slow. Takes him an hour just to get up the stairs, and when he does, he can't remember why more often than not."

"Enough, give it a rest, why don't you?"

"Why doesn't *he* give it a rest? Or They give him one?"

She heaved a sigh. "Well, maybe this new footman, he'll get on some better. Once he learns the ropes and all."

"And who do you think will be teaching him those ropes? Taking up the slack for him until he does learn them? Not a useless relic like Bennings; you can bet the house and cart on that. Because who do you think is also picking up *his* slack? No, mark my words, Mrs. S. it'll all be on *my* head, and *my* arse on the line." He ground out the cigarette butt on the heel of his shoe. "In fact——"

There was, from behind them, the soft sound of a throat being politely cleared.

They both nearly sprang from their skins. For a moment, the issue of Rupert's chair and its precarious two-legged balance was a teetering indecision. He lurched his body forward enough to bring it squarely down on all fours with a loud clack. Mrs. Sullivan, meanwhile, whirled with considerable dexterity for a woman of her age and girth, brandishing a long-handled spoon as if she were an aproned Boudica about to lead her army of Celts into battle.

"Please excuse the interruption," said the owner of the politely-cleared throat in a mild tenor. "Mr. Bennings sent me down. John Smithton."

Their startled—and not un-guilty—responses suggested that neither of them had any notion how long he might have been standing there, and what or how much he might have overheard. A silent moment spun out as they studied him, searching his gaze and countenance for some damning indication, but the gaze was even and the countenance composed.

He was some years younger even than Rupert, brown of hair, pleasant of feature, tidy of grooming, and neat of attire in traveling coat with hat held at his side. A small valise rested beside him.

"Lands, but didn't you give us a fright, popping in like that." Mrs. Sullivan hastily lowered the spoon, trying to look *not* as if she'd been about to brain an intruder. Her red face reddened further and she busied herself with spices.

"Terribly sorry. I'm told I have a very light tread."

"That, I'll believe."

"You must be the new footman," Rupert said, rising with a kind of careless nonchalance designed to make up for the earlier lurching and pinwheeling of arms. He'd already flicked away the cigarette butt with the speed of a stage magician, and now gave a brisk tug to the bottom of his waistcoat.

"Second footman. Are you Rupert?"

"Rupert Landrey, first footman, and I'd advise you keep that in mind."

"Of course."

Another silent moment of searching and studying passed, Rupert making an evaluating comparison of the other's person. Satisfied that he himself stood a bit taller, had the broader shoulders, finer backside, better-defined calves, and the overall advantage in handsomeness, he gave a curt nod.

"This is Mrs. Sullivan, the cook." Rupert didn't bother to introduce, or even glance at, the kitchen maid. "Bring your bag, I'll show you to our room. Don't snore, do you?"

"No."

"Good. Then we'll see about getting you into proper livery and putting you to work."

"Ah, Johnny, Johnny, there you are," Mr. Bennings said, when John entered the servants' hall the next morning. The aged butler pushed himself upright, or, as close to upright as his stooped frame would allow. Wisps of snowy hair were slicked to his balding pate with pomade. "Settling in, hey-what?"

"Yes, sir."

"Come in, sit down, have some breakfast." A bunched, liver-spotted hand trembled as he gestured around the table. "This is Mrs. Harte, our able housekeeper. These are the maids, Martine,

Edith, Sarah and Janice. Ladies, this is John Smithton, our new footman."

Nods were exchanged as John took a seat and the routines of pouring coffee and passing of cream and sugar were done. The housekeeper wore black-pinstriped dark blue, salted auburn hair pinned in a relentless bun. The maids ranged in age from perhaps sixteen to twenty, pretty girls in plain caps and aprons over print cotton day-dresses.

"You've already met Mrs. Sullivan and Alice, I take it," Bennings continued. "And Rupert, of course."

"Of course." John inclined his head to the cook as she set a plate of ham, eggs and porridge before him.

"Toast?" Martine, a sweet-faced brunette, offered him the basket. "There's butter, marmalade and jam. Black currant or strawberry."

"Thank you. Marmalade, please."

"What say you, Rupert?" asked Bennings, once they'd had a few moments to tuck in. "Is our Johnny all trained up? Fighting fit? Ready for the onslaught? Be a bit of a trial by fire these next few days. Hate to toss him in the deep end if he's not set for the swim."

Rupert, for his part, examined his neatly-trimmed fingernails. "He's got the gist," he said, in a grudging sort of tone. "Polishing the furniture, cleaning the silver, filling the lamps, at least. Have to see how he does waiting table, but, he might be all right. Oughtn't make us look *too* bad."

Bennings scoffed. "I should think not. In the blood, isn't it?"

"In the blood?" Martine echoed, tipping her head. "Are your parents in service, John?"

"They were, and for several generations back," he said. "Seven, at least."

"Seven generations?" Edith sniffed a bit. "Doesn't say much for anyone's ambition."

Janice, the senior of the housemaids, bristled. "Nothing wrong with being in service."

"Nothing wrong with wanting to better your lot, neither."

"Some of us, young lady, have considerable respect for tradition," Mrs. Harte told Edith.

Martine leaned toward John. "My family, too," she said. "On both sides."

"Mrs. Sullivan, you've been here a while—" Bennings began.

"Oh, donkey's years," she said, nodding.

"You must remember the under-butler we had, then. Back before the boys went off to university."

"That quiet chap? The one as we called Ghost on account of how he could come into a room without half seeming to open the door? I do remember him. What was his name?"

"Smithton," John said. "George Smithton. My father."

"Well, I'll be!" the cook said. "Knew there was something familiar about you the moment I set eyes on you, I did. How is Ghostie?"

"Passed on, I'm afraid."

"Oh, that is a shame. Didn't he marry one of the lady's maids?"

"Emma," Bennings said. "She looked after Miss Gertrude."

"I like that," Rupert muttered to Edith. "Forgets who he's announcing between front door and drawing room, but he can pull the name of some lady's maid twenty years gone out of thin air."

Mrs. Sullivan and Mr. Bennings, not hearing him, went on reminiscing. "Emma!" cried the cook. "That's right! And her sister as worked here too, didn't she?"

"Mrs. Forlen." Bennings shook his head in nostalgic admiration. "Finest housekeeper we ever did have."

At that, Sarah smothered a giggle, Edith and Rupert smirked, and Mrs. Harte's thin lips compressed into a pale line.

"Ah, that is," the butler hastily amended, "until you joined us,

Mrs. Harte."

"Indeed," said Mrs. Sullivan, though it may have lacked somewhat in sincerity.

"My mother and aunt always spoke very highly of Woadcastle," John said. "It was their fondest wish that I might find a position here."

"I'm sure they'd be quite proud," said Bennings. "Quite proud."

"Have they passed on as well?" asked Martine.

"My mother has," John said, finding her the easiest among them to talk to. Her gaze was both sympathetic and attentive. "My aunt's in declining health, and lives with my cousin and his wife."

Rupert made a show of trying not to yawn as he helped himself to another slice of ham. "Fascinating as this is…"

"Have you some important appointment to rush off to?" Mrs. Harte asked, with a touch of acid in her voice.

"Merely thinking of what Mr. Bennings said in regards to the onslaught and trial by fire these next few days. So as maybe we ought to get on with it."

"Oh," said Bennings. "Yes. Rather. Where was I?"

"You'd been introducing the staff, sir," Janice said.

"So I was." He peered around the table as if taking a quick headcount. "That's everyone here. The others, including His Lordship's valet, Her Ladyship's maid, and the driver, will be returning with the family. Now. Who am I forgetting?"

"Thaddeus, sir," said Sarah, dimpling in a manner that earned her a warning look from Mrs. Harte.

"Yes, that's right," said Bennings. "Thaddeus, our groundskeeper, and his boy. They have a cottage down by the back gate; we don't see them much below stairs."

"I do send them out a hamper now and then," Mrs. Sullivan said. The corners of her mouth quirked as she glanced from housekeeper to housemaid. "Sarah's usually good enough to trot it over without complaining, aren't you, girl?"

"Takes her sweet time about it, too," Janice murmured.

"Mind your own affairs," said Martine, giving her a nudge.

"You should talk; I'm not the one flirting with the new footman."

She went pink. "Janice!"

John kept his impassive demeanor, though a warm rush did tingle through him. He held to his father's training, reinforced by a lifetime of instruction—manuals such as *The Complete Servant, Beeton's Book of Household Management,* and *The Footman's Guide* had been, in their house, as much of the family Bible as… well… as the actual family Bible. If not more so.

Ignoring all this, Bennings moved on to the next orders of business, which concerned the various guests that Sir Roderick Fitz-Hughes would be expecting, the preparations to be made, and the planned schedule.

Woadcastle was a fine, grand country house, though with the various members of the family not currently in residence, it did have something of the museum about it, a sort of somber breath-held quality, looming with ponderous expectation. Having been largely closed up for the season, there was much to be done to have everything in readiness.

"It'll be a right carnival," Edith said. "How will we ever be ready in time?"

"By not dallying over your coffee or stopping work to gossip with every tradesman that comes to call," said Mrs. Harte, aiming the warning look her way this time. "Or taking a dozen smoking-breaks in the day, for that matter."

"Now, now," Bennings said. "We none of us need reminding that the honor of Woadcastle rests as much on the conduct of the staff as the reputation of the family. It's our job, nay, our sacred responsibility, to uphold both to the highest of standards. Hey-what?"

"Yes, Mr. Bennings," chorused the housemaids, with the kitchen maid Alice a mumbled beat behind them.

"And?" He looked at them paternally, or like a kindly old school-master.

"Always mind your place and station, and don't get above yourself," recited Edith, not without a faint curl to her mouth.

"Be as one both silent and invisible," Martine said, "so as not to upset or offend those of gentle birth."

"Keep confidences private, give counsel only when asked or invited to do so," Janice said.

"Don't go spreading about rumor or suspicions," Sarah chimed in.

"But be prompt to report all that is detrimental to the household," Mrs. Harte said.

"Manage your work with care and economy," said Mrs. Sullivan, "but don't scrimp, skim, cheat or cut corners."

"And, in all ways," finished Rupert, speaking as if by rote, "be attentive but unobtrusive, of the utmost discretion."

Bennings beamed. "Very good. That's what I like to see, right enough. A tight ship, Johnny, we run a tight ship around here."

"Yes, sir."

"Let's hop to it, then! Tally-ho!"

It was, indeed, a right carnival, an onslaught, a trial by fire, or being tossed into the deep end, however one cared to define the whirlwind of activity that marked the next few days at Woadcastle.

The Fitz-Hughes family returned *en masse*, Sir Roderick and Lady Jessica, the younger two of their five sons, a daughter, a son-in-law, a spinster great-aunt, and assorted nieces, nephews and more distant cousins. The fiancée of one of the sons came to stay as well, with her widowed mother and a brother in tow. More relatives would visit during the late spring and summer, including the older sons with their wives and children, and Sir Roderick's sister the countess. Frequent guests were expected from the peers and gentry, the clergy, a decorated war hero, and a celebrated opera singer.

John Smithton, however, was more than up to the challenge. Even Rupert found himself having to agree, however sullenly, that their new second footman was well-versed in his trade. A hard worker and well-groomed, he needed little training and never a reminder. He was all but silent in his movements, even upon the notoriously creaky back stairs. The rest of the staff remarked on how it was he seemed to be able to enter or leave a room unnoticed, with such subtlety of presence it was as if he materialized out of thin air. Mrs. Sullivan said again and again how like his father, the under-butler they'd called Ghost, John was.

"He's not near as good-looking as you, though," Edith told Rupert. "You, you're almost *too* handsome to be a footman, you are."

Which was, of course, the generally acknowledged truth; his fine features and figure as well as his manner of obsequious flattery made Rupert very popular. He was often shown off, not in an ostentatious way, but, displayed to the guests in much the same way that a particular piece of artwork might be, or a sleek motor-car. He also did well in the department of vails, gratuities, commissions and incentives from the guests and tradesmen frequenting Woadcastle.

There were garden-parties, and hunting-weekends, and an anniversary ball, and a concert-social to benefit a local home for the disadvantaged. There would be the autumn wedding of Mr. Henry and Miss Louisa, which really should have been hosted by the bride's family, but Lady Jessica insisted that it would be a kindness not to put such a great burden upon them, after they'd lost so much already, and wasn't it the happiness of the young couple that mattered most?

The staff could, in short, count on being busy from before dawn until well past midnight. Even with the addition of Sir Roderick's valet, the lady's maids, the driver, and what servants of their own the guests brought along, more than enough work remained to go around.

John would wake early in the room he shared with Rupert. He'd wash and shave, dress in his day-livery, and set to the many tasks that *The Complete Servant* described, not inaccurately, as 'multifarious and incessant.'

The house was fitted with the electric, sporting some edison bulb light-fixtures, but Sir Roderick preferred old-fashioned oil lamps. It was therefore John's daily duty to gather up all that had been in use the night before, bring them to the lamp-room behind the kitchen, trim the wicks, clean the brass bases and glass chimneys, and refill them so they would not spill or leak.

The tedious chore of cleaning and sharpening the knives was another that might have fallen to him, by virtue of his lesser status as second footman. But this, thanks to the purchase of a pedal-powered machine of rotating grindstones and brushes, was one that Rupert found too easy or enjoyable to hand off to a subordinate.

Care of the mahogany furniture fell under their auspices as footmen. So too were the gilded mirrors and picture-frames, and of course the silver, crystal and china. They were responsible for laying the table at mealtimes, in the breakfast-room and dining-room, as well as bringing in afternoon tea.

Then there were the myriad other matters requiring attention— messages to be delivered, the door to answer or dressing-bell to sound if Mr. Bennings were otherwise occupied, gentleman guests to assist when they traveled without valets, the newspapers to be iron-pressed, and the writing desks kept well-supplied.

And, of course, most important of all, they did the waiting at table.

Bennings, as butler, held pride of place behind Sir Roderick's chair. His was the privilege to select and pour the wine... but John soon saw that, unkind though Rupert's words may have been, there was some truth to them. The arthritis in his gnarled fingers clearly made it painful for him to grip the bottles, and the tremors of his hands turned the act of pouring into an ordeal of tense anticipation for all present.

To hear the bottle's neck chattering and clinking against the rim of the glass... to see the unsteady flow of liquid, sometimes gurgling... to cringe breathless against the moment that must soon occur, the moment when the wine would splash across the white damask tablecloth like a spray of shed blood...

With dining *a la russe* being the fashion, at least there was some mercy in the serving being handled by the footmen while the butler supervised. Rupert, as first footman, did the lion's share, presenting each course to the diners with the dishes balanced upon his left hand and the right tucked deferentially behind his back. John attended to the other myriad requirements of cutlery, sauces and seasonings, and otherwise kept to the background.

But, when it came to the wine, and the brandy after, Bennings would brook no suggestion that he let someone else tend to it. It was difficult to observe, and more difficult still to observe without displaying any emotion or reaction.

This went for family and guests as much as for the staff. If Sir Roderick was oblivious, or as unwilling as Bennings himself to face facts, Lady Jessica had been overheard expressing pity and an understanding of what it meant to the old butler to preserve his dignity. From others, however, there tended to be more of a thinly-veiled impatience, sometimes contempt... as if they shared Rupert's opinion that it was well past time Bennings was urged into retirement.

"They've got wagers running on it," Martine confided to John, one morning as he polished silver with a paste of powdered hartshorn and she sewed laundry marks into a new batch of bed-linens. "Wagers on how long he'll last, who and when he'll spill wine on someone, what a scene it'll make, how he'll go out... it's horrible. If only there was more that could be done to help him."

John smiled. "I've an idea or two. I'll do what I can."

"You're very kind," she said, also smiling. "After all, you haven't been here but a few weeks. You hardly know Mr. Bennings."

"Perhaps not, but he knew my parents, my aunt, my grandparents. He hired me on, gave me a place here."

"You *are* kind," she repeated. "And so good. They hardly notice you at all when you go in to clear away."

"I've been born and bred to this, raised to it, raised for it. In a sense, this is what I'm made to do."

"It's more than that," she said. "You're like those newts as can blend in with the wall-paper. Not to say you look like a newt, mind you!"

"Thank God for that. I may not be a show-piece like Rupert, but I'm glad I don't look like a newt."

"Oh, go on now," she said, blushing.

"And what about you?" he said. "I've yet to see you taken by surprise when a call-bell rings. Like you know what They want before They know it themselves."

Martine shrugged, tying off a thread. "Well, You can just tell, sometimes, can't you? When Her Ladyship's about to have one of her headaches and will be wanting a cold damp flannel, or when a guest is likely to upend an ash-tray over the carpet. I guess I'm born and bred and raised to it too."

"You'll be a housekeeper before you're thirty, mark my words."

"And you, you'll be a valet soon, and a butler some day, I shouldn't wonder." She glanced over her shoulder, ascertaining that they were still alone, and leaned closer. "Why, when Mr. Bennings does retire…"

"Didn't you just say how I'd only been here a few weeks?"

"Yes, but imagine if you got promoted past Rupert."

John did imagine that, for a moment, and suppressed a shiver. "He'd not be happy."

"Do him good to be taken down a peg or two, that peacock."

"Let's not get ahead of things," he said. "And let's not scratch Mr. Bennings from the lists just yet, shall we? A discreet helping hand now and then is all he needs."

There was, over the next several days, a subtle but decisive improvement in the old butler's wine-service.

Though still plagued by the painful arthritis, he no longer seemed in imminent danger of being unable to keep a firm hold on the bottle or decanter. Though his hands were still seen to tremble, his pouring became much steadier.

Not a drop was spilled to the tablecloth—or, worse, onto a guest. Not a single glass was chipped or cracked, let alone broken. When he brought in the after-dinner brandy for the gentlemen, the heavy-laden tray did not waver or tip in his grasp.

For most of the staff, it was considered impertinent to bring up the subject to his face, though it was the topic of some discussion amongst themselves.

"First he's quaking like an aspen," Rupert said to Mrs. Sullivan, "then he's the Rock of Gibraltar. Something's gone on."

"Well, it's not for *me* to poke my nose in," she said. "Should be glad for him, you should, that he's not declining further."

Mrs. Harte, however, did possess sufficient authority to inquire after Mr. Bennings' health in person. She did this late one night in the servants' hall, after those above-stairs had finally gone to bed.

"You know, it is a funny thing," he said. "I don't mind telling you, Mrs. Harte, that I'd been feeling rather out of sorts for a while there, rather not up to snuff, as it were. Thought I might be coming down with a touch of the palsy."

"A touch?" Edith murmured to Rupert.

"More like a slap."

"Lately, though, I dare say I've bounced back nice and sharp. Must have been a passing ailment."

"We're all right glad to hear it, Mr. Bennings," Mrs. Sullivan said, bringing a cake to the table for their dessert.

"That," Bennings added with a chuckle, "or a guardian angel has taken me under his charge. An unseen presence, an unseen hand or force lending support, don't you know."

"Oh, now, really, Mr. Bennings," chortled Anson, His Lordship's valet, who occasionally deigned to join the lower staff. "You'll have the maids jumping at shadows, saying Woadcastle's haunted."

"Is it?" Sarah gasped.

Rupert's lip curled in a malicious half-grin. "What, Sarah, haven't you *felt* it? That sense of being watched when there's nobody there?"

"Don't frighten her," said Janice.

"No, I've felt it, too," Edith said in a loud stage-whisper. "How often I've gone into the breakfast room or parlor, and I'd swear on my soul…"

"Tut and hush," Mrs. Harte said. "None of this foolishness."

"Don't you believe in spirits, Mrs. Harte?" asked Sarah.

"Strange sort of spirit, if you ask me," said Rupert. "A spirit of spirits, looking out for the brandy and wine?"

"Be skeptical if you like," Bennings said. "Remember Monday, at dinner? I went to put the wine on the sideboard, and I was sure I'd misjudged it, sure it'd come a cropper. Inexcusable. Would have gone smash onto the floor. There it was, teetering, about to topple over. But it didn't, and then I saw it was set a bit back from the edge after all. Safe and stable as could be."

Martine looked at John.

"Is that ginger-spice cake, Mrs. Sullivan?" John asked. "It smells divine."

"Why, that it is, me gran's own recipe. Will you have a slice?"

"Two, if you'll allow it."

She ruffled his hair. "One big one, to start with. We'll see how much is left later on."

The subject thus duly changed, they had their dessert, then went off to their respective rooms. A locked door, the keys in Mrs. Harte's sole possession, divided the fourth-floor hall of servants' quarters between men and women. The one John and Rupert shared was, like most of them, furnished with two narrow bedframes, small bureaus, a night-stand with lamp, a wash-basin, and wardrobe. The walls to either side were almost close enough to be touched at the same time with arms extended, but, it was not a place made for their languishing about.

"You wouldn't happen to have any ideas about what old Bennings was saying, would you, now, John?" Rupert asked.

"What makes you think that?"

"Don't know." He'd lit up a cigarette and puffed thoughtfully at it now, stretched out on his coverlet in shirtsleeves and undershorts. "Occurs to me that we're usually the only other servants in the room when he's pouring. You've not seen anything?"

"No." He shook out his livery jacket and hung it in the wardrobe. "Have you?"

"No."

"And no unusual experiences of your own?"

"Oh, I have plenty of experiences in this house," said Rupert, releasing a languid tendril of smoke on a chuckle. "Doubt as I'd call them unusual, though. I'm more talking about a different kind of… that which goes bump in the night."

"You mean, like what you were saying to Sarah?"

"Feeling watched, when there's nobody there? Phantoms and specters? Going into a room you'd swear on your life had been empty but finding an item not where it had been?"

"Something of the sort."

"If I said I did, Johnny-boy, would you know aught about *that*?"

"I can't say. I've never seen a ghost."

"Ghost. Right. Isn't that what they used to call your father?"

"Well, yes, but that was long before he died, and I assure you I've certainly not seen him since." John sat at the end of his mattress, removing his shoes.

"Hmm." Rupert hooked an arm behind his head and seemed to be tracing the ceiling-cracks with his gaze. "So, nothing much to it?"

"Seems not."

"Unless someone's playing pranks, snooping about."

"Why?"

"Why not?" said Rupert. "Overheard conversations. Secrets. Idle remarks."

"Aren't we privy to enough of those already?"

"Ah, even when They treat us like They don't know we're there, They know we're there. Doesn't leave much room for profit."

"Blackmail?" John asked, frowning. "Mr. Bennings would hardly approve."

"Perish the thought. All I'm saying is, suppose—just suppose—someone had a real knack for discretion. Doing more than fading into the background. Suppose someone could truly disappear."

"Disappear?"

"Vanish. Turn invisible. Gone from view. Before our very eyes."

"That'd be quite a trick."

"Wouldn't it, though? Imagine what a clever man could do with that kind of a talent. Be a shame to waste it on something menial. Like, oh, say, being in service."

"On the contrary," John said, "I think a talent of that sort would come in quite handy for someone in service."

"But such a man, he could get into anywhere, couldn't he? Bank vaults, jewelry shops, embassies, foreign capitols."

"As what? A thief? An assassin?"

"Or a spy."

"Not much better."

Rupert stubbed his cigarette against the wall, adding another charred spot to the constellation of them. He laughed. "You sound so offended, I'm glad I didn't suggest sneaking into ladies' boudoirs."

Tired as he was, at the end of a long day's work, the best of footmen couldn't have kept his disgust hidden behind an impassive servant's mask. John grimaced, and even let a revolted groan escape him.

"You see?" said Rupert. "Something to consider, though, isn't it?"

"No." John blew out the lamp, got into bed and drew the blanket to his chin. "No, Rupert. It isn't."

John stepped into the kitchen the next afternoon to find a moderate state of uproar. Mrs. Sullivan was near to tears, with Sarah and Janice trying to comfort her. Poor Alice was wringing a dish-rag and looking like her pet bunny had just been crushed by a motor-car. Martine stood by the door with a large laundry-basket in her arms, her pretty face fretful.

"Have Rupert do it, then!" Janice was saying, indignant. "He's the one who didn't check and ask. Surely he could just slip in without disturbing—"

"How?" wailed the cook. "You know what Her Ladyship's rules are about interruptions at tea-time! Not unless the house has caught fire, or a wireless comes saying war's broken out!"

"What's happened?" asked John.

"Rupert didn't take in the plate of petit-fours when he laid the tea-table," Martine told him. "They're in there discussing the wedding plans. I tried to warn him, but I was doing the ironing and couldn't get here in time."

"Maybe They'll overlook it," Sarah said, forcing a hopeful smile. "Maybe They won't notice. You sent up all those nice pastries. Who'll miss some silly little cakes?"

This did not improve Mrs. Sullivan's emotional state. "Miss Louisa's mother asked for them special!"

Janice pursed her lips. "And not having them, it'll give her something else to complain about. She's always after us for the way the household's run."

John bent to Martine's ear. "Where is Rupert?"

"*Helping* Edith turn the mattress in the Lilac Room," she replied. She hesitated, briefly biting her lower lip. "John—"

"No, there's naught else for it," said Mrs. Sullivan, sniffling, wiping her eyes. "I'll just have to admit me mistake and pay the piper. Her... Her Ladyship won't be... won't be *that* cross... surely..." Her chin wobbled, tears overspilled, and she buried her face in her apron, sobbing.

Timid Alice crept from the sink to pat clumsily at her shoulder. "Th-th-there-there, Muh-Muh-Mrs. Sullivan, it'll b-b-b-b -"

"It'll be fine," said John. "I'll take care of it."

"Oh, no, Johnny, I can't let you get in trouble!"

"He won't, Mrs. S.," Martine said. "He knows what he's doing."

"I hope so," he said, glancing at her.

"I believe in you." She held his gaze, and if he hadn't been lost already, he would have been then.

"Ih-ih-if you're g-g-going to—"

"Yes, Alice is right," Martine said. "Hurry. There's no time to waste."

He picked up the china plate with its arrangement of petit-fours, the tiny cakes piped with icing rosettes and sprinkled with glittering colored sugars. "Will you go with me, Martine? I'll need you."

"Of course." She pushed the basket of fresh ironing at Sarah, who blinked at them in surprise as she took it.

They went from kitchen to stairs, from stairs to upper hall, until they stood outside the drawing room's smaller second-door. It was shut, but the voices of the ladies within could be heard... if not their exact words, the pointed, sweet-poison edges and overtones.

"Tell me how it stands in there," John said. "When it's safest to go."

"How would I—?" she began.

"Martine."

She studied him, then nodded. They were far past dissembling, after all.

With a slow, deep breath, she tipped her head back and took on a faraway look, half-dreamlike. It was, he knew, the same look she got just before the front doorbell rang to announce an unexpected caller, or some impending catastrophe was about to unfold in the house. It was the same look she must have had in the laundry-room when Rupert left without the crucial petit-fours plate.

"They haven't fallen to, yet," she said. "Too caught up in the arguing. But, they will soon. You'll have to be quick."

"Is it opportune?"

"Wait... yes."

He saw himself reflected in the windowpane. Then he didn't. He saw Martine's eyes widen, her expression filling with wonder and delight. Knowing was one thing, but seeing—or not-seeing—was quite another. The doorknob turned without a click, the door eased open without a sound, and he slipped through the gap into the drawing-room.

Given the nearly-palpable levels of anger and spite in the air, a circus-clown could have passed through without attracting attention, as long as he did so without honking a rubber-bulbed horn. For a footman blessed with the gift of raising unobtrusiveness to an art form, it proved a simple matter indeed.

A group of men, meeting thusly and at this stage in the proceedings on such a hotly contested matter, might have been shouting and cursing by then, if not coming to blows. As, however, this was a gathering restricted to those members of the fair and gentle sex only… it was far worse.

The mothers of the bride- and groom-to-be squared off not in Marquess of Queensberry fashion or even a fisticuffs free-for-all, but exchanged their jabs in the form of well-chosen words and venomous smiles. Of the other ladies, some were enrapt as if watching a close tennis game, while some added their own choice innocuous-seeming barbs. Miss Louisa, the planning of whose special day this was, looked almost as stricken-to-tears as Mrs. Sullivan had in the kitchen.

None of them noticed the door open or shut. None of them detected the slightest disturbance as he crossed on silent steps to the tea-table, which stood against the wall beneath a gilt-framed oil painting of Sir Roderick's long-deceased sisters when they'd been bonneted young girls.

Rupert had laid the tea out with elegant precision. The silver gleamed. The china cups were arranged on their saucers so that their delicate handles made the suggestion of a clockwise spiral.

The serviettes had been folded into his personal variation on the 'Rose' pattern, with fresh petals from the garden artfully strewn. John preferred the 'Star' pattern himself, but the 'Rose' was appropriate for a wedding-plans discussion such as this.

Fragrant steam wafted from the teapot's spout. The plates held thin-sliced bread, chilled wedges of fruit, scones, and dainty pastries. One little dish was filled with curls of shaved butter, another with a whipped mixture of cream cheese and honey. The ladies had not yet, as Martine said, fallen to.

With a carefulness of hand that a surgeon or jeweler might have envied, John rearranged the repast just enough to fit the plate of petit-fours neatly among the edibles. He surveyed the table, decided it would do up to the most critical inspection, and glided back from it.

Just then, after a parry and riposte of particularly cutting faux-compliments from the two society matrons, Miss Louisa uttered an outburst of shocking vulgarity. She shot to her feet, fists clenched at her sides, glaring at her mother and her mother-in-law-to-be. Aghast astonishment filled the room.

"Stop it, just *stop* it!" Miss Louisa cried. "You're being vicious bitches, the both of you, and it *must* stop at *once*! This is *my* wedding, mine and Henry's! Not either of yours! Now, if you don't mind, we're going to have our tea, and then we are going to sit nicely and discuss this like *grown-bloody-women*!"

She thrust a commanding finger toward the tea-table, in a violent motion that missed striking John amidships by inches. The other ladies stared at her, thunderstruck. No one seemed able to speak, not even to muster a gasped "well-I-never" or "oh-I-do-say." Even Her Ladyship looked chastened.

He had never been gladder in his life for his rare talent. Of all the scenes that should *not* carry on in front of the help, this had to be rather high on the list.

Sliding sidelong, he eased past the young bride. The stirring of the genteel company as they rose from their seats—smoothing rumples from their skirts, primping their hair, unfolding fans—gave him the cover of distraction he needed to once again open the door and escape into the hall.

Martine waited wide-eyed, hands pressed anxiously over her mouth. John pulled the door shut. When he felt the latch engage, he let himself reappear to view, and leaned against the wall with a quavering exhalation.

"Well, They have petit-fours," he said. "I wouldn't be surprised if Miss Louisa starts throwing them, but, They have them."

She rose up on tip-toe to kiss him on the cheek, a kiss that lingered rather more than was proper, not that John was about to object. "That was wonderful," she said. "Saving Mrs. Sullivan's reputation, and the way you've looked after Mr. Bennings as well?"

His face felt warm, but he smiled. "Only doing my job."

"Still, we're so lucky you ever came to Woadcastle."

"I'm lucky, too." He brushed a stray lock of her dark hair under the edge of her white cap. "After all, you're here… and what would They do without us?"

> "Endeavour to serve with such good will and attention to the interest of your employers, that they know they are blessed in having gotten such a good servant." *The Complete Servant*, 1825.

NO ONE OF CONSEQUENCE

IT WAS DURING A NATURAL LULL in the after-dinner conversation that the drawing room door opened to admit, in a rustle of brocade and scented powder, Great-Aunt Gertrude with her immense silver-point Persian cradled in her arms.

"I don't mean to be a bother," she said, "but there appears to be a dead man floating in the swan-pond."

This pronouncement produced, as might be expected, a considerable disruption. Miss Caroline Eldridge struck a discordant jangle of notes on the pianoforte. Lord Fitz-Hughes choked and coughed out a sputter of brandy. Cards fluttered across the table as the players sprang up from their after-dinner bridge game.

"You know," the elderly dame said, stroking the cat between his pewter-colored ears, "I *did* think it was odd, seeing somebody like that. I was on my way downstairs and happened to glance out, and —well, I did think it was odd."

They paid her no mind in the general rush for the windows that followed. Ladies in satin and men in smart black jackets crowded together, jostling undecorously for position. Their voices formed a hectic babble, within which cries of 'who is it?' and 'oh my God!'

predominated.

"My first impression was, of course, that he might be swimming for some reason," she went on. "Though goodness knows I've never seen anyone swimming in the swan-pond before, by day let alone moonlight. Then I noticed the rather peculiar face-down way of his floating, and the fact he didn't move at all, or lift his head to breathe, and——"

Lady Fitz-Hughes staggered back with a hand pressed to her brow. She fell half-swooning onto a sofa, surrounded by a bevy of solicitous daughters-in-law. Salts and air were called for, and a glass of cold water.

The men, meanwhile, reversed their course from the window. They streamed into the hall, debating in excited tones their plan of action, whether someone should go fetch the doctor from the village, call the police, and so forth. The disruption had become a full-blown uproar.

"Such a fuss," Great-Aunt Gertrude said to Leopold, whose magnificent silver-banded plume of a tail flicked at the noise and activity. "I'm sure it's nothing, no one of consequence." Yet she, along with those ladies not occupied tending their hostess, moved in the wake of the throng.

Within moments, the great front doors flung open, spilling light down the broad stone steps. Lanterns were brought. Servants flooded from every corner—maids and footmen who'd been clearing the dining room, the butler, valets, the housekeeper and cook, even the kitchen-drudge popping her head out of the scullery.

Between the upper gallery railings peeped a host of little faces, the various children of the family and guests, like inmates of some mahogany prison. Sir Geoffrey barked orders to the nannies to keep them in the nursery until further notice. This was done, albeit over bleats and wails of protest.

Soon, most of the household stood outside, the ladies and female servants gathered on the eastern slope of lawn overlooking the pond. They murmured and whispered their anxiety to one another, fanned themselves, and held delicate handkerchiefs at the ready.

Lady Fitz-Hughes, recovered enough to join them, bemoaned this rude ruination of their hitherto quite agreeable evening, and despaired what *ever* in the world their esteemed guests must think, to which she was offered much polite assurance that the incident could hardly be held against her as any sort of blight upon Woadcastle's hospitality.

The gentlemen and senior male servants, meanwhile, clustered at the pond's edge as the younger footmen, gardener and groom's lad waded into the shallows. Their shoes sank deep into soft, spongy black muck, eliciting grimaces and squishy, squelching sounds. A green layer of algae some inches below the surface that, by day, gave the pond a most picturesque opacity, adhered to their pant-legs in a scummy manner the laundresses would no doubt find difficult to contend with.

"Does anyone recognize him?"

"Not from here, I don't."

"Not from this angle, either. Hardly a chap's best."

"Isn't one of the staff, is it?"

"Certainly not, m'lord."

"By the look of his clothes, I'd say he's no gentleman."

"That's a cert. From the village, do you reckon?"

"Must be, or traveling through."

A long pole-hook was fetched from the gardener's shed. It took some fiddling, and one unfortunate clonk to the drifting man's head, but finally they were able to snag his waterlogged clothing and haul him within reach. The footmen took hold of limp arms and legs and carried the body ashore.

"You might want to stay back," Lord Fitz-Hughes said to the women. By his expression, he wished he himself could do the same. By his expression, he also wished he could sit down, and perhaps finish that stiff slug of brandy.

His advice was, for the most part, hardly necessary. Only Rebecca, Sir Geoffrey's step-daughter, had inclination enough toward the morbid and ghoulish to attempt a closer look.

The servants set the man down on the grass and rolled him over. His hands flopped out pallid and wet by his sides. His head lolled. Pond-water trickled from his gaping mouth. A lily frond lay pasted across his cheek.

Gasps, small shrieks of horror, and little outcries greeted this glimpse of his slack, blue-grey face in the moonlight. Lady Fitz-Hughes swooned again and two other ladies followed suit. Eyes were averted, mouths daintily covered, pearls clutched. Some of the men shared grim looks. Others had to turn away. Old Bennings, the butler, tottered and pressed a palsied hand to his chest. Lord Stafford's valet was sick all down his shirtfront.

The man was, most decidedly and most definitely, dead.

He was also, most decidedly and most definitely, a complete stranger.

Sleep would be a rare and much-belated business that night, if in fact it arrived at all. For any of them besides the children, that was. They, at least, succumbed to a reasonable bedtime... if perhaps generously helped along by cups of hot chocolate laced with a tincture of something from a brown bottle the governess kept in a locked cupboard for just such occasions.

Well, perhaps not just *such* occasions. It wasn't every day, after all, that anything so noteworthy as a *death* took place at Woadcastle. The last one had been, oh, ages ago, the preceding autumn, that regrettable hunting accident with the poor Earl of Falloway. It had very much put a damper on the whole month. Of course, there had also been the matter of the actress a few years previously, the one young George found so fascinating, but her suicide had put quite the tragic end to their star-crossed love affair. Everything worked out for the best eventually, with George going on to a far more suitable engagement, though they all agreed it had been a most shocking breach of hospitality on the part of the actress. The stains would not come out of the porcelain; the entire bathtub had to be replaced.

These topics were uppermost on the minds of the Fitz-Hugheses and their houseguests, not to mention the servants. The temptation among the adults to seek a similar insomnia remedy as had wafted the children away to dreamland was not inconsiderable, but none of them wanted to be the first to make such a medicinal request. They contented themselves for the time being, therefore, with brandy, whisky and other spirits.

Besides, the doctor had been summoned from the village, and the police were on their way, and nobody wanted to miss any further developments.

"This isn't going to turn into another of those garish murder-mystery affairs, is it?" inquired Great-Aunt Gertrude, comfortably ensconced in a chair with Leopold curled on her lap. The cat's pale-sapphire eyes glimmered under drowsy half-lids.

"What, you mean with some inspector nosing about?" said William Stafford, Lord Stafford's brother. He threw back his third or fourth drink at a gulp, insulting to such a fine vintage of scotch whisky.

"Oh, I do hope not," fretted Lady Fitz-Hughes. "All that asking of impertinent questions—"

At that, several more of them chimed worriedly in.

"Not to mention making accusations and sinister assumptions

about motives!"

"Insisting no one's permitted to leave the estate, and so on?"

"Digging for secrets and scandals—"

"So uncouth. Not to mention inconvenient."

"A man has *died*!" cried Louisa, Henry's wife of a few months, silencing the rest. "Doesn't that matter rather more than our inconvenience?"

"Well, my dear, it's far too late for *him* to be troubled by it," Gertrude said. "Why should the rest of us be put out?"

"We don't know it's murder!" Lady Fitz-Hughes wrung her many-ringed hands. "We don't even know who the man is yet, let alone how he died. Let's resolve that before we go leaping to any melodramatic conclusions!"

"Melodramatic?" echoed her husband. "Oh, I say."

Their eldest son, Roddy, chuckled. "Besides, if this were one of those murder-mystery affairs Auntie mentioned, shouldn't it be Father as the victim?"

"To be sure," said Roger, Roddy's younger brother by only a matter of minutes. He grinned a wicked grin at the blustering reaction of Lord Fitz-Hughes. "He would have had to bring us all here to discuss changing his will, and then be found dead—"

"Several times over," said Roddy. "Shot, stabbed, cracked on the head *and* poisoned."

"*Then* pushed down the grand stairs for good measure."

Just like that, they were off to the races, exchanging rapid-fire remarks as their wives—they'd married sisters, of course, Lord Stafford's cousins—heaved identical sighs of chagrin.

"With the will then gone missing and none of us knowing what it had said."

"Everyone a suspect—"

"You having learned you'd been disinherited and furious about it—"

"Because he blamed me for something you'd done, disguising yourself, easy enough as my twin—"

"With some long-hidden bastard popping out of the woodwork —"

"I've half a mind to disinherit you both on the spot," Lord Fitz-Hughes declared.

"Capital!" Edmund tugged on his jacket lapels. "That's me next in line, then!"

"Rubbish it is," said Elizabeth, who was Roddy's wife. "I won't see my son passed over for the likes of you."

"What's wrong with Edmund?" Caroline favored him with a smile. "I find him quite charming."

Edmund preened. Rebecca muttered what might have been, "You *would*," but in so low a tone only those nearest to her heard.

Elizabeth glared icicles at Caroline. "Oh, of course you do, now that he stands to inherit and reduce my children to paupers!"

"What about mine?" added Adelaide, Elizabeth's sister. "How will Roger and I find good husbands for our girls? They'll need a fortune to back their prospects more than ever, with their father disgraced and a suspect in his own father's murder!"

"Need I remind you all," grumbled Lord Fitz-Hughes, refilling his drink, "that I am *not*, in fact, dead?"

"Weather's all wrong for it, anyway, of course..." Roddy went on, glancing out the window.

"Absolutely," said Roger. "Should be the proverbial dark and stormy night."

"Indeed. We'd lose the electric at a crucial moment."

"You see?" Lord Stafford shook his head. "Told you it was a mistake to rely too much on these modern williwags."

"That's when the next shot would ring out," said Roddy.

"Another murder, the killer eliminating someone who'd gotten too close to solving the crime."

"At that rate, half the household could be dead by dawn."

"More, if dinner had been poisoned."

"Or the brandy." Roddy raised his in a toast.

Great-Aunt Gertrude, who had been watching the interplay with the avid attention of a spectator at a tennis match, spoke up. "I thought, in those dime-novel situations, it was always the butler that did it."

"The butler?"

"Good God, old Bennings?"

"Given how he shakes, the safest place to stand would be wherever he was aiming—"

"Would you all *stop*!" Lady Fitz-Hughes, in her extremity of emotion, went so far as to make a throw-pillow live up to its name, hurling the small embroidered cushion across the drawing-room.

"Careful!" Roger caught it. "This might be the murder weapon itself!"

"He was suffocated as well?" asked Roddy.

The others, however, had the decency to be more duly chastened. A moment of polite silence passed, one for which idle chatter seemed discouraged. The awareness gradually returned to them that, murder-mystery fancies aside, a man was dead. A stranger, yes. Not a gentleman of quality—not a gentleman at all, judging by his attire. Not one of the household or visiting servants. Not one of the villagers that anyone could recognize, or a local tenant farmer. He was no one, really.

No one in particular, no one important, no one of consequence.

But still and all, a person. Some parents' son, possibly someone's brother, some woman's husband, some child's father.

"Perhaps it was an accident," Sir Geoffrey suggested, breaking that long moment of silence. "Perhaps the wind blew his hat into the pond, and he was trying to retrieve it, when he had a cramp."

"Perhaps a swan struck him," Henry said.

Edmund nodded. "They can do real damage, you know. Strength of their wings and all. They don't look it, of course. They look so regal, gliding about the way they do, but I wouldn't cross one."

"Met a bloke once whose arm was snapped in three places by a swan." Major Eldridge, Caroline's uncle, puffed on his pipe. No one had the heart to dispatch him to the smoking room at the end of the hall, him being a war hero and all, requiring a cane just to move about. "Vicious brutes, swans."

Louisa touched her fingertips to her brow. "I can't bear to think one of our swans might be a murderer!"

"Oh, for heaven's sake!" exclaimed Lady Stafford. "Listen to yourselves! How ridiculous you sound!"

"Or he might have done it himself, drowned himself," Edmund said. "Suicide, don't you know."

"In *our* pond?" said Lady Fitz-Hughes. "What kind of man would *do* that?"

"Well, but, Mother, I'm only saying, a man so deranged as to be suicidal wouldn't necessarily be bound by concerns of whose pond he chose. Not in the right mind, hey-what? Taken leave of the wit and wisdom."

"Nonsense. There is still such a thing as common decency."

"You do remember the actress—"

"Yes, but she was American."

"The moon's full," Rebecca said, nodding toward the white orb visible in the dark star-sprinkled firmament through the drawing-room window. "Suppose a werewolf got him?"

"A what?"

"A werewolf?"

"Are you daft?"

"Gracious!" Gertrude pursed her lips, stroking Leopold's back. "It's like living in the penny dreadfuls."

"Besides," said the Major, "if it was a werewolf, he'd be right torn up, wouldn't he? Throat laid open, gutted, eaten on—"

"Major!" several voices pleaded at once.

"No, the Major's onto it, he is," said Edmund. "Any sort of wild animal had done this—"

"Barring a swan," Louisa said.

Henry rounded on his young bride. "Would you forget the damnable swan!"

"Fine, fine, only *you* brought it up in the first place, the idea of murderous swans!"

"Not murderous, only…" He broke off. "Are we having our first fight?"

"Oh! Yes, I rather think we are!"

"Our first fight! Oh, darling!"

"Darling!"

They clasped hands and gazed at one another with lovestruck adoration.

"As I was *saying*," Edmund continued, raising his voice and giving an exaggerated roll of the eyes, "we'd be knee-deep in entrails, blood from Hell to Christmas."

"Edmund Chamberlain Hubert Fitz-Hughes!"

"Sorry, Mother. Ladies. Sorry." Stammering and blushing, he rubbed the nape of his neck.

It was hard to say which proved the more comical in the next instant—the cliché of the doorbell, or Edmund's pantomime of relief at the cliché of the doorbell.

Shortly thereafter, Bennings—who, to be fair, *was* on the far side of ancient; none of those present, even Gertrude, could recall the butler as a young man—tottered in with his usual unctuous discretion. "M'lords," he said. "M'ladies. Doctor Lenk has finished examining the, ah, deceased."

"Well, for heaven's sake, man!" said Lord Fitz-Hughes. "Don't bandy about... who is he? How did he come to be floating in our pond?"

"I believe the doctor would be better able to——"

"Yes, yes, show him in!" Lady Fitz-Hughes dabbed at her brow. "I honestly don't know how much more strain I can be expected to endure for one night."

Bennings, again with unctuous discretion, cleared his throat. "The police have also arrived, m'lady."

"Oh, God!"

"So it *is* murder!"

"What do they say?"

"Are they going to shoot the swans?"

"Here, now, that's hardly sporting."

"I agree. If anyone's going to shoot those honking black-banded blackguards, it should be done properly."

"Show in the doctor, Mr. Bennings," Lord Fitz-Hughes said. "And the police captain, when they've done... whatever it is they do."

The butler performed what, in earlier years, would have been an unctuously discreet inclination of the head. As it was, however, with time and palsy doing their work, it proved more of an impression of a nearsighted pigeon attempting to peck for seed. He stepped back into the hall and, moments later ushered in the village doctor.

Doctor Lenk looked as if he'd been roused from a deep slumber, and no doubt had been. He blinked around the well-lighted drawing room, at the well-dressed gentlemen in their dinner jackets and the well-dressed ladies in their evening gowns and jewels. If Bennings was the nearsighted pigeon of this nursery fable, Lenk was an owl, unceremoniously thrust into the midst of a gathering of songbirds.

He flinched from the barrage of questions peppering him like birdshot from all corners, clutched his sensible black doctor's bag to his stout frame, and wet his dry lips with a nervous little pink tongue.

"*Was* it the swans?" Louisa's clear voice rang in an opportune lull. She and Henry had mended their differences and sat side by side on a velvet settee, his right knee pressed to her left and her gloved hands clasped in his.

At this, Doctor Lenk blinked again, goggled, and said, "Beg pardon, mum?"

"Never mind that," Sir Geoffrey said from the mantle. "What can you tell us? What's going on?"

"Yes, please do, by all means, make your report," urged Gertrude. "It's far past Leopold's bedtime." On her lap, as if to second her remark, the Persian yawned to expose sharp pearl-white teeth.

"Blimey, Auntie," Roddy said. "You could send him up. It isn't as if the police will want to question the cat."

"Send him up? Alone?" She gave her great-nephew an affronted look.

"Alone, nothing," said Roger. "Ring for... what's-his-name. Bloody cat's got his own valet, might as well earn his keep."

"I'll have you know that Clarence very much earns his keep," Gertrude informed him. "He takes excellent care of my Leopold."

Rebecca leaned toward Edmund. "Her cat has a valet?"

"Oh, yes. Damned animal lives better than most anyone else in the house. I wouldn't mind sleeping half the day on silk pillows, eating from crystal dishes, and someone to brush my hair on demand."

"That *is* how you live, you ungrateful gadabout," his father said.

"What about tummy-rubs, then? He has tummy-rubs at his beck and call, hey-what?"

Caroline tittered. "Well, then, Eddie, maybe you should get

married."

"Would it trouble everyone unduly," began Lady Fitz-Hughes, with one of those sorts of tight smiles that would send sailors scurrying to batten down all hatches, "to let the doctor have his say?"

When he did, however, it turned out to be far less than enlightening. All that Lenk could tell them with certainty was that the man was dead, which obviously anyone with even a fraction of brain would have known. He showed no evident injuries or signs of violence or a struggle. For anything else, they would have to wait on a more thorough medical investigation.

"That's it?" Lord Fitz-Hughes said. "That's all you can tell us?"

"I'm not sure what else I could tell you."

"Who he is, for starters!"

"Doctor," interrupted a crisp baritone from the doorway. "Why don't you leave that... to me."

All eyes in the drawing room, even the pale-sapphire ones of Leopold the cat, turned to behold a tall man in a dark coat, returning their startled looks with a narrow, sharp, and flinty gaze.

The local constable, their village peacekeeper, lingered in the hallway, deferentially behind this striking new arrival. To carry on with the earlier descriptive bird motif, Constable Potter was more of the waddling gander, if ganders were possessed of muttonchops and made excessive use of moustache wax.

As for the striking new arrival, with his chiseled profile, sharp gaze, and erect carriage? An eagle, a peregrine falcon, a hunting-hawk.

"Isn't that Inspector Braithley of Scotland Yard?" whispered Caroline.

"Why, yes," Gertrude said. "I do believe so."

"He's famous! His picture's been in the papers!"

"Our own Sherlock Holmes." Edmund tugged at his collar. "What was it you were saying earlier, Auntie, about those murder-mystery affairs and whodunits?"

"I seem to recall saying that I hoped this wouldn't turn into one."

"We should all hope so, too," said Roddy. "God, King and Country help whoever *that* chap decides to twig for the crime."

"You were joking about it not twenty minutes ago," Roger said.

"So were you!"

"And you both should have known better," Elizabeth said, eliciting a fervent nod from her sister.

"Was there a crime, though?" Louisa clasped Henry's hands even tighter.

"Must be, if he's here," he said. "But don't worry, my darling. None of us have done anything wrong."

"Which won't matter a fart in church if he takes it otherwise into his head—"

"Roddy!"

"What? It won't. You know how these genius detectives operate. They make up their minds and that's that, and they find the evidence to suit."

"They can hardly find evidence if there's none to be found," said Henry.

Roger and Roddy gave him the kind of lofty, pitying, you-poor-fool kind of looks that only elder brothers can manage. Meanwhile, Old Bennings the butler stammered a mortified apology to Lord and Lady Fitz-Hughes, something to the effect of the inspector had not given him time to make a proper announcement but insisted on going right in. This was waved off, and Bennings retreated, though of course not so far as to altogether leave earshot.

Sir Geoffrey and Lord Stafford seemed acquainted enough with all parties to handle the necessary introductions, though it quickly became apparent that Inspector Braithley was not one for idle chit-chat and social niceties.

"Oh, but he's much more handsome in person, don't you think?" Caroline said.

"I think you've been tossed over," Rebecca said to Edmund.

"I'd only barely been tossed on in the first place."

"But what in the world is he doing here?" William Stafford wondered aloud. "He can't have come all the way out from London already, just tonight."

"He must be working some top-secret, exciting case!"

"Here?" said several of them together, equally askance.

"At Woadcastle?"

"Or the village? What could have happened there? Someone steal the vicar's pig again?"

"Scotland Yard's scraping the barrel if that's the state of things."

"He married one of the Durham girls, didn't he?" asked Gertrude. Leopold curled on her lap, setting his chin on his forepaws, and rumbled a low but steady purr. "I do think he did. Evelyn, the one with the red hair. Such a nice young lady. Quiet, pretty, mild. I know her mother."

Caroline's face fell. "He's married, then?"

"Lucky you," said Rebecca to Edmund, the words dripping sarcasm. "You might still have a shot."

"Shot?" cried Lady Stafford. "He was shot?"

"Who's been shot?"

"Someone's been shot?"

"We might have heard a gun——"

"Nobody's been shot!" Lord Fitz-Hughes struck the edge of a table with his heavy signet ring, the ring that surely would have been used to seal the envelope for his re-written new will, if matters had gone the way matters such as this were traditionally supposed to.

"Then would someone mind terribly explaining what *is* going on?" Gertrude soothed Leopold, who had twitched to full wakefulness at the loud rap of the ring on mahogany, hooking his claws into thick brocade. "There, there, don't snag my dress; my maid will have fits."

"If I may," said Inspector Braithley, moving to a spot that commanded the center of attention. The surrounding lamps managed simultaneously to highlight his features in a dramatic fashion and cast an imposing shadow.

"Oh, quite," murmured most of the Fitz-Hughes ladies, as Lady Stafford snapped open her fan and Caroline seemed to be having trouble drawing sufficient breath.

It wasn't that he was a particularly handsome man in the classical sense. But, the cut of his cheekbones, the set of his jaw, the backswept sleek and shining hair once he'd removed his hat, and those piercing eyes combined for a most riveting effect.

"To begin," he continued, with a cool glance at William Stafford, "I have not, in fact, come all the way out from London tonight."

The glance shifted to Gertrude's aged countenance.

"My wife and I, yes, Evelyn, were over at Durham House in Wilmingtonshire, visiting her family."

"Dear me," she said. "I do hope Lady Durham is in good health."

"Excellent."

"You will give her my regards, won't you?"

"Certainly." Next, the glance moved—cooling several further degrees as it did so—to Roddy. "And I assure you that if there has been a crime, it is my intention to determine the responsible party based on evidence, rather than take it into my head to *twig* anyone for it."

Roddy was by no means the only one to flush scarlet at the realization that the Inspector had overheard their every word. He was, however, the one to go the reddest… although Caroline was a close second.

"A local policeman, one of your Constable Potter's men, knew of my presence at Durham House and wired me there."

"Surprised the stuffing out of me, it did," Potter said. "I had nothing of it until he showed up, else I would've sent word."

"Wired you?" asked Sir Geoffrey. "Whatever for?"

"I can't imagine why something like this should require an emergency telegram to interrupt your visit," Lady Fitz-Hughes added. "We don't even know who the man in the pond is."

"As it happens," Braithley said, "the man in the pond had in his possession and on his person certain papers. Documents possibly pertaining to a complex and highly confidential case with which I am currently involved."

This revelation, with its implied deliciousness of secrecy and intrigue, thrilled through the drawing room. Anticipation had them, if not on the literal edges of their seats, at the very least figuratively hanging on his every word.

"My, isn't it exciting?" whispered Lady Stafford to the Major.

He harrumphed. "A spy ring, no doubt."

"The nature of the case being, as I've stated, complex and highly confidential," Braithley said, "you'll pardon me, Major Eldridge, if I do not respond."

"Spies?" Lord Fitz-Hughes looked thunderstruck. "Here? What in God's green earth would spies be doing *here*?"

"I'd guess it's political," Edmund said.

"Again, why *here*? We've nothing to do with politics."

"There was that fellow, the union agitator—"

"We've nothing to do with unions, either!"

"No, but, I mean to say, the way he died, that could have been political too."

"Who's this, then, that died?" Louisa asked Henry. "When?"

"Months ago," Henry said. "Well before the wedding."

"You never told me!"

"Why would I? And he died in a tavern brawl, that's what I heard. Nothing political about that."

Lord Stafford uttered a disdainful snort. "Any union agitator mouthing off in a public house about his cause deserves anything he gets."

"We seem," said Braithley, his right eye suffering a brief twitch of irritation, "to have drifted somewhat from the matter at hand."

"Indeed, yes." Lord Fitz-Hughes cast about a stern glower. "My apologies, Inspector. Please do go on."

"The papers in this man's possession were water-damaged from his immersion, the ink badly smeared and smudged. The post-marks enabled the policeman to recognize their significance, but it will take some time to dry and decipher them and reach a conclusion."

Lady Fitz-Hughes latched onto this. "You'll stay here, of course," she said. "For the night, and for as long as is needed. Bennings?"

"Yes, m'lady?"

"Tell Mrs. Harte to have the…" Her pause as she performed a quick headcount of her guests and compared that to the available rooms was incremental, but seemed eternal. "…the Spruce Room made up for the Inspector."

"Very good, m'lady."

"And reasonable accommodations for any other officers, staff or personnel. Inspector, you'll have full use of the study, the library, anything else you require."

"That is both kind and generous, Lady Fitz-Hughes. I do

appreciate such a gesture, and on such short, unexpected notice."

"Nonsense," Lord Fitz-Hughes said. "Whatever we can do to help. Upsetting to us all, yes, but, a man has died and…"

"…and that rather matters more than our inconvenience," finished Louisa, not without a hint of smugness at reiterating her earlier point.

"I will need to request," Inspector Braithley said, "that no one leave the estate until we've finished the investigation."

"No one would dream of it," Gertrude assured him.

The rest of the night, not that there was much left of it before dawn began to color the eastern horizon, passed in a blur of activity.

Outside, Constable Potter's men scoured the grounds for clues, poking into hedges and under bushes, dredging the swan-pond, trampling the gardens, tracking mud, and generally making nuisances of themselves.

Inside, below stairs, the kitchen bustled as the cook and her assistants put together an early breakfast, ran trays of sandwiches and tea out to the policemen, and did what they could to keep the body and soul of Woadcastle together. Housemaids and footmen rushed about their duties, changing linens, sweeping up, seeing everything was in order.

Inspector Braithley set himself up in Lord Fitz-Hughes' study, alternating telephone calls with interviews of the family, servants and guests. A mortuary wagon arrived and took the body to Doctor Lenk's little hospital in the village for further examination.

Rampant gossip was the lifeblood of the day. Might they be called upon to testify in court? When none of them knew anything? Would it be in the newspapers? How much of a scandal could they be facing?

To the great relief of Louisa, the swans were soon cleared of suspicion. They had been safely shut up in their swan-cote for the night, and the dead man bore no injuries consistent with being battered by powerful wings.

He had also, came the news by way of the gossip grapevine, been drunk. Very drunk. Very, *very* drunk indeed. No one in the village recognized him either, and he had not taken on such a skinful at any of the local pubs.

Who he was, where he'd come from, where he'd been headed, and why remained unanswered questions, much to Inspector Braithley's frustration. The man's clothes and calluses marked him as a common laborer, possibly a vagrant or a veteran or both. He had no money on him, no identification of any kind.

More and more it seemed apparent that he must have made a drunken stumble-blunder into the pond. There, perhaps unable to swim or simply too impaired to do so, he'd drowned. A stupid and senseless accident, but, an accident nonetheless.

Except, of course, for the matter of that sodden, ink-smeared papers he'd been carrying. Papers which, despite great care and attention in handling, proved all but illegible.

Had he been delivering a message? From and to whom? Did the post-marks have actual significance to Braithley's case, or was it some sort of strange coincidence? In his line of work, he was not much of a believer in coincidence… but, try as he might, he could find no connection.

Two more days passed, during which the other policemen finished up. The restriction against anyone leaving Woadcastle was lifted, allowing the Straffords and Eldriges and those Fitz-Hugheses who had other residences of their own to depart. They all did so with an odd mix of relief and reluctance, and only after obtaining sworn promises from their friends to share any new developments.

Inspector Braithley lingered to press on with his investigation.

He proved, in his working capacity, something less than an ideal guest... not one for idle after-dinner chit-chat, or billiards, or bridge. The offer was extended to invite his wife to come over from Durham House to join him, but he refused, limiting his communication with her to brief telephone calls.

Lord Fitz-Hughes and Sir Geoffrey seemed to find his company agreeable enough, terse though it was. The initial blush and flutter his chiseled profile had occasioned among the ladies did wane somewhat at his continued reserve and coolness of manner. The Fitz-Hughes sons, Edmund and Roddy in particular, suffered a certain awkwardness in his presence.

All in all, however, it went tolerably well and without further incident.

Until it was that, one night in the dining room, the Inspector suddenly uttered a gasp, interrupting a discussion between Lady Fitz-Hughes and her daughters-in-law about their upcoming holiday plans.

"Gracious," said Great-Aunt Gertrude.

"Inspector?"

He commenced coughing, thumping a curled fist against his breastbone while attempting to quell the outburst of concern with an apologetic waving of the other hand.

"Inspector, are you all right?"

"Something down the wrong way, no doubt."

"What ever is the matter?"

Rather than clearing his breathing, the fit worsened into a whistling wheeze. His face went the most alarming shade of red, deepening toward burgundy. His eyes watered, his mouth gaped, and in a sudden surge of movement he lunged from his chair with such force that it overturned.

"Oh, my God!"

"I don't think he can breathe."

"Give him a glass of water."

"Clap him on the back."

"Have him bend over and breathe into a bag."

"That's for hiccups, you fool."

"Well, someone do something!"

"He must've caught a bone in his throat!"

"It's a roulade; there's no bones in it!"

"Well, he's caught something, no bones about it!"

"I said clap him on the——"

"I'm clapping, I'm clapping! I clap much harder, I'll knock him over!"

The Inspector lurched away from the helpful clapping. He bumped into the table hard enough to make the dishes jump. Several wine glasses tipped with a crash and a splash. Those few of the ladies who had not yet risen to their feet did so with cries of alarm.

"He's choking!"

"Look at his face!"

The face in question had gone from burgundy to a purple-verging-on-plum. He clawed at his neck, which strained and bulged. His lips, and his rudely protruding tongue, seemed to be swelling before their eyes as if inflated by a bellows.

"Get the doctor!"

"Give him some air!"

"He can't breathe!"

"That's why he needs air!"

"But he can't bloody breathe!"

"Open his wind-pipe!"

"With what, a dinner knife?"

Footmen and housemaids rushed to and fro. Old Bennings, the butler, had to steady himself on the back of a chair. The family dithered about in frantic helplessness.

Inspector Braithley staggered a few steps, both hands clamped to his neck. His watering eyes rolled madly in their sockets, exposing vein-burst whites. His shins struck the jutting legs of his own overturned chair and he went down with thrashing, bucking convulsions.

Some days later, Gertrude Fitz-Hughes arranged to have herself driven out to Wilmingtonshire to pay a condolence call at Durham House. She found the place subdued, as was proper for a time of mourning, but was still warmly received by Lady Durham.

A lovely afternoon tea was laid out for them in a corner parlor overlooking the garden. Gertrude duly admired the china and silver, and how well the flowers were doing. Inquiries were made after mutual acquaintances, the weather was discussed, the polite small-talk was done.

Gertrude also spoke with effusive appreciation that, amid the delicacies, a dish of flaked whitefish, a portion of cold salmon mousse, and a tiny pot of caviar were sent up for the pleasure and privilege of Leopold. Who was, as a gesture of respect, wearing a collar of black velvet dusted with diamond chip.

Soon enough, the servants went on their way and left the ladies in genteel privacy to enjoy their tea, and the conversation was able to turn to more personal matters.

"How *is* your Evelyn?" asked Gertrude, spooning a selection of delicacies onto a saucer.

"Well, it's been a terrible shock to her, as you might imagine. A man his age, so fit and healthy… if he'd fallen in the line of duty, that would be one thing, but… like this, so sudden, so unexpected."

"Yes, very." The dryness of her tone was not lost on her hostess.

Lady Durham forced a pained smile as she poured. "I suppose I needn't talk on *that* point, should I? After all, it must have been a shock to everyone. I'm so sorry for Lady Fitz-Hughes. Is she well?"

"Rather shaken, of course. It was something of a scene."

"I can only imagine."

"She's gotten it into her head now, I'm afraid, that Woadcastle is bad luck, or some such nonsense. Wouldn't go so far as to say cursed, of course, let alone haunted—Sir Geoffrey's step-daughter was kind enough to put forth those options; morbid girl—but Lady Fitz-Hughes does worry it will give the house a difficult reputation."

"Hardly surprising, after what happened with the Earl of Falloway."

"Fortunately, his widow doesn't hold it against us."

"I understand they'd not been on the best of terms, anyway."

"Oh, you know how these things go." Gertrude glanced around approvingly at the furnishings. "I must say, I love what you've done with this room. The new wallpapering brightens it so."

"You mean," said Lady Durham, stirring her tea, "that the old stuff was atrocious, and I'd be the last to argue. I'm thinking we'll re-do Evelyn's suite next. It might help her feel better, particularly now that she'll be spending more time here."

"Has that all been decided?"

"Well, there's no reason for her to keep the Watson Street house now, is there? And I'll be glad to have her home. I don't believe she was very happy in London."

"The poor girl. I remember her as being so lively before she married. So sweet and vivacious in those days."

"Marriage can change a person." Lady Durham went to the mantle, where there stood several small, framed photographs arranged in progression. The change in Evelyn, from rosy-cheeked bright smiles to a wan, withdrawn reserve, was slight… but it was there to be seen by the discerning eye.

"For better or for worse, as they say," said Gertrude. "Or so I've been told."

"And not all husbands are created equal, are they? Not all marriages are the same from within as they might appear from without. Sometimes, years can go by before even one's nearest and dearest realize the whole truth."

"I do hope she won't face too much trouble in the settling of the Inspector's affairs."

"No, I don't expect so." Turning from the mantle, Lady Durham sat again at the tea-table. "He was very organized. Meticulous and thorough. I'm sure it must have annoyed him dreadfully, dying in the midst of such a baffling, unsolved case."

"He certainly kept to himself, didn't he?" Gertrude helped herself to another dainty scoop of jellied salad. "Close to the vest, as I believe the young people call it."

"And impressed upon Evelyn to do the same. Most firmly. I doubt she had a soul to confide in; he worried she would spill a vital secret or some clue or another. Even so simple a detail as that matter of the post-mark, for instance."

"As if anything so small as that could do any damage." She tutted and fed Leopold a morsel of fish.

"Why, even his personal physician was unaware of that dangerous mango allergy," Lady Durham went on. "His own *wife* wouldn't have known, had he not fallen ill in her company on that trip to India."

"Indeed... speaking of something so small doing such damage... who would have suspected that even the tiniest amount could cause a fatal reaction?"

They paused for a quiet moment to reflect upon the fickle and capricious nature of life.

"What I do wonder, though," said Lady Durham, stirring her tea, "is... who *was* the man in the swan-pond? The one upon whom those post-marked papers were found."

"Just some drunkard, some vagrant, they tell me," Gertrude said. "No one of consequence. These cakes are superb, by the way. Do give my compliments to your cook."

"Oh, I certainly shall. You must try the scones as well. A new recipe. Which reminds me, I heard there was a most interesting pork roulade served at Woadcastle the other evening. With an apricot and bread-crumb filling?"

"Normally, yes, but I understand certain substitutions can be made to spice it up. With, oh, say, a nice fruit chutney, for example."

"That does sound exotic. More tea?"

"Yes, thank you."

She refilled the cups, musing. "And that man... no one of consequence, you say?"

"Quite."

"So, then, there won't be any additional charge?"

Gertrude reached across the table and patted the other woman's hand, Leopold purring in her lap as she did so. "My dear Lady Durham, don't be silly. Our arranged-upon fee will more than suffice."

THE TERRIBLE SECRET OF TETLEY HALL

IT CAME AS SOMETHING of a surprise to me, upon the lifting of the lids, to discover Great-Aunt Beatrice standing at the foot of my bed.

A surprise severalfold, might I add. The door was locked, for one. We Tetleys, as a rule, don't go barging in on each other at midnight, for another.

But what was most pertinent, I thought, was the fact that the old bird had some thirty years agone shuffled off ye mortal coil. Passed on, I mean to say. Died, if you wanted the cold hard hammer-blunt truth.

Yet, there she stood. Looking every bit as I remembered her, though I'd still been in pinafores and pigtails when I'd last clapped the oculars to her upright and mobile presence.

Here was the same finely-creased countenance, the skin like faded silk that had been wadded into a tight clump and then laid flat, the crimped ivory-yellow hair, the austere dress of dusty taffeta with velvet trim and a spot of lace at the collar. The posture was severe and ruler-straight, absent of any dowager's hump or stoop-shoulders. The hands, bunched and be-ringed, gripped the heavy cut-glass knob handle of a walking stick.

But it was the eyes that most riveted my notice, intense, dark pinholes glittering bright. I know how that sounds, the inherent contradiction, dark and bright. Still, there you have it. And, dash it all, in a discussion of the greater scheme of things as it were—this apparent appearance of an apparition and all—it's rather silly to quibble over the simultaneous brightness and darkness of eyes.

I rubbed my own, which were likely far more muddled than bright, and hitched up on the pillows. Only the dim glow of a night-lamp from the adjoining bath illuminated the room. Thus shadow-shrouded, we stared at each other.

Silence stretched. I expected the vision to disperse as some remnant of the dreaming mind. It did not. I realized that the outlines of wardrobe and wash-stand were discernible through her, and that the soles of her high-buttons were firmly planted three inches above the carpet, on absolutely nothing.

Something, it seemed to me, should be done. Something should be said to mark the occasion. The moment all but demanded it.

Thus, I spoke. "What-ho, venerable ancestor!"

I did my best to come off cordial, as if there was nothing unusual about this late and unannounced visit. Which isn't to say, of course, that I'm one of those unmarried women who's in the habit of entertaining company at such hours in the privacy of her bedroom.

Company from beyond the grave, no less.

I suppose a more rational response would have been to scream the head off, rouse the household, and make with the hue and cry. Perhaps if I'd been more in the full clear frame of mind, I would have done. Deprivation of the most blessed elixir, that steaming life-sustainer to which I was accustomed—addicted, as certain of my friends would be quick to mention—had taken its toll. Left the good grey-matter somewhat not up to par, don't you know, but one must make the best and soldier along.

So, to the jovial greeting, I added a chummy smile. It may not have been my strongest-nerved best, this manifestation having reduced me in spirit—so to speak—to that scampering pigtailed and pinafored girl of yore.

I'd thought her an ancient even then, Great-Aunt Beatrice. And, though by now the maidenly flush of youth had begun to bid farewell to the bloom of my own rose, she was ancient still. She must have been nearing ninety when the Reaper knocked. To be fair, she hadn't aged a day since, the circs being as they were.

There was, however, nothing of the decrepit about her as she swung up that walking stick and jabbed its cork-capped end in my direction. Indeed, the old notable was practically brisk in her movement. Brisk enough to startle me into recoiling against the headboard, giving the back of the noggin a thump that should have wakened me had I in fact merely been suffering some nocturnal cinematopia of the brain.

She then swept the stick—briskly!—toward the door. One did not have to be a prodigy of the *cognoscenti* to get the gist. I popped from beneath the blankets like a jack-in-the-box, and before I could gather a single wit, let alone the trusty robe and slippers, I found myself ushered out into the hall as if I were late for school.

I mean to say!

That I felt reduced to girlhood was one thing. To be marched through the house in my pajamas, for all the world to see, was rather quite another. Not that there *was* all the world to see; Tetley Hall slumbered under the heavy coverlet of its own stately-manor reputation. All the same, I mean to say! If any of the kith-and-kin happened to stir for a late ramble of his or her own, I'd be hard-pressed to explain myself.

"Oh, just following the ghost of Great-Aunt Beatrice," I could say, with a nonchalant wave of the hand.

Yes, that'd have someone on the wire in no time, ringing up one of those spas where the well-off stuck the hopelessly goofy. Half of them already thought that of me, given my general habits and my unthinking critical lapse at dinner. Wouldn't do to add coal to the boiler.

Fortunately for me, Tetley Hall stayed slumbering as the taffeta-clad specter led me along. I noticed that she further had the benefit of passing through solid objects, a neat trick, and one I was soon to envy as I had to dodge the occasional occasional table, tall vase, or figure of statuary that lined the route. As she moved, she held aloft the walking stick, and the cut-glass knob emitted a faint and eerie radiance. It helped me avoid coming a complete cropper against some odd bit of furniture, at least.

The initial spark to the system upon awakening to see her there had begun to wear off by the time we reached the central gallery. What I wouldn't have given for a generous cup of the fog-clearing, piping hot, black as Darkest Africa, strong enough to kick-start a motor-driven and with sufficient sugar as to capsize a tramp-steamer. That would have done the job, all right. That would have gotten heart and head clacking along like a steno-typist.

Aside from a single stubbed toe—mine, obviously—we made our way along the gallery without incident. The only scowling gazes were those of various other long-gone Tetley relations, none of whom seemed compelled to join the party. Interspersed with their gilt-framed oil paintings were glass-fronted cabinets and display cases that held the family history, dating back to 1837. There were maps, advertisements, newspaper articles, labels, pots, cups, strainers, infusers, and just about every odds-and-ends piece of associated paraphernalia or memorabilia that could be thought of.

This was the museum of the Tetley legacy, of course. The

business and fortune had their origins here. So too was the future…
some New Yorker had been selling the stuff in hand-sewn silk bags
that his customers discovered could be steeped as-was without
fussing with the loose-leaf and all that rot.

It was also the reason we'd been summoned to Tetley Hall from
our various far-flung corners of the globe. Uncle Ned, current
patriarch-in-residence, was opposed to the company jumping on
the mod-con bandwagon. His wife was in favor. Their sons were
divided and of shifting alliances… in short, you know, identical to
that whole mess with King Henry and Eleanor of Aquitaine.

They wanted input from rest of us, as if more opinions chucked
into the pot ever settled anything. And so, here we were. Packed
together under one not-always-convivial roof.

My cousin Abigail, a young and silly creature with a flair for the
romantic, said it was like living in a novel, don't you know, one of
those fraught and torrid affairs filled with fraught and torrid affairs.
I had to wonder, as we ascended to the third floor, what Abigail
would say if she knew it had turned into more of a penny-dreadful
on us.

The fourth-floor servants' quarters were also under the gentle
sway of Lady Sleep. Doubtless they were worn down to the nub
from having so many of the flesh-and-blood or by-marriage
disrupting the normal routine. Just as well, as far as I was
concerned. I didn't need some insomniac maid or footman
catching sight of me and bearing tales. Household gossip did have
a way of getting around. A good juicy one to do with Miss
Primrose—you know, *her*, the spinster-in-training, almost forty and
not so much as a fiancé in sight, well on her way to becoming one
of those dotty old maids who collect doilies and talk to the cat—
why, that would be cash currency to the domestic set.

I opened my mouth to ask if that was how come the restless soul
had sought *me* out. After all, she had never yoked-up with some

fellow in matrimonial harness either. Over the years, I'd heard theories advanced on the subject: pining for a lost love, a distaste for the male of the species in general, some shameful secret or other blotch upon the respectability, the usual stuff and nonsense. Whatever her reasons had been, it *was* something we had in common.

However, I managed to catch the words on the tongue and not break the somnolent hush. I'd not heard a peep from her, anyway, or even so much as the rustle of taffeta. Whatever it was she wanted me for, I therefore gathered, was more *show* than *tell*, as it were.

In the attic, no less.

I must admit, the prospect did not exactly thrill me to the innermost. When I'd been a little girl, romping about Tetley Hall with the assorted cousins, the attic had been one of *those* locations, if you catch my meaning... not outright forbidden, but not outright approved... not dank, dingy and dangerous like the cellar, but decidedly musty and strange... not thick with thorns and beetles like the abandoned greenhouse but very cobwebby, and prone to rat-scufflings. To venture up there into that daunting gloom was a badge of honor, but it often required the goadings and dares of others. To go up there by one's self was just not done. Besides, with no witnesses, any such claims would have been laughed out of court.

To go up there now should not have given much pause to a grown woman thirty years older than that inquisitive pigtailed child. Then again, I was a grown woman thirty years older, in my pajamas. And socks. Following the ghost of a dead great-aunt. That would, I daresay, have given any right-thinking person something of a pause.

When, as a result, I hesitated at the foot of the narrow flight of attic steps, Great-Aunt Beatrice turned. Those glittering-bright dark pinhole eyes fixed on me again. Her lips, always a tucked drawstring purse, seemed to tighten. She raised the walking stick as if to do another jab at me with it.

I proceeded up the stairs. I proceeded into the attic. It had lost none of its musty, strange, daunting gloom. If anything, those qualities had redoubled. Dustcloth-draped furniture loomed everywhere. Crates had been stacked in a manner so precarious it looked as if a sneeze would set off an avalanche. An old-fashioned dressmaker's dummy gave me a start—ghost!—until I remembered that I was already following a ghost, and felt like a dunce.

See how well a body functions without a good steady supply of the potent caffeinated? I needed that welcome jolt on a many-times-daily basis; otherwise I wandered in a mental haze.

I resolved that, at breakfast, I would bite the proverbial bullet and slug down a stiff cup or two of what was available. If I sweetened it enough, it might be tolerable, no matter how insipid. So I told myself. Like taking one's medicine. Needs must when the devil… something something… I couldn't even recall the rest, which only further proves my case.

Furthermore, I told the self to bolster the sagging mood, I would seize the earliest possible opportunity to vacate this groaning mausoleum in favor of a hearty sojourn to some comfortable establishment where I could hobnob with like-minded persons of sense. Until I ruddy well *sloshed* with it! If sleep therefore eluded me for a few days, and my nerves danced a perpetual jitterbug, I deemed it small enough price to pay.

Great-Aunt Beatrice led me to a corner where several angles of wall, dormer and ceiling met with a geometry that wouldn't have looked out of place in that house the rifleman's widow was reputed to have built… all windows opening onto blank brick, and stairs that went nowhere, and cupboards within cupboards, you know.

I don't think I'd ever noticed this architectural oddity before, on those childhood forays with the cousins. If I had, it hadn't stuck in the memory. I noticed it now, though. A bit hard not to, what with the ghost shining the cut-glass walking stick knob at it like an electric torch.

Upon this close inspection, I discerned a thin crack, an outline. I also discerned a very shallow, very subtle depression in the paneling. And possibly other concealed workings that, in short, convinced me that I stood looking upon a genuine concealed door.

Well, naturally, there was nothing to do but open it! I dipped the fingertips into that shallow depression and gave an experimental sideways pull. Sure enough, it moved, though only a slight begrudging budge at first. Motes whirled in the eerie radiance. I saw that the crack had widened, and deduced—even bereft as I was—that it must have been years since this door had been opened.

Thirty or so of them, as a matter of fact.

I tried again, giving it a stronger heave-ho. It slid, with a groaning of warped wood and a gritting of dust in the track. And, if this was a genuine concealed door, behind it was a *bona fide* secret room.

Not much of a room, to be sure. Not really a room at all; one of those new telephone boxes that were becoming all the rage was what came to mind. If, that was, said telephone box had been made for circus folk. Midgets, I mean to say, or contortionists.

But, there was space enough in it to hold a small, lovely cherrywood chest. Dusty, of course—everything up here was—but ornate and polished, and fitted with a sturdy brass lock.

I raised the gaze to Great-Aunt Beatrice. She, in turn, leveled the walking stick at the chest. The lock clicked as if key-turned.

This, I took as an invitation. Indeed, even instruction.

Within the chest was the usual litter of feminine accouterments one might expect—a jewelry box, some gloves, a fan or two, a vanity set with brush and mirror, perfume bottles, handkerchiefs, a slim volume of poetry, trinkets and bows, that sort of thing. But, beneath those, and beneath a folded cashmere, I found that which made my eyes widen.

Was that an original Madame Vassieux? The pewterware piece, I'm sure, was a James Dixon. The silver service, probably Rockford. The ceramics looked to be Wedgwood and Staffordshire.

Tucked against the inside of the chest, tied with a length of ribbon the way a girl might safe-keep letters from her sweetheart, was a sheaf of thick papers. I took this up for examination and the eyes did not merely widen but nearly popped.

I flipped through them. Stockholder's certificates, good for... I tried to count, but mathematics remained beyond the purview. A *lot*, that much I could tell. A lot of shares. While I was not familiar with a Mr. William H. Bovee, or any such company calling itself Pioneer Steam anything, the other name displayed prominently upon the later certificates was one that I had no trouble recognizing in a wink.

My unpardonable sin of the evening prior came back to me. The looks I'd earned from a table full of Tetleys! As if I'd committed some heinous offense, whether done thoughtlessly or with malice and deliberation.

Then, without so much as a nod of farewell, the aged spirit whiffed from view and was gone.

I now understood why it was that I, of all the assembled descendants, should be the recipient of this message from Great-Aunt Beatrice. I knew the shameful secret that had distanced her from the rest of the family.

I knew it, and shared it.

I shuffled through the stock certificates again. With the light gone, I could no longer see to read what was inscribed there, but I no longer needed to. The words had, as it were, made their impression.

J.A. Folger & Co.

After all, at dinner with tea-barons, I *had* been the only one with the temerity to ask for coffee.

CINDER'S TWELVE

See how it glitters, Castle Bezaubernd. See how it shines. Torches in gilded sconces, silver candelabras and crystal chandeliers, the brilliant golden flicker of myriad bright flames. See how the stained glass windows glow, colored panes like jewels. See the mirror-gleam of polished marble, and alabaster's pale radiance.

Everything is light. Everything is splendor.

Hear the music, flutes warbling, chimes ringing, the liquid trill of harpstrings, a tapestry of melody weaving through the rooms. Hear the murmurs of conversation, whispers, and sweet laughter. Hear the fountains plink and plash their delicate cascade.

Oh, and smell the fragrances in the air, roses, honeysuckle, perfume, pastries and wine! Feel the evening breeze waft in, cool and mild from the terraces. Behold the lavish centerpiece, the castle in icing and sugar, recreated in precise detail!

At the top of the sweeping stair, heralds in fine livery attend the open doors. Medals sparkle upon the chests of dress-uniformed guards. Servants circulate among the crowd, trays of champagne deftly balanced.

And the crowd... oh, the crowd! Has there ever been such a

crowd?

The prince's summons has been answered. It is *the* event, the event of a lifetime, of a thousand lifetimes. From all corners of the kingdom have the ladies come in droves, eligible maidens of good family or wealth, sisters and daughters, each seeking to outdo the others.

Gowns of silk and satin, lace, velvet and brocade. Starched ruffs and seed pearls, flowing trains, feathered fans, long gloves, dainty slippers. Cheeks flush and lashes flutter. Corseted bosoms rise and fall. Ornaments bedeck hair worn upswept, or in ringlets, or styled into fanciful designs sprayed stiff and pastel-powdered.

Outside, the carriages roll up, one after another. They, too, seek to outdo their rivals, richly curtained, garland-draped. Sleek horses prance-step, plumes nodding from their spangled harnesses. Footmen spring forth to assist the occupants as they alight, these glorious butterflies, upon the red carpet that awaits them.

Now, see this next coach as it draws to a stop. See the black horses, manes and tails rippling like ebony ribbons, tossing their proud heads so that the tiny bells on their bridles prettily jingle. See the coach itself; just as the banquet's centerpiece castle was wrought from sugar, so too does this seem to be, with wheels of white-willow wickerwork and gossamer hangings.

Out from it, when the footman opens the door, emerges a lady more magnificent than any who've come before.

Her gown is a wonder. It has the lambent hue of moonlight, sewn with silver and sapphire thread. The skirt falls in ruffles over a crinoline frame of thin hoops and lace-trimmed petticoats; its bustle and flounced hips making her waist look even narrower than does the nipped whalebone of her corset. The collar is modest, the bodice very flattering. The gown's sleeves are puffed and slashed to the elbow, inset with opalescent silk to match her long gloves. Her dancing slippers, glimpsed as she lifts the skirt's hem to step down, appear to be diamond-encrusted.

But it is not merely her attire that has the onlookers stunned. She herself is a creature of phenomenal beauty, her movements supple, the tilt of her head and the line of her throat a delight of grace. Her hair is the color of honey mixed with cream, done up in an elaborate arrangement and twinkling with gem-studded pins. Loosed, it would spill down her back in a lush river; half the men there go weak-kneed at the very thought.

The rest of them are rendered weak-kneed by the blush-pink fullness of her lips, by wide eyes so blue the summer skies would be jealous, and a smile outshining the whole of Castle Bezaubernd in its splendor.

She turns to the coachman. "Midnight," she says, her dulcet voice also honey mixed with cream.

He nods. He flicks the reins. The black horses move on, hooves clip-clopping in unison, tiny bells jingling, the carriage's white-willow wickerwork wheels rolling.

The magnificent lady pauses on the red carpet and raises her gaze to the ornate bronze clock-faces set into the four sides of the high spire above the castle's steeply-peaked rooflines. The hands indicate a quarter past eight.

The prince's feminine guests soon become aware of this new arrival in their midst. While some react with admiration, most regard her with the smiles of icy, polite hatred that only the fairer sex can muster. Unaffected, she glides through the entrance and down the grand, sweeping stairs to the splendidly-lit and appointed ballroom.

No one knows her. Curious speculations abound. She must, they whisper, be a princess, a foreign princess, visiting from a far land's exotic imperial court. Hopes sink and hates blossom in the hearts of those who'd thought themselves above all competition.

The prince, as they fear, is captivated at once. Nothing will do but that he brush aside the light chatter and present himself to the lady to request the next dance.

She consents. The musicians oblige. See what a pair they make, what a sight to behold! The prince is handsome, if perhaps a trifle well-fed and with an indulgent pout to his sensualist's mouth. His garments are of expensive but understated elegance, the better to display the gold-and-ruby circlet adorning his brow. He dances well. He presses his partner most intimately close.

Oh, and how the spite shines like the myriad candle-flames from all corners! Ladies who'd been bitter enemies mere moments before are united now in a shared mind against the intruder. The stranger. The interloping usurper.

At last, after many dances, she pleads weariness. She sips champagne with the prince, then begs leave to sit out a dance or three. And, if there might be a quiet salon where she could take a brief respite from the revelry…?

He immediately offers to accompany her. She, however, conscious of the piercing glares aimed her way, demurs. The prince should not, she says, neglect the rest of his guests. She adds, with a maidenly downcasting of her eyes, that she would welcome the chance to, ah, powder her nose.

His pout briefly deepens until it resembles that of a spoiled child, but he agrees. A snap of his fingers brings a prompt page-boy in velvet knee britches, with matching cap and silver-buckled shoes. The page, he tells the lady, will escort her and wait attendance. While he, a hardship though it may be, will suffer other company in the meanwhile.

She thanks him, offering a gracious curtsy. He watches her go the way he might watch one of his royal confectioners carry away a decadent cake it is not yet time to eat, then heaves a sigh and surveys the clusters of maidens vying boldly or shyly to catch his eye. They are at their utmost efforts now to be pretty, and witty, and make memorable impressions.

Leave him to it, the prince, as he goes on to dance with a buxom auburn-haired beauty dressed in emerald-green, and a tall slender brunette of smoldering manner, and a giggling apple-cheeked blonde. Leave him to it as he samples these other sweets, for he is a man not easily sated. A taste here, a nibble there, only whets his appetite.

See here, instead, the mysterious and magnificent lady. The page guides her to a small but luxuriously-appointed private salon. She thanks the boy, and gives him a coin—how he beams!—and asks that he make certain she is not disturbed. This he will most readily do, the young page assures her. He takes up a sentry's post outside the door, thin chest puffed and chin lifted with the importance of his duty.

The strains of the music reach but faintly here. Soft shadows drape the walls, a reprieve from the bright dazzling splendor. The arched window overlooks an inner courtyard, dark now, stirring only with what small night creatures rustle in the gardens.

The lady removes her long gloves. She loosens her collar and draws a deep breath. An upholstered divan promises comfort. She regards it, but does not recline. She moves to a corner of the room.

She lifts off the elaborate arrangement of coiffed honey-cream hair held with gem-studded pins—a wig!—and carefully places it aside

Then she... what is this?... she reaches for the side-seams of her bodice and skirt. Rows of clasps and hinges are concealed there, hidden by clever design. She undoes them in a trice and the gown entire opens like a clamshell tipped up on end.

Slipping her arms from the sleeves, she steps out of the garment. It stays in place, the hoop-skirt frame holding it upright on its own, an empty iron maiden made of silk and satin and lace rather than hammered metal and spikes.

What is this, what is this? Oh, what a peculiar scene to unfold in this shadowed salon!

Here now is a lithe young woman clad in snug black hose and a close-fitting jerkin, the outfit nigh as revealing as a second skin! Beneath the wig, her own hair is a short-cropped chestnut brown. With a handkerchief, she wipes the blush-pink from her lips. She opens a pot of cinder-ash and soot-blacks her face.

She looks out the window, craning her neck to catch a glimpse of the clock-tower from this angle.

Almost ten.

Right on schedule.

Plenty of time.

After all, she has until the stroke of midnight.

"Come and meet the team," she'd said, heaving aside musty hay bales and folding back a straw-strewn sheet of canvas. Under it was a trap door, the planks scarred and warped. A length of rope had been knotted through the rusted ring. She seized it and pulled.

The door came up easily. Not to mention silently; he'd been expecting a hideous screeching creak. Motes of dust and chaff drifted in the square hole below, stirred by a draft of earthen-smelling air.

"Here?" he'd asked, astounded, with a furtive glance back over his shoulder. Only one wing of the manor house could be seen from the barn. An overgrown fruit orchard stood between them, further obscuring any view.

The girl scoffed. "Where else?"

"But, your stepmother—"

"You think *she* comes out *here*? She or her wretched daughters, for that matter? Not on their lives would they be caught dead in such a shabby, filthy place."

"I suppose you're right."

"Of course I'm right." Nimble as a cat, she preceded him down the wooden stairs. "They'd as soon sit grubbing in the ashes of the chimney corner, or anything else they prefer to leave to me."

With a shrug, he followed. The barn cellar was low and cobwebby, still smelling strongly of cow though it had been years since the last of the herd had been sold off.

A shame, really. This had been a fine estate once. A fine, productive estate. But, once the lord of the manor had passed on, his widow hadn't seen the sense in keeping up the dairy, the orchards, the winery... even the mill. It cost too much, she'd claimed. That money could be put to better use. She had daughters to support. The same claim was her reasoning for closing up half the house, selling off much of the furnishings, and everything else she'd done.

Including her decision that they no longer needed huntsmen, galloping hither and yon with their baying, flea-bitten dogs... hence his own family's sorry state of unemployment, his father the former hunt-master whiskey-soused more often than not, his brothers conscripted into the prince's army, one of them already killed. It was all a youngest son could do with the odd job here and there to keep the old man and the faithful hounds fed.

He was, therefore, not adverse to earning a bit of coin on the side. On the other hand, if they were caught, he was fairly adverse to swinging from the gallows in the execution yard in front of Castle Bezaubernd.

As they made their way along the tunnel connecting the barn-cellar to a warren of caverns, he said as much to the girl. She spared him a look but would dignify it with no other response. He held his tongue for the rest of the way to the cave being used as a hideout. Several people, half a dozen or so, were busy there by lantern-light.

"This is my dress-maker," the girl said, introducing him to a spinster hunched over her sewing like a crone from a nursery tale. "She worked for my mother, but my stepmother dismissed her from service."

Next he met a wizened, gnomish little man, applying jeweled pins to an elaborate wig of honey-cream hair. Paste jewels, the girl explained, but very convincing.

The hunt-master's youngest son had to agree. He, at least, would have believed them to be genuine.

A broad-shouldered man was at work on the wheels of a coach, while a red-faced woman in kerchief and white-sprinkled apron stirred an immense copper vat with a long-handled wooden paddle. The thick, bubbling contents gave off a cloyingly sweet steam.

"You really are making it out of sugar?"

"Why not?" The girl laughed. "We pilfered the stuff from the prince's larder, bag by bag. Cartwright's wife is the royal confectioner's assistant for the centerpiece miniature of the castle —which is where, also, we came by the floorplans, from the original architect."

"But... sugar..."

"As long as it doesn't rain. And, it'll be easy enough to get rid of afterward. Roll it into the lake..." Her fingers flicked in a dispersing gesture. "Pff. Nothing left but the wheels and undercarriage."

"Fine and well," he said. "Nice dress, nice hair, nice coach. You'll be the belle of the ball. But what about the rest of it?"

She smiled. It was a very impish smile. "For that, we've got the mice."

"The mice?"

"The Maus brothers, our inventors. They may be eccentric, but, they're geniuses in their way. Practically magicians. The next best thing to having a fairy godmother."

Examining the various devices and gadgets the gangly twins had assembled, he acknowledged she was certainly spot-on about their eccentricity. He'd withhold, however, judgment on their genius for now.

"For those on the inside," she went on, "we've got three more. A guard, a chambermaid, and a page-boy."

"You're sure you can trust them?" he asked with unease. He himself might have no great fondness for the prince, after seeing his brothers marched off to battle, but...

"The guard and the chambermaid are in love. The prince refuses to grant them leave to be married, and they can't afford to elope. This will give them the chance they need to start a new life together, somewhere far away. You must have heard the saying, *if you pay your servants poorly, then they will pay themselves.*"

As a matter of fact, he had, though he'd more taken it to mean that the disgruntled servant would abscond with some of the silverware.

"And the page?"

"Grandson of an old friend of my father."

He nodded. "So, then, what's this to do with me? You seem to have it all well in hand."

"Almost," she said, and indicated a portly man who sat dozing with one plaster-bound foot propped up on a cushion. "Our hostler got us the horses, but has had a mishap and broken his leg."

"Nothing I can do about that. I'm no doctor, and even if I was —"

"No, no." She turned her impish smile upon him. "It means I need a coachman. A driver, one who also can ride. What do you say?"

See what she does now, the mysterious lady, the girl garbed in close-fitting black with her face all soot-smeared… see how she reaches into the opened side of the ballgown.

The skirt stands like a lampshade, its ruffles and flounces and petticoats supported by the wire crinoline frame. The stiff whaleboned corset holds up the bodice, the puffed sleeves dangling, the high collar drooping. The gown has the look of a headless scarecrow, or unfinished work upon a dressmaker's dummy-form.

Inside the skirt, attached to the wires, are numerous objects and items that the girl swiftly collects. She hangs them from a belt that girds her slim waist. She removes her dancing-slippers and pulls on soft-toed ankle-shoes instead.

The slippers are not truly diamond-encrusted. Most of the gems are, as are the ones on the wig's hairpins, made of paste. But, set into the heel of the left *is* a real diamond. This slipper, the girl also hangs from her belt.

She goes to the window. On the clock-tower, the great brass hands point to just past the hour of ten. The great bells have struck the hour, their bonging notes resonant in the night. The wall stretches upward, stone bricks embroidered with ivy. It offers good purchase to grip as she climbs.

Which she does with such ease, such speed, such agility… a scurrying squirrel could do no better in its ascent. Once the ivy gives out, her pace slows with caution. There are ledges, crevices in the mortar, niches and fingerholds.

And what is this, taking place in the shadowy salon that the girl in black has just vacated? A panel quietly opens, admitting another figure, a pretty young woman in the uniform of a castle chambermaid. She gets into the empty ballgown, puts on the wig, and settles onto the divan in a posture of napping. One leg is bent, the foot hidden by lacy petticoat hems. The other peeps out, dainty in its sheer stocking, while the remaining slipper rests upon the carpet as if it had simply slipped off.

The ruse is, to a casual inspection, quite effective. It would seem that the mystery lady must have been more weary than she thought. Even a man so ardent and eager for her company as the prince would scarcely have the heart to disturb her.

Outside the salon door, the page-boy stands watch just in case. Though, as a glance at the ballroom will prove, a princely disturbance is unlikely. His Royal Highness is swamped by the fair sex. It is as if a conspiracy has spontaneously arisen, the ladies determined to distract him from the mysterious beauty. At his every effort, however slight, to excuse himself from the festivities, he is beset by still more of them. They demand, and dominate, his attention.

Why, he is kept so occupied, he fails utterly to notice that certain, ah, *key* items may be missing from his person.

Where could they have gone? Were they lifted by some deft and surreptitious touch? Might they be, even now, in the possession of a certain black-clad maiden as she scales ever higher on the wall?

They might be, and, indeed, they are. So enraptured was he by her beauty as they danced, he never noticed her fingertips dipping lightly to relieve him of the keys to the castle.

When the purchase afforded by niches and fingerholds is no longer so sure, she takes from her belt a length of thin but strong cable with a pronged metal grapnel affixed to the end. This, she whirls for momentum, then throws. It clinks once on a stone ledge, missing the mark. She throws again. This time, it flies true. The cable winds around the pole of a weather-vane. The grapnel holds firm.

Higher now she climbs, and yet higher still. The view is breathtaking in more ways than one. She reaches another window, jimmying the latch with a thin iron rod. It opens. She boosts herself through. She shakes loose the grapnel, coiling the cable again to her belt.

The room, as expected, proves to be a small parlor where the queen had been known to spend her mornings, embroidering with silken threads on fine linen while the morning light streamed through leaded-glass panes. It is not dusty, but disused for some years. At the door, the girl pauses to listen.

The guards pass by, right on schedule, just as she was told. It is half-past ten. They will not pass this way again for three-quarters of an hour. Moments later, her soft-toed boots tread silently in the dark hall. The oil eyes of royal portraits alone observe her progress.

She passes through into an antechamber and strikes a stub of wax candle alight with a match. The clerks' tables stand in neat rows, each with its blotter and inkwell and leather-padded stool. Shelves of ledgers line the walls. At the far end is the Lord High Treasurer's desk, and behind it a passageway.

Here now are three gates, one after the other, impeding the way. The first is of copper, the second silver, the third plated with gold. They are locked, but upon the ring of keys she obtained from the prince, are three—one each of copper, and silver, and gold.

The girl in black lets herself through the three gates and into Bezaubernd's treasury, a round and dome-ceilinged windowless room. Candlelight twinkles on coins by the stack and the pile. Gems gleam and glitter.

A railed gallery rings the upper level, where recessed niches hold goblets and platters, swords with jeweled hilts, statuettes, other large valuables. In the center of the room is a raised octagonal dais supporting a large glass display case. The floor around it is a starburst mosaic of lapis, malachite and carnelian. A wary eye can readily detect the fine trip-wires and pressure plates. Within the case—

Well, but, all that, for now, she ignores. She places several gold coins on soft cloth, rolls them up so that they will not clink, and tucks them away. She fills small pouches with loose lesser-gemstones—garnets, opals, amethysts, blue topaz and green peridot, pieces of honey-smooth amber.

It is not much, not compared to the immense fortune around her. This is a royal treasury, enough to ransom a king many times over. Even so, and even after being divided into twelve equal shares, what she's already gathered will keep them living in comfort and luxury for years.

Then she turns to regard the display case. Oh, and see how she smiles as the light from the candle plays over its contents!

"You aren't worried your stepsisters will recognize you?" the hunt-master's son had asked. "They will be there, won't they?"

"Of course they will," she said, unconcerned. "Just try and keep them away, those greedy gold-digging she-devils! My stepmother, too."

"Isn't she a bit…?"

"Old for such things? Because the rest in attendance will be the kingdom's eligible young maidens? As if that would stop her. She'd be the first to point out that she is a widow, after all." Her voice took on a snooty society note as she mimicked her late father's wife with cutting accuracy. "Vibrant and healthy. In the prime of her life. The prince might benefit from a wiser, more experienced woman."

The hunt-master's son made a face. The girl did the same, then laughed.

"I know, I know," she said. "Believe me, her daughters are none too pleased about it either. They'd rather it was one of them, not their mother. Whereas she, well, she wouldn't mind being mother-in-law to the future king, but better than that would be landing him herself."

"Speaking of which," he said. "That's something I have been wondering... why go to all this effort, risk and danger? The gown and the coach, all right, but why bother with the rest?"

"What do you mean?"

He'd gestured at the work-table, where the Maus brothers and the dress-maker were putting the finishing touches on concealing the gadgets and devices within the hoop-skirt's trick frame.

"If you're already going to be the most beautiful lady at the ball, capturing the prince's attention so thoroughly, why not capture his heart as well? Marry him? Be queen?"

"Oh, I see," she said. "Have the entire treasury at my disposal? More money than anyone could hope to spend in a lifetime? Not to mention sticking it to my stepmother and stepsisters. Imagine how they'd hate it if I, whom they've sneered at and treated like the lowliest servant, became queen!"

"Exactly. So, why not?"

Her wide blue eyes blinked at him. She spoke the way she might have spoken to a dull-witted child, with slow and gentle patience. "Because then," she said, "I would be married to the *prince*."

After considering that, he had to admit, she did have a point.

Behold how she goes about the next part of the plan... a strong line strung like a tightrope from one side of the gallery rail to the other... the grapnel hooked over it and the cable affixed to her belt... see how she slides out along the line and then lowers herself in careful increments.

When she is just above the top of the glass case, she stops, suspended there like a spider on a strand of web. She tilts the candle to dribble a puddle of wax, then presses the sole of the left dancing slipper into it.

She sweeps the shoe's heel around in a circle... the heel with a real diamond set into it, the diamond from her dear mother's engagement ring, left to the girl when that good lady died, and hidden all these years from the avaricious stepmother.

The diamond cuts into the glass with a brittle, scraping scratch. She lifts away the cutout circle with the wax stuck to the sole of her slipper, leaving a hole more than large enough to reach through.

Inside this case, of course, are the crown jewels, the pride of the kingdom. The gold and ruby circlet the prince chose to wear to the ball is a cheap trinket by comparison. She takes them, putting them into a sack.

She replaces the cutout glass circle, sealing the edge with more melted wax. It will not last long, but, it will hold for a while. Long enough to give them a shock when they see the case empty but seemingly undamaged.

Then she returns the same way that she came.

The clock strikes eleven as she locks the last of the three gates behind her. She hurries from the treasury's antechamber to the hall, and from there to the queen's morning-parlor. She eases the door shut just before she hears the approach of the guards.

Out the window she goes, and down the wall. Despite her extra burdens, she makes the descent with quick ease and slips through the window to the private salon.

With the help of the chambermaid, she gets back into the gown and wig. The cinder-ash is cleaned from her face, the blush-pink reapplied to her lips. She emerges, looking perhaps somewhat less than well-rested, and thanks the page-boy for waiting so dutifully.

She returns to the ball.

The prince is delighted to see her, but crestfallen when the mystery lady declines another dance. She is thirsty, she tells him—this is no lie—and faint from hunger. Let her have a few minutes to take some refreshment while he continues attending to his other guests, she beseeches, and from then until dawn they can dance the night away.

The prince is amenable to this, and does as she suggests.

The lady takes her champagne out onto a terrace. Light from the windows glimmers on the river below. How splendid it is, Castle Bezaubernd, as the music plays on. Everyone else has gone in, awaiting the prince's midnight toast.

No one seems to have noticed the slight difference in her walk, a difference brought about in part by the extra weight of sacks and pouches attached to the inside of her skirt's crinoline frame, and in part because now she pads in stocking feet.

Her mother's diamond, pried from the heel of her left slipper, is hidden away in her bosom. The sole of that shoe still bears a patch of sticky candle-wax. She leaves it on the marble stairs, as if it slipped from her foot and she could not go back to retrieve it.

The other, she gave to the page-boy, who went to the cloakroom to hide it in the pocket of a particular fur-trimmed wrap.

What may come of all this, as the theft is discovered and the pieces put together, she does not yet know. Nothing good, that much she is certain. Shame, and suspicion, at the very least. Questions, to be sure.

Let her stepmother, whose fur-trimmed wrap it is, answer for it.

Below, on the path beside the river, two black horses and one rider appear. Their manes and tails ripple like ebony. The tiny bells no longer jingle on their harnesses. They no longer pull the coach made from sugar.

The great clock begins to strike the hour of twelve.

Her impish smile returns. In a flurry of petticoats, lace ruffles and satin flounces, she vaults over the balustrade.

See how they ride, see how they gallop away, laughing, together. Soon, they will rendezvous with the others, divide up the take, and go their separate ways.

And let them all, henceforth, live happily ever after! ✗

ABOUT THE AUTHOR

Christine Morgan recently relocated from the Pacific Northwest to her family's ancestral home in the suburbs of sunny Southern California. There, she hopes to finally take the plunge of making it as a full-time writer. Her works span the horror gamut from historical to cosmic to extreme, including the Splatterpunk Award winning Lakehouse Infernal. She was a longtime contributor to The Horror Fiction Review and occasionally dabbles in freelance editing. Her other hobbies include weird crafts and baking, when she's not being bossed around by her cats.